'Are you try

'I think it is inco[illegible] [illegible] you could tell me anything more unsavoury than you already have,' Dominy said, lifting one slender eyebrow at Beau.

'Shall we say, rendering a subtle warning? The coast is full of men far worse than me. If you learn to recognise them, you won't get your fingers burned so badly.'

'I have no intention of getting them burned at all,' she replied, forcing a smile to stiff lips. 'Besides, it would take a gentleman to do that, and, by your own admission, sir, you cannot claim that honour.'

Valentina Luellen began writing at school—mainly because she loathed maths! It took her twelve years before she had a book accepted, but she has since published regularly. Historical romances are her favourites, because she loves researching into so many different countries.

She and her husband moved to Portugal when he became seriously ill, and there his health improved. Her hobbies are restoring antique furniture, decorating, cooking and dressmaking.

TO PLEASE A LADY

Valentina Luellen

First published in Great Britain 1992
by Mills & Boon Limited

This edition 1992

ISBN 0 263 77639 5

Masquerade is a trademark published by
Mills & Boon Limited, Eton House,
18–24 Paradise Road, Richmond, Surrey, TW9 1SR.

Set in 10 on 10 pt Linotron Plantin
04-9204-94140
Typeset in Great Britain by Centracet, Cambridge
Made and printed in Great Britain

CHAPTER ONE

'THIS is yours. You must never—*never*—part with it.'

Dominy stared down wide-eyed at the magnificent necklace of rubies and diamonds which had just been pressed into her hands, before lifting her eyes to the face of her grandmother, bright tears glistening in the green depths.

'How could I? It has been in your family for generations. It is an heirloom. . .and I have no right to it, even though it is the most precious thing I have ever been given,' she breathed.

'*Pourquoi pas?*' Louise Sablon, Comtesse de Chauvignon, asked as she reached for the porcelain cup at her fingertips and regarded her granddaughter over the rim of the delicate china as she sipped the herbal tea. 'I gave it to your mother on her wedding-day, and now it rightfully belongs to you.'

'But I cannot keep it, you know why,' Dominy protested, although she dearly wished she could.

'Do I? Tell me, *mignonne*, why should you break with a tradition that has been in the Sablon family for over three hundred years?'

'I know about the money Father borrowed from you before he sailed for America. It is unforgivable after all you have done for us over the years. Mama gave you back the necklace to try and repay some of the money you had given us. She would turn in her grave if she knew what Father had done. I overheard him asking—no, begging you to help us. . .' Dominy's lips trembled as she recalled the humiliating incident. 'I never thought, even after all he had been through, that he would. . .'

'Sink so low as to ask for money from a woman he detests?' The Comtesse gave a soft laugh, but there was no amusement in the gaze which considered the pale, serious face so torn with indecision. 'I did not agree with your mother's desire to marry Edwin Granville, but she was in love and headstrong enough to have disobeyed me had I withheld my permission. You have inherited that from her. Beneath the carefully cultivated young lady I have taken pains to mould and nurture these past years, there is a devil waiting to be unleashed. *Bon Dieu*, what fine great-grandchildren you will give me. Hopefully before I die. But your father. . .' She shook her grey head sadly. 'He is a weak man. His gambling has ruined his family, his drinking has almost destroyed his health. He has lost all his friends, been disinherited and forced to leave England. Personally I think it is the best thing that has ever happened to him. Now he must stand on his own two feet. All he has left is a useless title which could not be taken away from him as the eldest son.

'However,' the Comtesse's voice softened, 'my offer to you still stands. Stay here with me, Dominy. Let me take care of you. Give up this foolish notion of following him. His letters have been so vague of late, and he never seems to remain in one place for more than a month or two. That is no life for someone of your background.'

'I cannot stay, Grandmère, even though it will break my heart to leave this lovely place. Even more, I think, than it did when I left England. Everyone had become so horrible to us there.'

Dominy looked wistfully around the room in which she sat, regretting her decision the moment the words were uttered, even though she knew in her heart it was the only one she could make.

The furniture was Louis XV, the walls decorated in pastel shades which, she thought, reflected the gentle nature of the woman who sat opposite her. The château was set in beautiful grounds and surrounded by woodland, which separated it from the small village two miles away on the road to Paris. She had spent two happy years here under her grandmother's wing, being groomed and educated to the highest possible standards.

Here she had never been considered a Granville, the daughter of Lord Edgemont. She was the granddaughter of the Comtesse de Chauvignon, a member of the Sablon family, who in the past had boasted they were descended from the Kings of France. Yet nothing she had been taught could ever have prepared her for the predicament in which she now found herself: penniless, deprived of her home, forced to leave England along with her father or remain at Granville Manor, which had once been her home and now belonged to her uncle and his large family—of none of whom she was very fond—completely dependent on his charity. She had not considered such a suggestion.

'Father will need me,' she added, as much to convince herself as her grandmother. In two days she would sail away from the shores of France, never to return, and join him on the other side of the world, where she planned to make a new life for them both.

The daring of the venture made her heartbeats quicken for a moment. America! This time she would not be crossing the Channel, but an ocean! The Comtesse had insisted she take a personal maid with her as was befitting a lady, but Dominy had been stubborn on the subject. She would have little enough money for the journey, and that only due again to her grandmother's kind heart, and she could waste none of it on such a luxury, even though she wondered how she would manage without one. And so the Comtesse had declared that she would pay a full year's wages for her. Dominy had almost weakened, then refused that offer too. In the end they had compromised and Dominy had agreed to travel with a couple well known to her grandmother who would be sailing on the same ship. As they were childless and the wife was in poor health, the reason for their departure, they were delighted to have her accompany them. Dominy suspected she would become nursemaid and companion, but this did not trouble her; after all, she would have to find work as soon as she rejoined her father. It would be a good experience and, she knew, the only way she would be allowed to travel otherwise.

'I wish I could believe that. Mark my words, within six months he will be up to all his old tricks again and you will wish you had stayed here. He will give no thought to you so long as he gets what he wants.'

'You are very hard on him. He suffered deeply when his friends deserted him because he had no money. And to be disinherited in favour of his younger brother. . .the shame was unbearable for him.'

'Rubbish! If he suffered it was because he could no longer borrow from all those who had supported him in the past. As for being hard. . . I suppose I appear so to someone of your tender years. I am seventy-two years old, Dominy. I have borne three sons and watched them all die before they reached manhood. I have lost a husband in the prime of his life. I live alone in this huge old house because it is full of memories for me and I prefer these to the people who live outside its walls and only come to me when they need a favour.

'Don't look so shocked; I know what they say about me in the village. The Comtesse is old and lonely. . .go to her with a sad story and she will press money into your hands, use her influence to lessen your troubles. Once that was true, but not any more. The three servants who remain with me have been here for over twenty years. When I am gone they will want for nothing. No one else will get a *sou*. Everything I have will be yours.'

'No, Gramdmère! And do not talk of dying,' Dominy protested.

'Why not? It comes to us all in time. Not that I intend to depart from this earth yet. I want to meet the man who will make your eyes shine with love and bring a glow to those pale cheeks. Will you bring him to me when you find him?'

'Yes, Grandmère.' It was a promise easily given. She had no intention of throwing herself into a loveless marriage as an escape from poverty. She had pride and determination. First she would find her father, then work that would provide sufficient money to keep them. They would never again live in the grand style in which she had been raised, but they would have their independence—a new life in a place where no one knew them.

'How I wish. . .' The Comtesse began, then smiled

with a shake of her head. 'One day perhaps, but not now. You have your mother's stubbornness and I must not try to change your mind. But promise me you will never sell the necklace. Not even if you are in desperate circumstances. It must never be sold!'

'I promise, Grandmère. I shall wear it at my wedding and you will be there too,' Dominy whispered, leaving her chair to plant an affectionate kiss on the lined cheek offered to her, knowing it was what the old woman wanted to hear.

'I shall hold you to that promise, *mignonne*.'

A smile touched Dominy's lips as she thought of the necklace safely concealed in her reticule. It was never out of her possession. In the evenings before she had gone to sleep on the long, often tedious Atlantic crossing she would take it out and gaze at it, imagine how many beautiful women had worn it before her as she'd laid it against her bare skin, closed her eyes and pretended she was back at the château, in a room full of exquisitely gowned women and elegant men. She tried so hard to be sensible and accept the new way of life which had been thrust upon her, but sometimes it was so difficult.

The Comtesse had paid her passage and insisted she took with her all the Parisian gowns which had been made for her by the family dressmaker, ignoring Dominy's protests that she would have little use for such finery. She was reminded that, no matter what the circumstances, a lady always dressed well. It was the mark of good breeding, of which she had more than her fair share.

She was right, of course, Dominy mused as she began a leisurely promenade of the deck and was aware of eyes turning to follow her progress. By her appearance, no one would ever suspect she was penniless apart from the small amount of money given to her before she left France. She had accepted only enough for her needs until she reached her destination. What she needed after that she would earn.

Leaning over the rail, she stared down at the water

frothing and churning beneath the wooden paddles of the boat. A slow but pleasant way to travel, giving her time to catch her breath after the somewhat hectic sea crossing, during which most of her time had been occupied with duties as a companion and nurse to the woman with whom she had been travelling.

And then, immediately after their arrival, there had been the hustle and bustle of making the arrangements for transport to take them to the cattle ranch where, it was hoped, she would in time recover her health. Endless days spent in stuffy, crowded trains, which, although the fastest method of reaching their destination, had been uncomfortable, with few amenities.

And then, at the end of the long journey, to discover her father was no longer residing in Virginia City. . . Had she not had the company of a ranch hand who had decided to leave his present employment to seek his fortune in the gold fields, Dominy wondered if she would have had the courage to go looking for him. Even now the memory of the towns she had visited on the way to the west coast made her shudder in distaste. She could not leave them fast enough!

The last place had been the worst of all and she had been at her wits' end about how to escape from it when she had seen the steamboat pull alongside the rickety dock. The only other choice had been to retrace her steps and take a train, but she had eagerly seized on the one which had presented itself like a miracle from heaven.

Only after she had boarded had she realised the reason for the Captain's reluctance to give her passage. The decks were laden with cargo, and the full sacks provided beds for the passengers who had watched her climb the gangplank with curious eyes. This was no place for her! She had been given a small but comfortable cabin, although she had been told that cabin space was not usually made available for passenger use, causing her to wonder who had been so chivalrous? When she had asked how long it would take to reach their destination she had been told, providing the engine did not fail, the paddles break or the seas grow rough, whereby they would be forced to take shelter in some safe cove along the way, they would reach San Francisco within two days.

The side-wheeler, as she had discovered such a vessel was called, was a rare sight on the open sea, but because of its capabilities for close inshore manoeuvrability it was ideal for delivering supplies and for eager men heading for new strikes to reach their destinations. And it was taking her to her father! She would endure any discomfort to reach him. So little distance separated them now.

She became aware of a pall of dark smoke wafting under her nose, which was whipped away by the wind, leaving behind it a not unpleasant aroma reminiscent of chestnuts roasting over an open fire. The fireplace in the great hall at Granville Manor had been an enormous size, stretching the length of a whole wall. At Christmas-time, as a child, she had crouched beside the hearth while the grown-ups had clustered around the tall pine tree which always stood resplendent in the centre of the room, its branches laden with glittering decorations, presents piled high beneath the lower branches, awaiting permission to join them and open hers. She would never know those times again. And it was no use dwelling on the past!

A pair of long, elegantly trousered legs with a large expanse of highly polished boots blocked her path as she turned to go below. Another long cloud of sweet smoke drifted past her.

'Excuse me, may I. . .pass?' Her voice trailed off as she encountered the gaze of a dark-haired man she had been conscious of staring at her in the dining-room the evening before. He had been in the company of another young, attractive man, who had also shown an interest in her. From the looks which had been directed her way throughout the evening, Dominy had been very aware she was their source of conversation, but she had pointedly ignored them. They had both worn clothes of the best quality, and expensive; men whom she would probably have once associated with, but not now! And certainly never alone. The laughter which had come from their table had seemed to indicate they might consider her to be approachable, as she was alone. And if they had seen her board the steamboat from that awful little mining town there was no knowing what manner of person they considered her to be!

The man lounging in a chair in front of her, a thin cigar between his lips, was totally relaxed and, although very aware of her presence, in no hurry to remove his legs from the rail and allow her to pass.

Close to, she discovered his eyes were of the palest blue and very disconcerting as they slowly considered her, framed against the brilliant midday sunshine. After a long moment he inclined his head in her direction.

'*Bonjour, mademoiselle.*' The low tone sounded amused. Dominy wondered why.

'You are mistaken, sir. I am English, not French,' she replied, intending the coolness of her tone to imply she was not accustomed to being spoken to by a complete stranger. As indeed she was not! A year ago no man would have dared to be so bold. She had never confessed it to her grandmother, but there were times when she doubted her ability to survive the change in her lifestyle, despite the determination to overcome whatever obstacles presented themselves.

'Forgive me—my mistake. I overheard you conversing with the waiter at dinner last night. You were so fluent in the language that I naturally assumed——'

'You assumed incorrectly.' Dominy's green eyes darkened with annoyance as they flickered to the obstruction blocking her path, and still the man did not move. 'But I have lived for some considerable time in France.' Now whatever had prompted her to add that little piece of information? She owed him no explanation as to her background. 'Will you please remove your legs so that I can go below to my cabin?'

'My apologies. I did not realise my presence was so distasteful to you.' Over six feet of well-built body came out of the chair with the litheness of a cat and was removed to one side. A derisive smile touched the lean mouth as Dominy gathered up her skirts to pass him. 'I assure you I have nothing contagious, Miss. . .?'

An icy stare met the mockery in his eyes. She left him without supplying an answer to his question, her heart pounding as she hurried to the sanctuary of her cabin. When she closed the door behind her and glanced into the mirror it was to discover that her cheeks were glowing profusely—and not because of the fresh breeze which had prevailed on deck.

She could not recall any man before making her feel so uncomfortable—so lacking in poise. She, who had been raised to accept that a lady never allowed herself to become flustered, but at all times, no matter how difficult the situation, remained calm and dignified. All the strict schooling beneath the critical eyes of her grandmother, the hours of being under rigorous scrutiny as she dealt with guests at the château, at soirées and balls, had apparently not been sufficient to prepare her to deal with a man who obviously thought she would welcome his attentions.

She would remain well out of his way until she disembarked, she decided as she sank down on to the bed, dropping her reticule and parasol on the floor at her feet and waiting until her heart grew calmer.

It was some considerable time before it did. She had just decided to rest for a few hours—the heat had been increasing noticeably over the past few days and by the early afternoon she began to feel quite drowsy—when there came a knock on the door. Quickly she drew on a wrap over her petticoats and belted it around her waist, before easing the door open just a fraction. There seemed to be few passengers on board, apart from herself and the two men she had seen the previous evening in the dining-room, and those were the kind she had found in the mining camp—rough, raucous individuals who stared at her with rude eyes, whistled at her and made crude suggestions under their breath. The journey across the bay to San Francisco, although only a short one, could not end quickly enough for her.

The bearded uniformed man who stood smiling the

other side of the door she recognised as the Captain, who, although at first had told her there was no cabin space available and had showed little sympathy with her plight, had suddenly reversed his decision before she had left the dock and agreed she could travel with him. She had not wondered why, too grateful that she could leave behind her the horrid, miserable encampment where men were scrabbling out a meagre living from the ground, most of the time looking, and smelling, like dirty animals. After only a few hours there she had begun to fear for her life. To have been forced to remain there another night. . .

'Miss Granville, I've brought you a message. From Mr Austen LaMotte. An invitation, actually, to dine with him this evening.'

'Mr LaMotte?' Dominy repeated, a vision of the dark man and those mocking pale blue eyes instantly springing into her mind. 'I know no one by that name.'

'You must have seen him on deck, ma'am. Good-looking, well dressed, brown hair.' The Captain wondered at her hesitation. Most of the women he knew would have jumped at the chance to be in the same room with the man, let alone have dinner with him. But this one did have the appearance of a lady. She walked like one, dressed like one, and addressed those she spoke to in a manner that indicated quite plainly that she was accustomed to having servants do her every bidding. What puzzled him was why such a creature should be in a mining camp full of gold-hungry men—only one kind of women usually frequented those places.

'Thank you, Captain, but I am not in the habit of dining with strange men. Please convey to Mr LaMotte my apologies and my refusal.'

'He thought you'd turn him down, ma'am, which is why he sent me—to speak up for him. Well, you know what I mean. . .convince you he's quite respectable. That he is. The LaMotte family is one of the most respected in San Francisco. He owns the city's largest property developments and a fair-sized bank as well. If you want to get into San Francisco society, ma'am, he's the man to know. And he said to bring your companion too. He's a gentleman, is Mr LaMotte. He knows the right way to do things.'

And, having seen her walking alone on deck, he knew very well she did not have a chaperon. A word with the Captain had probably supplied him her name and the fact that she had come on board alone. Again she opened her mouth to refuse, then changed her mind. What harm would there be in dining with him? Respectability could cover a multitude of sins, but what harm could she come to in a few hours? And it would be a great help not to have to delve into her rapidly dwindling money.

'Very well, Captain, I am convinced Mr LaMotte is respectable. I accept.'

And a bet had been won, the Captain mused as the door closed behind him. He wondered what her reaction would have been to the amount of the wager that had been staked on her answer!

Dominy's choice of gown for the evening was of burgundy silk, which clung to the slender body it sheathed, moulding itself to her breasts and waist like a second skin. Still inept at dressing her own hair—at such times she despaired at her own incompetence and wished she had agreed to her grandmother's suggestion to have a maid accompany her—she brushed the glossy brown hair, which reached almost to her waist when loose, high on to the crown of her head and secured it with pins, then wound a strand of pearls through the mass of curls. The effect she found rather pleasing. It made her look older and more sophisticated as well as accentuating the fine bone-structure of her face and shoulders.

She pondered on the array of jewellery in the box before her, selecting at long last a single red ruby on a silver chain and wishing as she laid it against her white skin that it could have been the ruby and diamond necklace. She slid a matching ring on to one finger, her eyes thoughtful as she took a last lingering look at her reflection to satisfy herself on her appearance. No one would ever guess that the clothes packed in her trunks were the only possessions she had in the world, apart from two framed miniatures of her father and mother. That the jewellery she wore was imitation. Her mother had sold the real articles and replaced them with paste copies, which she continued to wear whenever the occasion demanded. The money had gone towards repayment of their debts, but it had not saved them from ruin, or her from an early grave.

Picking up a black velvet purse and black elbow-length gloves, she left the cabin, wondering as she did so how long the interest of the respectable Mr Austen LaMotte would remain if he knew she was a pauper? He would discover the truth soon enough when they arrived in San Francisco. And she would probably discover that he had a wife and family awaiting him.

She had never dined with a man alone before in all her nineteen years. She had no chaperon peering over her shoulder, telling her what to do or how late the hour was. No mother to remind her that a young lady did not show an interest in a man, no matter how deeply she wanted to meet him. She could not recall the number of eligible young men who had been turned away from the house because one of her parents considered them unsuitable. Not that she had found any of them particularly interesting. Life had been too full to consider marriage, even though she knew that was intended for her once her parents agreed on a husband of suitable background and wealthy enough to support her in the manner to which she was accustomed.

A few of the tables were already occupied, but none across the far side of the room, where two men were seated, deep in conversation. Dominy swept across the carpeted floor with eyes for no one but the well-dressed man who broke off to rise and greet her, although she was very aware of eyes turning to follow her progress.

'Miss Granville, there is not a man on board who is not envying me tonight.' Austen LaMotte took her hand and touched it to his lips, admiration in the brown eyes surveying her and which he did not attempt to conceal. With a smile he turned to his companion, who rose, she thought, somewhat reluctantly to greet her also. 'Don't you agree, Beau?'

'I am sure it will be an evening to remember,' the dark-haired man replied as he inclined his head in Dominy's direction. His words were accompanied by a mocking smile, which immediately reminded her of the uncomfortable few minutes she had spent in his company earlier. If he thought he would embarrass her again so easily he was mistaken! She would ignore him if necessary.

A smartly attired waiter hovering at her elbow drew out a chair upholstered in gold velvet, which matched the drapes around the room. The comfort she had encountered surprised her. She had been totally unprepared for such luxury everywhere on a simple river-boat. It far surpassed that of the ship she had sailed on from France.

'We shall look at the menus now, Pierre. And serve the champagne while we decide. Beau and I will have two mint juleps.'

'Mint—what?' The words slipped out before Dominy could contain them, intrigued by the strange-sounding name.

'It's a southern drink, Miss Granville. Bourbon whisky, crushed ice and mint leaves. Rather harsh for a refined palate as your own perhaps,' Austen explained, examining the large bottle of champagne which had been brought and indicating his approval. Dominy watched it being poured into tall crystal glasses, the bubbles sparkling in the candlelight, remembering she had not drunk from anything so delicate since leaving the château. 'Beau has given the recipe to most of the bartenders in San Francisco.'

'I hope you like champagne, Miss Granville. Most women do, I find,' the man called Beau murmured as she accepted one. She sensed his words were double-edged, as if he was hinting at something she should comprehend. She wondered why he had not been properly introduced—and if it had been intentional. As before, she began to find his presence discomfiting, and turned her attention to Austen LaMotte as an escape.

'I believe you live in San Francisco.' She sipped from her glass and then put it to one side, conscious of pale blue eyes following her every move. 'I confess I know little about the place that is to be my new home.' She wondered if it would be too bold of her to ask if he knew of her father. A man of his connections might have access to information she did not.

'I live on Deacon Hill. I suppose you would call it the respectable side of the city.' A smile passed between the two men as if they shared some secret. 'You will find San Francisco a place of contrasts, and the people come from all over the world. The first gold rush in '48 brought sailors swarming off their ships in the harbour, shopkeepers from England, sheepmen from Australia, Mexican peons and Chinese—the population doubled overnight. Fortunes were found—and lost the next day at crooked gambling tables. Unfortunately many of those who found gold never went home, as was their first intention. They stayed, hoping to find more, and where there is an abundance of money there will always be lawlessness. San Francisco went through some very difficult times before it began to grow. I think I can truthfully say we are quite civilised now,' Austen added proudly.

'Providing you stay on your own side of town,' Beau remarked drily. 'Miss Granville would be out of place on Market Street, although that red dress would draw customers to the Devil's Rest like wildfire,' he commented, eyes gleaming as they centred on the huge jewel nestling between the rise of Dominy's breasts.

'And what is your side of town?' Dominy asked, sparks of emerald-green springing from the grey depths of her eyes at his uncalled-for rudeness. It was not her imagination—he was being deliberately provocative.

'Let us say Austen and I don't have our business premises on the same street,' he replied with a deep chuckle. The mint juleps arrived, and she watched the men consume almost half of the dark honey-coloured liquid immediately. 'I think at last I have taught Pierre to make a julep,' he commented in appreciation, and Austen nodded his agreement.

'Are you a banker too, Mr. . .?' Dominy looked across the table enquiringly.

'My friends just call me Beau, Miss Granville. My, the Captain did fill you in, didn't he? No, I'm in a similar business, you might say, except that money changes hands across a card table or roulette wheel instead of a polished desk. I'm a gambler.'

Dominy chose to ignore the insulting inference that she had been supplied with information on both their backgrounds. As if she would find *him* interesting! The very idea.

'Oh.' The luxury on the boat was suddenly clear to her. It was a floating gambling house. He had probably been to the mining camps in the hope of cheating the miners out of their hard-earned diggings. She knew what misery could result from the turn of a card. She had watched her father squander all they had possessed in his feverish attempts to recover his losses, and, once he had won even a little back, to continue on and on, day after day, in the hope of regaining everything. She had seen her mother's health destroyed, watched friends turn from them, eventually even their own relatives. His weakness had deprived her of everything she had known and plunged her into a world of poverty. Her only salvation was the inner strength she possessed, which decreed she fought back—and survived.

'I am what the English would call, I believe, a "black sheep". I killed a man in a duel and my family disowned me.' There was no contrition on the suntanned features. How could he speak of such an act so callously?

'The subject of gambling disgusts me. I suppose it was over a game of cards.' She had never been so close to anyone so outrageous before. Such things happened in England, of course, but they were not a topic to be discussed over dinner as one might comment on the weather.

'No—a woman.' Dominy averted her gaze from the smiling face.

'There is nothing noble in involving one's family in a scandal,' she said icily.

'A sentiment shared by my father. The woman was married and the man I killed was her husband.' Beau reached for his mint julep again. His gaze narrowed as he looked into the pale face of the elegant young woman opposite and wondered if it would be worth the slap he would probably receive if he kissed those inviting soft lips later on. 'It provided the county with the biggest scandal since the Mayor seduced one of his parlourmaids and she took a poker to his head. I was given the option of marrying the grieving widow or taking my disreputable presence elsewhere. As neither she nor I was of a mind to spend the rest of our lives in misery, I chose the latter.'

'I had heard southern gentlemen were the epitome of good breeding. You, sir, appear to be the exception.' Dominy could not contain her anger at the cold-blooded confession. Did he have no feelings at all? 'Such matters are suitable only for gentlemen, discussed over port and cigars.'

'Blame it on the war, Miss Granville. Most of us southern gentlemen had our manners knocked out of us,' came the infuriating reply, but the pale eyes had grown cold at her remark.

'Take no notice of the man,' Austen broke in. 'Beau has forgotten more about manners than most men could learn in a lifetime.'

'Don't try to shield her—she'll meet worse than me on the Barbary Coast.'

'I think it is inconceivable that you could tell me anything more unsavoury than you already have.' Dominy finished the champagne in her glass, and immediately Austen refilled it. She could feel its potency and decided not to touch the second glass until the food had arrived.

'Oh, there is much more.' Muscles rippled beneath the tailored jacket as Beau shrugged broad shoulders.

What he hoped to achieve by recounting more she could not imagine. Austen settled back in his chair, nursing his julep and looking amused by the whole proceedings. 'I was in the war; I fought on the side of the Confederacy, of course, and there are people who will be only too pleased to tell you I resigned my commission under something of a dark cloud. I will not bore you with the lurid details. I don't live on Nob Hill alongside my friend. I gamble, I admire pretty girls and I enjoy a drink or two. I like the way I live and I would not change it for anything on this earth.'

'Are you trying to shock me?' Dominy asked, one slender eyebrow lifting at his words.

'Shall we say, rendering a subtle warning? The coast is full of men far worse than me. If you learn to recognise them you won't get your fingers burned so badly.'

'I have no intention of getting them burned at all,' she replied, forcing a smile to stiff lips. The arrogance of the man! 'Besides, it would take a gentleman to do that and, by your own admission, sir, you cannot claim that honour.'

'*Touché*, Miss Granville. Well done,' Austen applauded. 'You asked for that, Beau.'

Beau raised his glass in Dominy's direction.

'I think the lady will be able to take care of herself quite well in San Francisco.' He made the word 'lady' sound almost insulting. But then, Dominy decided, he was unaccustomed to being in the company of one.

When Austen suggested he order for her, Dominy agreed. Secretly she was finding it pleasant to be cosseted and waited upon once more. Beau ordered separately, a rather sparse meal, she discovered when it arrived—plain meat accompanied by a salad, nothing more, whereas their plates were full with the most succulent thin slices of beef, swimming in a wine sauce, accompanied by potatoes and fresh vegetables.

She drank a glass of the excellent claret, which Austen also chose, and left only two small potatoes, determined to make the most of what the evening had to offer, for she suspected it would be a long time before she ate so well again.

When Austen suggested pancakes *flambéd* with liqueur she shook her head with a soft laugh.

'I could not eat another mouthful. That was delicious. And I must not stay much longer, although I have enjoyed the evening, Mr LaMotte. I think tomorrow will be a very long day.'

'Austen, please.' Austen's gaze lingered on the cabochon ruby on the slender hand that covered the glass as he went to refill it. 'Is there any way I can assist you when we dock? Are you being met?'

'You are very kind, Mr. . .Austen. I would be most grateful for the name of a respectable hotel. After that I must find my father. I confess I am at a loss to know where to start. He should have been waiting for me in Virginia City. I wrote to him the moment I left France, telling him when I would be arriving, but to my horror he was not there. Someone told me he had mentioned going on to that mining camp, where I came on board, but they must have been mistaken. Besides, I cannot imagine what my father would be doing in such a place. It was one of the crew from this boat who remembered the name of Granville and seemed to think Father is living in San Francisco. I pray too that he is not mistaken.'

'Granville. . .can it be? Devil take me for a fool! Your father—cannot be Edwin, Lord Edgemont.'

The reply which sprang to Dominy's lips died unspoken. Her father had every right to use the title, even though he had been disinherited. What he did not have was the money to support the lifestyle which accompanied it! An icy hand clutched at her heart. She had hoped for a change in him, prayed for him to settle down and help her provide a home for them both, but this alarming news indicated he was still living in the past, pretending nothing had changed. Here no one knew him or what had happened in England. People trusted him easily, for he had a friendly personality, and this, accompanied by the manners and bearing of a gentleman, would open many doors to him. Suddenly she wished tomorrow were a thousand years away.

Had she travelled so far to be involved in another scandal? To be the object of gossip? Her grandmother had been right. Better she had remained in France, under the protective wing of someone who loved her.

'Edwin Granville—is my father.' She chose her words with care.

'We have never met socially. I have been away on business for the past month and the moment I returned Beau whisked me away on an errand of mercy. We were looking for a couple of husbands who had disappeared in the mining camp across the bay. Their respective wives feared they might be dead. Those places can be very rough.'

'And I am susceptible to a pretty face,' Beau added with a crooked grin as he produced a cigar and lit it.

Dominy somehow could not imagine him being so gallant without there being some profit in it for him.

'But you know where—where he is now?' she asked hesitantly.

'I believe he was enquiring after a property on Wilmington Avenue. A fine old house which had just come on to the market. The details were sent to him the day I left. Your worries are over, Miss Granville. I think you will find you have a new home and a father waiting for you.'

'You don't know how wonderful that sounds,' Dominy breathed. If it was true. Where had her father found money to buy a house? The loan from her grandmother would have dwindled considerably by now. He had been gambling again—and won! But at the back of her mind was the frightening thought that he was obtaining credit on the strength of a meaningless title. 'I expect he wrote to me after I had left France.'

'Then it will be a delightful surprise for him.' More like an unpleasant shock, Dominy thought. He believed her to be thousands of miles away. Now she understood the reluctance she had sensed in his letters to talk of the new places he had visited, people he had met. Never once had he spoken of settling down in one particular place. If he was obtaining credit not rightfully due to him then that would be impossible. She could not find him a moment too soon. He needed her! 'With a favourable wind, which Beau assures me we have, we shall arrive in San Francisco early in the morning. My carriage is at your disposal. You must allow me to drive you directly to your father's house.'

'I—I cannot put you to so much trouble,' she protested, secretly horrified at the thought of his being present when she found her father. It would not be the joyous reunion Austen was expecting.

'Nonsense. Nothing could give me greater pleasure.'

'Then you must forgive me if I retire early.' Dominy gathered up her purse and gloves, glad of an excuse to leave the table. 'I want to look my best. You understand.'

'My dear Miss Granville, you would shine dressed in sackcloth and ashes,' Austen declared as he lifted her hand to his lips. 'May I walk you to your cabin?'

'Thank you, but that will not be necessary. It was a very pleasant meal, Mr. . .Austen. Goodnight.' She quickly withdrew her hand, smiled politely at Beau and left them.

The latter relaxed visibly as she disappeared from sight, signalled for Pierre and ordered two more juleps, then lit another cigar. Through a haze of grey smoke thoughtful eyes rested on his companion's face.

'She went through that door three minutes ago,' he remarked drily. 'Did you hear what I said? Are you going to say anything to her?'

'The poor girl would be devastated!' Austen exclaimed. 'Can it possibly be the same man? How could I break it to her?'

'That her father is a liar and a cheat—and a fraud? And in the short time he has been in San Francisco has made more enemies than I have in four years? That's quite an achievement.' Beau flicked ash from his cigar. There was an angry glint in his eyes which his friend did not understand. Or did he? Beau was very particular about his women. They came and went from his life, leaving little or no impression on him. Scars from the past had made him vulnerable, although he had never succeeded in dragging the whole story out of him. He was an expert on diversions. The last time he had tried it, he remembered, he had ended up telling Beau his own life history, complete with all the grisly skeletons which had a habit of popping out of the family closets at the most inconvenient times.

Beau was interested in Dominy Granville! What other explanation could there be? However, that theory was dashed when Beau said, a hard edge to his voice, 'I wouldn't worry too much about our pretty wide-eyed damsel. She can take care of herself. She is already sharpening her claws to dig them into you.'

'There are times when I find it hard to know when you are serious. She is a perfect lady! Well mannered, well educated.'

'Who travels the countryside looking for her father?' Beau scoffed. 'If you took her out into the moonlight and kissed her she'd enjoy it. Just like any other woman. Don't tell me she got to you? Heaven forbid. Take my word for it, you are her next mark. She has to be working with her father. The man has already run up bills in every restaurant that will let him in the door. He's using this so-called title he says he possesses to get a foot into San Francisco society—and he does not have a dollar to his name.'

'That is easily explained. His letters of credit had not all arrived from his bankers in England. Everything will be settled by the time I return. He has travelled extensively, Beau. These things take time.'

'For health reasons, of course.' Beau was not convinced. 'Since you are a banker I should expect you to show more caution. Perhaps the innocent-faced daughter is intended to be a distraction.'

'I intend to see a great deal of that young lady, so get used to the idea. Unless you are. . .'

'Interested in her?' Beau's amusement at the suggestion immediately dissolved Austen's fear that they might become rivals for the attentions of the charming creature he intended to monopolise. 'This afternoon I wagered you that she would jump at your dinner invitation. You thought she would refuse because she is travelling alone. Think on that, my friend. Someone of her supposed background does not travel without a chaperon. I would not let my daughter—or my sister—wander around a mining camp full of men who haven't been in the company of a decent woman for months. Would you? Of course, she will probably give you a satisfactory explanation. . .it's what you want to hear. Me? I'll bet you she is up to those pretty eyes in larceny with her father. You name the stakes.'

'The thoroughbred mare you bought from Mulligan last month. She's fine breeding stock,' Austen replied without hesitation. 'This is one wager you are going to lose.'

'Don't rely on it. If I win you give me a stallion for my mare. Agreed?' Beau's confidence was momentarily shattering; then his companion nodded.

'Agreed. Shall we set a time limit of two weeks?'

'I shan't need that long to expose Miss Granville for the little gold-digger she really is.'

Dominy was awakened by a movement in the cabin. The sound of something falling to the floor roused her from a deep sleep, and it was several seconds before she realised where she was—and that there was an intruder in the room. She could hear heavy breathing in the darkness at the end of the bed, and then a shadow materialised almost at her side. She opened her mouth to cry out, but was so gripped with fear that no sound escaped her lips. Then with a supreme effort she screamed, at the same time throwing herself backwards, away from the hands reaching out towards her.

Stale breath and the sickening aroma of spirits invaded her nostrils as the man launched himself across the bed, a rough hand smothering another cry for help. His free hand was wound into the cloud of loose brown hair tumbling around her shoulders, painfully jerking back her head.

'Quiet, girlie, and you won't get hurt. All I want is

those baubles you're carrying. Hand them over and you'll live to see tomorrow.'

Dominy's senses swam. The weight of his body held her immobile, crushing the breath from her lungs. She felt as if she was suffocating, and grew limp in his grasp. After a moment the hand relaxed about her mouth, slid down to her throat and over the contours of her shoulders. Her skin crawled in fear and disgust as searching fingers explored the firmness of her breasts beneath the silk nightgown she wore.

'In the jewel case—on the table,' she gasped. Let him take everything—there was nothing of value. Her grand-mother's necklace was well hidden in a separate place.

'Now there's a good little girl. Saved me spoiling that lovely face, you have.' Thick lips searched for and found hers in the darkness, while one hand crudely continued to move over her breasts. Dominy raked at his cheeks with her long nails, knowing he would no longer be content with taking just her jewels. As he drew back with an oath that made her shudder she screamed again and again until a savage blow rendered her almost insensible. Swearing profusely, the man stumbled back from the bed, groping his way across the room towards the table where the jewel box lay beside a perfume bottle and pots of scented salve. A chair crashed to the floor and was kicked aside.

The door was flung open without warning. Light flooded into the cabin. Dominy had a brief glimpse of dark hair and a hard brown face framed in the doorway before Beau flung himself at her attacker, who, taken unprepared, had no time to defend himself against the clenched fist which thudded into the side of his face. As he reeled backwards, crashing into the closet, Dominy's jewel box flying from his hands, the contents spilling out in all directions, Beau followed, giving him no time to retaliate.

She shrank against the back of the bed, hands pressed against her mouth at the grunts of pain intermingled with the sickening sounds of blow after blow.

'Get him out of here.' Beau moved back from the inert

form at his feet, wiping the back of his hand across a split lip, and immediately two men were at his side, hauling their unconscious burden through the door and out of her sight. 'Leave the lamp, Weng. Make sure he is chained below, out of harm's way,' he added to the silent Chinese man who stood at the end of the bed, his face impassive at what had just taken place.

For some reason as Beau turned to look at her Dominy found herself reaching instinctively for the bedcovers and pulling them around her bare shoulders. The gesture brought a smile to the bruised lips.

'You are in no danger from me, Miss Granville. Are you hurt?'

'Frightened. . . If you had not heard me scream. . .' She broke off with a shudder. Beau placed the lamp on the small bedside table, frowning as the light illuminated the bruising on her mouth, the tear in the sleeve of her nightgown from wrist to shoulder.

'You have had a very unpleasant experience. You need something to help you sleep.' Before she could protest he had turned on his heel and left the cabin. Almost immediately he reappeared, a bottle and glass in one hand. She stiffened visibly as he closed the door behind him and approached the bed. 'Brandy. This will chase away any gremlins. Drink it down like a good girl.'

'Don't—that's what *he* called me. . . He was after my jewels. . .' Dominy stared apprehensively at the glass thrust out towards her. 'I—I don't think I am going to like that. It smells terrible.'

'In life we cannot always have what we like.' Tentatively she took it from him. He smiled as she sipped it and immediately grimaced as the fiery liquid seared her throat. 'All of it, and then you will sleep like a baby.'

Turning away, he bent to retrieve the jewellery scattered over the carpet and dropped the items one by one into the box from where they had come.

'Was it worth it?' There was an odd note in his voice as he dropped it on to the table and sank down on the edge of the bed, despite her frown of disapproval. Dominy had only just become aware that he was without a shirt or shoes! He had been roused from sleep, as she had. She kept her eyes averted from the bronzed chest matted with dark hair, but not before she had seen the wide scar which arced across the dark skin, from the left shoulder until it disappeared amid the black matt. There was another, long and much thinner, which stretched from one wrist to his elbow. Duelling wounds most likely, she assumed, embarrassed by his lack of concern at his nakedness. Her grandmother would have had a fit to see her now!

'I don't understand you.'

'Was it worth getting bruised over those?' He indicated the jewel box. 'Paste, all of them. As phoney as you are. No wonder you were so anxious to meet Austen. Are you hoping to replace them with the real thing?'

Dominy gasped as if he had struck her.

'You are insulting, sir! You have been since the first moment I laid eyes on you. How dare you suggest that I——?'

'You play the outraged lady well, and the accent is impeccable.' Beau lifted suntanned shoulders in a shrug, and once again she was aware of the strength in those rippling muscles, which intensified her embarrassment and her growing consciousness of him as a man. . .a very attractive man. Far too sure of himself. She took a little more of the brandy and had to admit to herself that it had settled the unsteady feeling in her stomach and that the warmth stealing through her body was beginning to relax her in a not unpleasant way.

Beau leaned forward. His fingers lightly touched her bruised lips. She flinched away from him as if his touch had been red hot. He made what should have been an impersonal gesture feel like a caress!

'A little powder and paint and that will not show. But all your finery and airs will not get you past the "dragon lady",' he added, a deep chuckle rising in his throat. 'Austen's mother—Elizabeth—the most formidable woman on Deacon Hill. She's the uncrowned queen of society and she scrutinises every woman he is ever interested in. There have been quite a few in the past, but when the competition started to get too much she would find some fault with the poor things. I doubt if you have the necessary credentials to get your dainty feet through the door. You are no different from the hundreds of girls who flock to San Francisco looking for. . . What are you looking for, Miss Granville? A rich husband? A good time?'

Dominy's lips compressed as she fought to keep a tight rein on her temper. After what she had just been through his insults were the final straw to break the camel's back.

'In my book you are just another little girl out for what you can get.' Her indignation only served to increase the mockery in his soft voice. 'My customers would love you. If you need money I'll always find you a job.'

It was possible, despite her anger, that he could have said anything and she would not have lowered herself to his level by retaliating. . .but the mention of money. . .that hated subject that had ruled her life for so long, had brought about her mother's bad health and, Dominy believed, her premature death, had shamed her father, ruined his life and hers. . . It was too much to bear. . . Without thinking, she flung the contents of the glass she held into the smiling face.

Beau did not move. With wide, horrified eyes she watched the brandy run down his face, over the wide shoulders and arms. After a long moment he wiped a hand across his mouth, still without a word. A chillingly cold gleam sprang into the pale eyes, frightening her more than any abuse, which was what she had expected from someone of his unsavoury character. She was totally unprepared for what happened next.

Her wrist was seized in a vice-like grip. The empty glass fell from her lax fingers on to the carpet. She gave a cry as the protection of the bedcover disappeared and she was pulled unceremoniously against his bare chest. The warmth of his skin penetrated the thin material of her nightgown, momentarily numbing her senses with a strange new, alarming sensation, then instinctively her nails arched towards the handsome face. Beau averted the danger with a low chuckle that made her blood run cold. She had roused a devil in him which she had no possible way of controlling—she did not know how!

Her mouth was crushed beneath his. Livid with humiliation and indignation, she was forced to endure the angry kisses which seared her lips. She would make him pay for this! No man had ever treated her with such contempt. She made a feeble attempt to protest as she was lowered back on to the pillows, but, pinned beneath him, she was unable to move—and, as he continued to kiss her, rapidly losing the ability to think.

After the terrible experience she had just undergone she should have been fighting for her life. He was no better than the man who had come to rob her. Yet, even with that thought uppermost in her mind, she found her lips softening beneath his, her taut limbs relaxing beneath the weight of his body.

A hand brushed away the loose hair from her face and she realised her wrists had been freed. His lips trailed burning kisses from her mouth to the shoulder, where her nightgown had slipped away from smooth white skin. She trembled at the sensation which was growing stronger, willing her to enjoy what was happening.

'You really are very beautiful,' Beau murmured. His lips followed the line taken by his fingers, trailing over the rise of her breasts. His touch was as light as a breath of wind caressing her, yet it made her feel as if she had drunk several glasses of heady champagne.

'Let me go—please. . .' She had never begged anything from anyone in her life—there had never been a need.

'You don't mean that. . .do you?'

The lips which took command of hers again, silencing her answer, no longer bruised them with the relentless pressure that had brought her so quickly to the point of surrender, but were gentle, teasing, cherishing them with an expertise she knew she should have found alarming. It had to be the brandy, she thought. Why had she not been warned how pleasant it was to be kissed?

Unconsciously her hands reached up to his shoulders. The hair they encountered at the nape of his neck was unexpectedly soft and curled about his ears. She trembled as Beau lifted his mouth from hers and allowed his hands to follow the contours of her body beneath the silken material. Her eyes flew open as she felt him draw back from her.

'You will do well in San Francisco, Dominy Granville, although not necessarily on Nob Hill. All cats are the same in the dark, as I've just proved, and, believe me, you have nothing new to offer. Take my advice and peddle your wares elsewhere.' His words slammed into her like an iron fist. The mists of pleasure were washed away on a tidal wave of sheer horror as he continued pitilessly, 'Austen is not as gullible as he leads everyone to believe, nor as soft. Like me, he is man enough to take what he wants.'

'You! You are an unbridled savage! A conceited egotist.' Dominy fought against the tears which flooded into her eyes. She would not give him the satisfaction of seeing her give way to the confusion and the anger which was engulfing her. Her eyes unleashed emerald fire at him, contrasting vividly with cheeks that had become chalk-white. 'You are without shame!'

'I could say the same of you.' Beau's amused gaze considered the bare shoulders, her breasts showing taut and proud beneath the nightgown. 'Be honest—you liked it. Enjoyed it. Shall I stay?'

She flinched away from the hand that touched hers. To his surprise the rage seemed to fade away. She looked at him with an expression of contempt on her lovely face such as he had seen only once before—on the face of his own father the day he had fought that stupid duel and alienated himself forever from the affections of the only person he cared about.

'If you do not leave this cabin immediately I shall scream until someone comes, and when they do I shall tell them you stayed behind and forced yourself on me, wanting some reward for your help.' The heat of Dominy's rage had ebbed away with the realisation that he had used her, as he might have used any one of the notorious women who frequented the Barbary Coast. She had overheard snatches of conversation from some of the miners on board about the shameless lives such women led in houses of pleasure and low gambling dens which catered as much for the needs of the men who frequented them as they did for the desire to gamble. And he dared to place her alongside them!

'Call away. . .' Beau rose and flung open the door. Just outside Dominy saw the Chinese man and caught her breath, realising he had overheard everything that had taken place. 'I am sorry to disappoint you, but Weng will disprove that story, and I do not think it would go down too well with Austen. Shall we chalk it up to experience? One you should reflect on in the short few hours before we reach our destination.'

'Get out,' Dominy cried, her hands clenching into tight fists. Beau knew if she could have reached for something heavy she would have thrown it at him.

He sketched a mocking bow in her direction and, despite the hardness of his voice, there were still the mocking undertones to remind her what had passed between them. And she had enjoyed it! For a few brief foolish moments she *had* enjoyed his touch, his kisses, and for that she would never forgive herself. Or him for the indignity she would never be able to erase from her memory.

'Weng will remain outside the door for the remainder of the night to ensure you are not troubled by further unwelcome visitors. By the way, Austen has offered me a lift in the morning. I look forward to meeting the illustrious Lord Edgemont and to seeing over your fine new home. Goodnight—milady. Sleep well.'

The parting remark left her sitting bolt upright in the bed, stunned, incapable of gathering together her confused thoughts. . .and dreading the coming of morning. He had ensured she would not know a moment of peace. . .

CHAPTER TWO

'WENG tells me you played Sir Galahad to our charming passenger last night,' Austen remarked as they made their way down the gangplank to the landing stage. A carriage stood waiting a few yards away. He was relieved his mother had not put in an appearance. As yet he preferred she did not meet Dominy Granville. This relationship was going to be on his own terms. 'Lucky you are a light sleeper. I didn't hear a thing.'

'Weng talks too much,' Beau replied with a grin, knowing only the barest details would have been supplied. The faithful Weng was the guardian of many secrets. Although to most people he was only a servant, to Beau he was a trusted friend, as well as being a most formidable bodyguard. He had relations throughout San Francisco who were always on call when help was required, and his knowledge of what went on in every quarter of the city, from Nob Hill, where the gentry had their fine houses, to the vice-parlours on Telegraph Hill, never ceased to amaze him.

'Are you turning the man over to the police?'

'No. I let him go an hour ago. Weng had a talk with him and he knows what will happen if I see his face again. You know how persuasive he can be. I did not think Miss Granville would want the embarrassment of charging him with attempted theft. She was frightened, but not hurt. And it does not look as if the experience was too traumatic,' he added, motioning with a nod towards the figure who had appeared on deck.

Dominy had selected what she should wear with great care, desperately in need of bolstering her shattered confidence. Her dress was of jade green, the skirt slashed to expose a profusion of Brussels lace. Her shoes and gloves were of the softest goatskin, dyed a matching colour. She wore her hair as she had the previous evening, and perched on the top of the abundance of dark brown hair was a neat little hat with a bright yellow ostrich feather that caressed one cheek. As she descended towards them she opened a silk parasol to shade her face from the sun. Despite the early hour, it was surprisingly warm.

'Perhaps she will get a foot in the door after all,' Beau muttered, his gaze narrowing as they concentrated on the elegance and poise that radiated from her. She could have been out for a stroll in the Bois de Bologne, he mused as Austen moved forward to greet her and took the outstretched gloved hand to help her on to dry land. He had to admit she had been well coached. The 'dragon lady' would have a fight on her hands if she tried to get rid of this one.

Like himself, Austen enjoyed more than a fair share of female company and had on more than one occasion decided to settle down, but at the last moment either he had changed his mind or his mother had changed it for him. He was by no means a weak man, but Beau suspected he was seeking perfection—and he did not know of a woman who had been created who was that! They were all full of flaws, and, the deeper you dug, the worse they became.

Beau led a full life and had no wish to change his status as a single man. He was free to choose company or be alone. No strings, no ties, no heartache.

'My carriage is waiting.' Austen tucked Dominy's hand beneath his arm in a possessive manner that made Beau's eyebrows rise quizzically.

'I do not want to cause any inconvenience—to either of you,' she said, glaring pointedly at the silent man walking beside her. How dared he inflict his odious company on her after his conduct of the night before?

'It's no trouble or inconvenience. I am going to personally deliver you into the hands of your father. Besides, I want to make sure everything is to his satisfaction, as the purchase took place while I was away.'

'And I just love to see how the idle rich live,' Beau drawled as he climbed into the carriage, seating himself opposite her and crossing his long legs. She quickly pulled her skirts aside from the booted foot that rested against the green silk. He was impossible! 'I might even buy a house up there myself. But Weng is so particular about the choice of neighbours.'

'Damn!' The muttered exclamation of annoyance made Dominy look at Austen in surprise. His gaze was fixed on a small carriage heading towards them. It pulled across in front of them, completely blocking their path. 'I think I have just been waylaid. My mother,' he added. 'Excuse me.'

After Beau's description of Elizabeth LaMotte as a 'dragon lady' Dominy had expected a woman who breathed fire. She had encountered possessive mothers before, who scrutinised every girl their sons looked at, demanding impossible standards both before and after marriage, which often turned out to be loveless affairs where both parties were miserable for the rest of their lives.

Had she wanted to marry Dominy knew her grandmother would have selected a suitable husband from the many young men of excellent families among her acquaintance, but she had been firmly against it. Her life had become so unsettled that it was not the answer to her problems. She was finding her independence frightening at times, but it was also exciting to make her own decisions.

Elizabeth LaMotte could have been in her mid-thirties—she certainly did not look more than five years older. Beneath a wide-brimmed hat Dominy glimpsed blonde hair. She was dressed in pale blue with accessories a shade darker. A magnificent sapphire graced the long slender throat. Two more hung from her ears. As she laid a hand upon her son's shoulder to lean forward and allow him to kiss her cheek the sun flashed and sparkled on the rings on every finger.

'Why—she is lovely,' Dominy breathed.

'And—like you—every inch a lady,' Beau chuckled. 'If you get to know her—really know her—then you'll discover why I think that remark so amusing.'

'You seem to find many things amusing, if they are at the cost of someone else,' she returned coldly.

'The world would be a dull place without a touch of humour.'

Austen came hurrying back to where they sat but did not climb back into the carriage. He looked annoyed, although there was no sign of it in his voice as he said apologetically, 'I have just been reminded I have a meeting with the board of directors of the bank in half an hour. It completely slipped my mind. Beau, will you take care of Miss Granville and deliver her safely to her father?'

'I have been thinking it will be better if I could find a room in a hotel for today.' Dominy seized the opportunity to escape from what she feared would be an embarrassing situation. 'Perhaps you would be kind enough to find out for me if Father has indeed bought the property he was interested in. If so then I can surprise him in the morning. I do not want to appear on the doorstep of a complete stranger. . .'

'Of course not; I should have considered that.' Austen lifted a gloved hand to his lips, his eyes silently conveying his regret at the unexpected departure. Was the meeting really that important, Dominy wondered, or was Elizabeth LaMotte's domination of her son stronger than Beau had indicated? 'My mother bids you welcome to San Francisco and would like you to call on her as soon as you are settled.'

'I shall be delighted. Please thank her.'

'Poor Austen,' Beau said as Austen and his mother were driven away. 'If she gives out an invitation at this early stage that means she wants to give you a look-over before she passes judgement. Right at this moment he is being inundated with questions about you. I don't think the news that we picked you up at a mining camp will impress her.'

Dominy ignored him, difficult though it was, and turned her head away to concentrate all her attention on her first sight of San Francisco. After the appalling conditions in the mining camp she had thought of it as little more than an accumulation of wooden houses and gambling dens, with no law, no comforts and no hospitality.

The waterfront area, which, she was to soon discover, was in no way indicative of what to expect, momentarily seemed to bear this out—narrow streets, teeming with people of every race and colour. Austen had not exaggerated. The carriage progressed at little more than walking-pace behind carts laden with fruit, clothes, household effects, slowed almost to a standstill until the driver, whose patience was infinite, succeeded in clearing children from his path. The buildings were huddled close together. Many looked unsafe and badly in need of repair. There was great poverty here, Dominy realised as Beau reached into his pocket and tossed a coin to a one-legged beggar supporting himself against a pile of empty wooden boxes.

It landed in the dirty cap beside him, but before he could pick it up a barefoot boy of about ten darted from behind him, scooped it up and vanished into the milling crowd. The stream of abuse which followed him made Dominy inwardly wince.

'Did you see that? That horrid child stole the poor man's money.'

'It will probably buy his mother a loaf of bread.'

'Are there no charities to take care of such people?' Dominy asked.

'That I would like to see. You won't change anyone or anything on the coast until you start to clear some of these slums. If people live like animals they act like animals. The church does what it can. . .very little.'

'Are you an expert on human nature?' Dominy asked. 'A change of clothes—or money—does not alter what a person is inside.'

'How true.' Beau's eyes rested challengingly on her face. 'We are what we are, no matter where we are. But I still believe, if these fire-traps were pulled down and decent houses erected in their place, people would have a chance to decide for themselves what kind of lives they wanted to lead. Most of them have known only poverty from the day they were born. Some have been deprived of the right to work, like that beggar we just passed. He was just eighteen when he lost that leg at the Battle of Cedar Creek. When he returned home after six months in an army hospital it was to find the Yankees had burned his home. His mother, his only surviving relative, had been forced to walk three miles in pouring rain to seek shelter with a neighbour. She died a week before he got there.

'He came here seeking to make his fortune, go back home and buy a farm, but claim jumpers robbed him of everything one night and left him half dead in the street. After that he did not consider life worth bothering about. He does odd jobs, enough to keep himself going on a bowl of soup and a bottle of whisky. The boy has become an old man before his time. That's life on the Barbary Coast, Miss Granville.

'Of course, where you are going it is different. Clean linen, servants, good food and a roof over your head that isn't going to collapse on you if there is a quake or it rains for more than two days. Life on the other side of town is paradise compared with here.'

'Yet you prefer it here.' She was determined not to be intimidated by the implication behind his words, the veiled suggestion that she was something other than she claimed to be.

'This place is the heartbeat of San Francisco. It throbs with life every minute of every day. Even the do-gooders who sit up on Nob Hill and shake their heads at the way of life here can't resist the lure of the gambling houses—my own in particular. The scent of violence excites them. They come looking for thrills on the coast because their own lives are so dull. I think you are going to find it very uninteresting up there too.'

'On the contrary, once I have settled down again life will be anything but dull,' Dominy returned with a toss of her head. 'And I am sure Mr LaMotte will be glad to show me around, don't you?'

She watched his lips tighten at the implication that she intended to continue the friendship with Austen.

'Do you like the opera, Miss Granville? Austen does and so does his mother. She is a patron of the new opera house, which opened here last year. Just a small place at the moment, but there are plans for an extension. There has been so much interest shown in it. And we have many fine restaurants and fashion houses for you ladies to spend our money in.'

Beau settled back in his seat and lit a cigar. Then, to her surprise, he began to expound on the amenities provided in the city. Dominy smiled politely and tried to appear interested at his comments, but it was difficult. She still could not accept that her father had bought a house, especially one in a part of the city where they could not afford to live. That kind of lifestyle would cost a fortune to maintain. Neither Austen LaMotte nor his aristocratic mother would want to know her if the truth was ever discovered, and the nearer they drew to the other side of the city, the more her apprehension grew.

She was barely aware of Beau's chatter, the pavements crammed full of people who turned to watch the fine carriage pass, or the hats which were doffed in the direction of the occupants, or the raucous noise that came from the gambling houses even at this early hour of the day. There seemed to be street after street filled with nothing else. Painted signboards in vivid colours swam before her eyes—'THE PURPLE PIG', 'GIRLS', 'DANCING,' 'LIVE ENTERTAINMENT!' She did not want to think what that meant! 'DICK'S DIVE'—'KELLEY'S PARLOUR'—'MULLIGAN'S!'

Chinese laundries and restaurants were almost as plentiful, squeezed side by side down narrow alleyways. Occasionally the delightful aroma of baking infiltrated her nostrils, but mostly there was an overriding smell of rotting vegetation and sewage.

A man and a woman passing close to the carriage caught her attention. The latter, although perhaps middle-aged, was still very attractive, with black hair that gleamed in the sunlight, and large almond-shaped eyes that looked up momentarily into her face, then were quickly averted as she hurried past, tightly clutching the arm of her companion. Or, rather, supporting him, Dominy realised, seeing how she steadied the frail, bent figure when he stumbled on the uneven cobbles. The man lifted his head slightly and smiled wanly into the face close to his. Dominy had a brief glimpse of an unshaven chin, gaunt cheekbones and an unhealthy tinge to the skin that told her he had been ill for some while. . .and then it was as if her heart stopped beating.

Unconsciously a hand flew to her mouth, stifling a gasp. She felt the colour ebb from her cheeks as her disbelieving gaze followed the man and the woman until they disappeared around a corner.

'You look as if you have seen a ghost, Miss Granville. Is anything wrong?' Beau asked, and when she looked at him it was to discover that his attention was not on her at all, but focused on the point where the couple had vanished from sight.

'Nothing, thank you. I find the flies troublesome, that's all.'

How Dominy retained her composure for the remainder of the short drive she did not know. Her mind was still reeling with the shock of seeing her father on the street, looking so ill, so destitute. He had been dressed in a rough homespun shirt and trousers such as were worn by the Chinese men. Had the face not been so dear to her it would have gone unnoticed among so many others, but it had rarely been out of her thoughts, her dreams, since they had parted in France. No matter what had happened in the past, he was still her father and she loved him with all her heart. The most disturbing thought uppermost in her troubled mind now was how to find him.

She stood in the foyer of the Majestic and realised she had been brought to the most luxurious hotel—and probably the most expensive. She could not afford to remain for more than one night. She would go out later on and find cheaper lodgings, and at the same time try to remember the name of the street where she had seen her father and his companion. Had it been Wilson or Maple? How would she find her way around that maze of streets? It was a daunting prospect, but what choice did she have? She had to find him—and quickly.

At the reception desk there seemed to be a lengthy discussion ensuing between Beau and whom she supposed was the hotel manager, a thin man with a fussy little moustache that drooped over his top lip. He reminded her of her music teacher at the château. . .fussy, impatient and very short-tempered. The latter cast a long look in her direction. Beau leaned forward and whispered something in his ear. Immediately the man stepped back and called loudly for a bell-boy.

'Is there some difficulty in finding me a room?' Dominy decided it was time she discovered what was being said about her. She did not like being discussed behind her back—or stared at in such a rude manner. If the hotel was full it would be a relief and enable her to find somewhere cheaper, but Beau turned to her with a disarming smile.

'Not at all. You have the best suite in the place.'

'That—that really was not necessary.' She winced, thinking of the cost even for one short night. 'Anything would have done for such a short time.'

'I promised Austen I would look after you. The manager will provide you with anything you require, and there is a quiet dining-room just off to your left. Try the sole. . .it is the cook's speciality. I will have the rest of your trunks sent over this afternoon after lunch. I don't suppose you would consider having lunch with me?'

'You are correct.' Dominy did not warm to the sudden change in his manner. His friendliness was suspicious. She wanted him out of the hotel—and out of her life.

'No—I can see why Austen's company would be more preferable to mine. You will probably hear from him within the next few hours. But if you should need anything you can reach me at the Devil's Rest. I'll even give you a personal tour of the place.'

'That is a pleasure I shall deny myself.' Dominy picked up her skirts and turned in the direction the bell-boy had taken towards a flight of broad stairs covered in orange carpet. 'Goodbye.'

The suite of rooms Dominy had been given were as comfortable and as luxurious as in any English hotel, which surprised her, and the enormous four-poster bed immediately brought back memories of her room at the château. Had circumstances been different she would have been delighted to stay here, but as she tipped the bell-boy and sat down in a chair, staring at the single overnight bag she had brought with her, she realised how little time she had.

Her feet sank into the deep-pile carpet as she rose and went to the window and drew back the pale lilac curtains there to look out over the city. The hotel was in a street full of restaurants and coffee-houses. Men and women sat outside on the wooden walkways, served by immaculately dressed waiters in spotless white shirts and black trousers, the women no doubt discussing trivialities with their friends, the men deep in debate over politics—as they did outside any of the cafés on a Paris boulevard.

The hotel was situated on higher ground and gave her a panoramic view of San Francisco, without the noise and bustle which had at times almost deafened her in the carriage.

From the bedroom window, she discovered, she could see Nob Hill, as it was called by the less fortunate. The place where money resided. Tall, imposing houses of grey stone rose on the horizon, flanked by bright green lawns and gardens flooded with a multitude of colours. She could imagine the monogrammed carriages standing in the driveways. She would be as much at home there as she was here in the Majestic—but neither was for her now, and she allowed the curtains to fall back into place with a sad smile.

She had just finished unpacking her overnight bag when there was a knock on the door. The young bell-boy stood there, a large bunch of roses in one hand.

'A gentleman left these for you, miss. There is a card. And he's reserved a table in the dining-room for you at lunchtime,' he said, thrusting the bouquet under her nose with a cheeky grin. 'Gave me a large tip too. Nice gent, that.'

He was gone before she had a chance to answer. It had to be Austen, of course. Nestled among the yellow rosebuds was a small white card. The kind gesture momentarily lifted her spirits, but the smile faded from her face as she read what was written there.

Welcome to San Francisco. Enjoy—while you can. You can reach me any time at the Devil's Rest.

There was no signature. None was necessary. Beau! The insufferable arrogance of the man! And what did he mean—enjoy while she could? It was as if he knew more about her than he had intimated. Was it possible he knew her father? Beau owned a gambling house and her father was a compulsive gambler—and one on a losing streak, from the look of him. Did he frequent the Devil's Rest? If so she knew where to start looking for him, but the prospect of setting foot inside such a place—and having to endure more insults and mockery—was not an appealing thought.

Her first impulse was to hurl the roses against the far wall, but as she inhaled their fragrance she relented and went in search of something to put them in.

At first she had no intention of going downstairs to the dining-room, but as noon approached she realised how hungry she was becoming. She had eaten no breakfast, remaining in her cabin until it had been time to disembark. She could find no ulterior motive for Beau's reservation of a table. Perhaps, after all, he was simply looking after her, as Austen had asked. And she would spite no one but herself if she ignored his action. 'Enjoy while you can' had been his instructions. She would do just that!

She was heading towards a small table in an alcove, when a waiter waylaid her and directed her to another beside the window, where the sun flooded across the white linen tablecloth and gleaming cutlery. One place only had been laid, which she found reassuring. She had been half expecting Beau to make an unexpected appearance and force his company on her again.

A single yellow rose had been placed in a frosted vase to one side of the napkin. Her lips pursed as she sat down and then deliberately moved it further away from her. She looked up as the waiter reappeared, expecting the menu; instead she discovered that a trolley had been pulled up beside the table. On it were two silver serving plates with delicious smells coming from beneath the high domed covers.

'I did not order this. There must be some mistake.'

'There is no mistake, miss. Lunch was ordered for you by the gentleman—Mr Beautrellis,' the man added as she stared at him blankly. 'We had very clear instructions that you were to be served the cream of tomato soup.' He removed one cover with a flourish to reveal a tureen of soup, the surface scattered with fresh parsley. 'The sole in wine sauce, accompanied by sliced mushrooms, new potatoes and vegetables. The speciality of the cook. He is from Paris, and Mr Beautrellis thought you would appreciate the dish as you are acquainted with that city.'

Dominy was beginning to wonder what had been told to the manager during that tête-à-tête? Beautrellis—so that was his name. And, despite his profession, he seemed to be well known here.

'Mr Beautrellis appears to have thought of everything.' All she could think of was how much this would cost her!

'Indeed he has, miss. That's his way.'

The soup was delicious, made from fresh ripe tomatoes with just a hint of oregano. The cook at the château had always added a dash of garlic, which she had never found to her taste. The sole melted in her mouth and was so large that she could only manage half of it. Reluctantly she refused the pears soaked in sweet red wine and ordered black coffee. As she lingered in the warmth of the sunshine, mellowed by the unexpected excellence of the meal provided, the fussy manager appeared beside her. He had been hovering in the background since her arrival, noting everything that had come and gone from the table. Now his eyes scanned her empty coffee-cup, the untouched dessert and the three liqueur-filled chocolate bon-bons beside that.

'Madam was satisfied with her meal?'

Dominy smiled up politely into the enquiring face. She felt he did not like her. Or was it Beau he did not like? She was struck with the sudden alarming thought that perhaps she was not the first female guest he had installed here—and paid so much attention to. The waiter did stare at her a great deal, and the maid she had passed on the stairs had hurried past, giggling to herself.

'My first meal in San Francisco was very pleasant. I enjoyed everything.'

'And your room? Do you require the services of a maid? I notice madam has no one travelling with her. Perhaps you will not be here long.'

He made it sound as if he could not wait to see her leave, Dominy thought, putting aside her napkin. She squashed the inviting notion of engaging someone to take care of her personal needs, and shook her head.

'The remainder of my luggage will be here this afternoon, but I shall not unpack. I shall probably leave tomorrow to rejoin my father.'

'Ah—Lord Edgemont, is he not?'

'You know him?' The words were uttered before she gave thought as to how her father could have stayed in the most expensive hotel in San Francisco.

'He stayed here several weeks ago. A visit I am doing my best to forget—as are the guests from whom he "borrowed" money. If your bill had not already been taken care of by Mr Beautrellis I would never have allowed another of you to set foot inside the door of the Majestic.'

As Dominy struggled to find words to answer him the man turned on his heel and strode from the room.

How long Dominy sat in a stunned silence she did not know. Everything had been paid for! The relief that she was not to be presented with an enormous bill was short-lived as she realised the interpretation the manager and his staff had placed on her association with Beau.

Stiffly she rose to her feet, gathered up her purse and left the room with as much dignity as she could muster. She passed under the nose of the manager as if he were invisible and went upstairs. Only when she was out of sight did her composure begin to crumble, and she found herself trembling with anger and humiliation.

They all knew what her father was and thought her to be from the same mould. He had vanished from the hotel, leaving unpaid bills behind him, had borrowed from other guests, probably to continue his gambling—an unforgivable sin. And now he was somewhere out in one of those narrow, twisting alleyways—hiding.

On the thick carpeting her shoes made no sound, so that when she passed the half-open door of a linen closet the two giggling maids inside were unaware of her presence. Her step faltered, and she froze as she heard one declare maliciously, 'Did you see Miss High and Mighty in the dining-room? She's as fancy as that crafty old reprobate of a father who had the nerve to pass himself off as a gentleman of means. Sneaking out of here in the middle of the night like a thief. . .'

'At least he left his fancy clothes behind. They fetched a fair bit.'

'Not enough to pay back those two guests he borrowed from the night before he left. Caused quite a row that did. Gives the hotel a bad name.'

'Did you see *her* clothes? I wonder who paid for those? That gorgeous Mr Beautrellis maybe? We know how she'll pay him back, don't we?'

Dominy flung the door open so violently that it crashed back against the wall. Two startled, red-faced young girls swung around to find themselves confronted by the very person they were so carelessly discussing.

'Chambermaids do not discuss the personal affairs of guests. If I related this conversation to the manager you would both lose your jobs,' she snapped, barely able to keep her temper under control. She had never encountered such insolence before.

'You ain't no better than us. I don't have no fancy man paying my bills for me.' The eldest of the two girls, who could not have been more than eighteen despite the hardness of her features, flung the words at her with a shrug of her shoulders. 'Besides, the manager ain't fond of anyone by the name of Granville. Come on, Annie, she can't do a thing to us.'

She flounced past Dominy, her arms full of clean linen. The other girl hung back as Dominy blocked her path.

'Please, miss, we didn't mean any harm. Don't say anything to the manager; I've only been here a week and me mum needs the money awful bad. If he tells Mr LaMotte I'll be kicked out for sure.'

'Don't you mean Mr Beautrellis?'

'It's Mr LaMotte's hotel, miss. And he'd have me given the boot if he knew I'd been talking about the guests. Oh, lawd. . .'

A look of horror registered on the girl's face, causing Dominy to turn. She expected to find the fussy manager, but instead found an even larger bouquet of flowers than the first one she had received, held out towards her with a flourish. Behind them was the smiling, rather curious face of Austen LaMotte. The maid's eyes almost bulged from her head as he kissed Dominy's ringed fingers and then, still holding them firmly, drew her out into the corridor.

'You have some problem with the staff?'

'None at all. I was just asking this girl for some directions. . . I thought I would like to take a walk this afternoon—after the excellent meal I have just eaten I need it,' Dominy replied, forcing a smile to her lips.

'Alone? I will not hear of it. Unfortunately I have only come by to tell you I shall not be free until this evening, but I will leave my carriage at your disposal. The driver will take you anywhere you wish to go. Perhaps I could call about seven to collect it and we could dine together? Good. That is settled, then.' He gave Dominy no time to reply.

She would have to find some excuse to refuse, Dominy

realised as he left her. The maid came slowly out of the linen closet, a look of awe on her face as she stared at the flowers Dominy was holding.

'Good luck to you, miss, that's what I say. He ain't an easy mark. Your old man could pick 'em too. . .' She broke off as Dominy raised a hand as if to strike her, and fled along the corridor.

Within an hour the whole hotel would be speculating which of the two men she had really set her cap at, Dominy thought, infuriated by their stupidity. The sooner she found her father and left the Majestic, the better!

Dominy shaded her face with her parasol, as much to protect it from the afternoon sun as to hide it from the inquisitive glances directed her way as Austen LaMotte's carriage progressed through the streets. The liveried driver had not even blinked twice when she had directed him to take her to the Devil's Rest. She relaxed back against the velvet-covered seat, aware of how her heart began to beat faster as the black and gold monogrammed carriage left behind it the atmosphere of prosperity which prevailed about the Majestic and the smart restaurants and the cafés frequented by people who had nothing to do all day but indulge their slightest whims and entered the part of San Francisco where every day was a struggle for survival and life was cheap and often expendable.

She had been raised in a rich world and was now forced to survive in another where poverty, squalor and hardship prevailed. This was now her father's world. He could never return to the one he had once known—no more could she. But could she live here with him, amid people she shuddered to brush shoulders with? What work was she suitable for that would earn sufficient money to keep them both?

'Shall I accompany you inside, Miss Granville? This is not the kind of place a lady should frequent alone.'

She became aware that the carriage had stopped and the driver was looking at her enquiringly. She shook her head, not wanting him to overhear anything that passed between herself and the man she had come to see—come to beg for help. The situation was humiliating enough without him relating the conversation to Austen LaMotte.

'I am sure Mr Beautrellis will take care of me. Will you please wait? I shall not be long.'

She had no idea what to expect the Devil's Rest to be like. From the outside it looked no different from buildings on either side, built of dark red brick, except that in front of the bright yellow door was a long awning which covered the entire area of the house. At the top of the steps stood a powerfully built Negro in a smart uniform. A man who not only opened doors, but kept out all undesirables, she suspected.

Had she come to the right place? This did not look like a common gambling house, although she was in ignorance as to what they should look like, never having set foot inside one before. And then above the awning she saw the large sign that caused her eyes to widen.

An attractive woman in a skin-tight scarlet dress, clutching in one hand a wicked-looking pitchfork, the prongs of which emitted tongues of orange-red flames, lounged seductively beneath the boldly painted words, 'Devil's Rest'.

'That red dress would draw customers to the Devil's Rest like wildfire.' The mocking comment Beau had flung across the table at her on the river-boat came unbidden into her mind, to bring the colour surging into her cheeks. Was that how he visualised her—half naked? As she had been in the cabin when he had seized her in his arms and forced burning kisses on her mouth.

Her legs felt like lead as she mounted the steps, passed through the open door, responding to the doorman's polite greeting with a nod of her head. Beyond the interior it was pleasantly cool and took her breath away. She had never expected anything like this! She stood in a large foyer decorated in pale grey and gold. The upholstered chairs were of saffron-yellow with grey or gold tassels. The curtains that divided the area from the two rooms beyond were of heavy matching velvet. The same luxury as she had found on the river-boat. What would she find next?

To the left of her she saw a long bar, which stretched the length of the room. It was backed by mirrors that reflected everything taking place in the room. The furnishings were a little more austere—heavy pine tables and benches, in some places high-backed chairs. From the noise and smoke which prevailed, she realised it was not a place used solely for entertainment in the evenings.

She glimpsed girls serving drinks, with dyed hair, low-cut dresses and painted faces, like the girl coming towards her. Dominy squashed the impulse to turn and leave as cheap perfume invaded her nostrils. Where was her courage? Her determination?

'I wish to see Mr Beautrellis.'

'Do you, now? He turns away half a dozen of your kind a week, do you know that?' The girl's tone was derisive. 'Take my advice and go back where you belong.'

'You are mistaken this time, Maisie. Miss Granville is expected—although we were not quite sure when she would arrive.'

Weng, the Chinese man, stood to one side of them, his slippered feet making no sound on the thick carpet to give warning of his approach. Expected? Dominy looked at him enquiringly. How could she have been?

'Will you not take a seat, Miss Granville?' He waved a hand towards one of the chairs. 'Mr Beautrellis will not keep you waiting long. I shall inform him you are here immediately. Maisie, perhaps our guest would like some refreshment. Something non-alcoholic.'

'No, thank you,' Dominy said firmly as she seated herself. This was not a social visit.

The girl called Maisie turned back into the room behind her with a flounce of her tiered dress that revealed very shapely legs, and joined a man drinking at the bar. Weng bowed and like a silent shadow melted away behind a heavy pleated curtain. Dominy had a brief glimpse of a staircase before it fell back into place and she was left alone.

The minutes ticked by so slowly that she found herself beginning to fidget nervously with her purse and gloves. Was she being kept waiting deliberately? 'Miss Granville is expected.' The words kept running through her brain. It meant Beau knew all about her father. Did Austen also know? Was he too much of a gentleman to tell her the unsavoury truth, or was there another reason for his kindness? The hotel staff thought her to be Beau's kept woman. Did Austen LaMotte want more from her than gratitude? Why—oh, why had she not stayed in France with her grandmother?

The moment of self-pity was abruptly shattered by the sound of loud voices coming from the other side of the curtain, followed by what she instantly recognised as the sickening thud of fists connecting with some solid object. A grunt of pain turned to one of alarm, and then before her disbelieving eyes a man came rolling out into the foyer and sprawled almost at her feet.

The swarthy face was bruised and bloody. She leapt to her feet, backing away from the disgusting spectacle as people crowded from the bar-room to see what was going on.

'Go back and enjoy yourselves,' Beau declared, straightening a crumpled shirt as he came into view. 'The show is over.' Dominy saw that the only mark of a fight he bore was a slight graze on one temple. The pale blue eyes rested momentarily on her startled face before slowly inspecting her from head to toe. She was surprised that no comment followed. Instead he motioned to Weng, hovering in the background. 'Have Jason remove Mr Gascoigne—and tell him not to be too gentle about the way he does it. Now, Miss Granville. . .'

Beau turned to Dominy with a smile that would have charmed the angels, extending a hand towards the staircase. It was hard to believe he had just been involved in a vicious fist fight. As the doorman appeared and bent to drag the insensible man away no one gave them a second glance.

'That man is hurt,' she protested indignantly. 'Have

you no feelings at all, Mr Beautrellis? He must be seen by a doctor.'

'If he shows his face here again he will be seen by an undertaker,' came the chilling reply. 'Don't waste your sympathy on a man like Philippe Gascoigne, Miss Granville. He's the lowest of the scum on the Barbary Coast, and when someone like that tries to drag me down to their level I am inclined to lose my temper. Shall we go upstairs? I take it your business is of a private nature?'

She ignored the gibe and the inscrutable face of Weng watching her with slanted almond eyes.

'Your servant seemed to be under the misapprehension that I am expected,' she said coldly.

'Weng is not a servant. He is my friend. If you are very lucky one day he could be yours too.' He made the idea sound very unlikely. 'And you were expected.' Now the laughter was back in his voice as well as in those piercing eyes. Lean brown fingers closed over her arm, propelling her gently but firmly through the curtain to the stairs. 'I knew it wouldn't take you long to find me.'

As she was led upstairs Dominy felt as if she were walking into the jaws of hell—on the arm of the devil himself!

CHAPTER THREE

THE room where Dominy sat was comfortable, but typically a man's room for a man's needs. Nothing ostentatious or frivolous. Beau sat behind a large carved mahogany desk, the polished surface littered with papers and books. Behind him two walls were lined with bookshelves. There was not a space to be seen. She would have liked to look at the titles and discover what interested this man who lounged at ease in a leather-backed chair, one booted foot crossed over his knee. Since he had asked Weng to bring them refreshment, ignoring her protest that she required nothing, he had not spoken a word.

'Mr Beautrellis——' she began and was immediately interrupted.

'Only people who want to pick a fight with me call me that. And I am sure that is not the case with you. We are two of a kind.'

'We. . .' She choked over an answer. 'If I were one tenth as callous as you I would throw myself into the bay,' she declared at last, and the words brought a ripple of laughter from deep in his throat.

'That would be such a waste. If you are not here to ask me for a job then why? Is it because you know that by this evening at the latest Austen will have discovered the truth—as I have? Being a gentleman, he will not have you tossed out into the street, where you belong, but you cannot expect him to come calling again with flowers.'

Dominy opened her mouth to ask how he had known and then thought better of it.

'And what is the truth, Mr Beautrellis?' she demanded with quiet dignity. 'That my father is being maligned, hounded unfairly? To suggest that he would swindle anyone is outrageous—and untrue. May I remind you, your own background leaves a great deal to be desired, whereas he comes from a respected English family, the son of a titled landowner who certainly has no need. . .to defraud anyone, as has been suggested.'

She faltered beneath the narrowed gaze focused on her. She did not hear the door open behind her, yet suddenly Weng was at her elbow. A tray was placed in front of her. There was a pot and one cup and a plate of some strange-looking fruit.

'Lychees,' Beau told her. 'Try one, they are delicious. Did you attend to that matter I mentioned, Weng?'

'It is taken care of. Will you deal with it now?'

'No, later. Perhaps it will resolve itself, though I doubt it. He moves very quietly, doesn't he?' Beau added as Dominy glanced around and found they were alone again.

'I find him rather—sinister.' It was the only word that sprang to mind. And frightening, but she did not say that.

'Weng would not harm a fly—unless someone tried to injure one of his relatives, of which there are many, or me.' Beau indicated the tray. 'Lemon tea. Isn't that what the English drink in the afternoon—or am I carrying the charade too far? Perhaps you would prefer whisky? I'm going to have one.'

'No, thank you.' Dominy poured herself half a cup of tea, and tentatively tried one of the lychees while his back was turned and found it like nothing she had ever tasted before and beyond description—yet very pleasant.

Beau splashed whisky from a silver-topped decanter into a glass and leaned back against the oak sideboard, watching her sip her tea. Perhaps somewhere in his dark and murky past he had known a better life, she surmised. He could play the gentleman when he chose and he surrounded himself with the best of everything.

'You live well, Mr Beautrellis. Does it not worry you that your lifestyle is built on the misery of those who lose money gambling here?' she asked frostily; he looked down his nose at her father, questioned his morals, when he knew nothing of the circumstances.

'My life is not built around a web of lies; it is an open book,' Beau retorted.

'With some very lurid pages.'

'I cater for those people who can afford to lose. Their losses are my gains.' He shrugged indifferently and returned to his chair.

'That makes you as much a snob as they are,' Dominy said, setting aside her empty cup. 'And as much of a hypocrite.'

'My lurid past, as you put it, is what brings them here. It alleviates the boredom of their rich lives. But, unlike your father, they do not walk out of here owing me large sums of money. There is a house rule that credit is never given. I don't care how influential they are, or whether their women are dripping in jewels. Cash across the tables is all I am interested in. IOUs are issued to a select few, and settled within one week. Failure to comply means I pay them a visit, and some of those aristocratic chins could be bruised by my knuckles. No one does me any favours. Is this where you arranged to meet him?'

The question was so totally unexpected that Dominy found herself floundering for words.

'Who?'

Beau opened a drawer in front of him and took out a bundle of paper. He tossed it across to her with a contemptuous look.

'He was gambling here the night I left for the mining camp. And winning. His luck changed the following night and every night after that. The man I left in charge decided to repay me for a slight. . .disagreement we had last month—and allowed him credit. Don't you recognise the signature, Miss Granville?'

Recognise it! It leapt at her from the paper, searing her brain. Edwin Granville—and in his flourishing hand, which she had always admired—Lord Edgemont.

'The man was an impostor.' Why did she continue to defend him, to lie? Everyone knew the truth! 'This looks nothing like his signature.'

'Liar! Austen has already confirmed it. It is the same

as that he used on bank documents, which by this evening will have been proved worthless. You came here hoping to contact your father. You knew where he would be, didn't you? Was it pre-arranged? You should be on the stage, Dominy Granville. Perhaps in England you were. Is that where you perfected the accent?'

'My grandmother would have you whipped for such insolence.' Dominy sprang to her feet, eyes blazing.

'Sit down,' Beau ordered, 'or I'll come around there and put you over my knee. You've had your say; now you will hear me out.'

Dominy sank slowly down into the chair again, not liking the look in his eyes.

'In the short space of the few hours since I've been back in San Francisco I've discovered more than I need to know about the smooth-tongued, yarn-spinning Lord Edgemont. I can make you out a list of more than a dozen people who would like to see his hide nailed to a wall. And that includes me. Not that I shall ever see the money he owes me—any more than anyone else will. He's gone to ground. . .but when I find him I'll have my pound of flesh before they lock him away in a cosy cell for a couple of years.'

He paused, watching the effect his words were having on Dominy. She sat bolt upright, her hands locked tightly together in her lap, her lips compressed in a tight line. Begrudgingly he admired her composure. He thought she would have turned on the charm by now. . . What was going through her mind behind that mask of pretended indignation?

'If you are considering Austen as a possible solution to your problems forget it. He's too conscious of the weight the LaMotte name carries here. Besides, he can buy any pretty bed-mate he wants for less than the price of a dinner, so why should he want to part with three thousand dollars to keep your father out of gaol?'

'Three thousand dollars!' Dominy echoed, thunder-struck by the amount. She had six hundred in her purse. How could she begin to pay off such a sum?

'He still owes the Majestic around a thousand, and the

sum would probably double if you include everyone else he's swindled. *Now* would you like a whisky? You probably need it.'

'No, Mr Beautrellis, I require nothing more from you.' She had come with the idiotic notion of asking his help. She would die first! She rose to her feet, shoulders stiff and straight, head held high, and stared at him across the desk, her eyes smouldering with hatred. 'You are the lowest, most contemptible creature it has ever been my misfortune to encounter. My father is—is the victim of a cruel hoax intended to blacken his name. . .' She broke off, the lies choking her. 'You shall have your money—every single dollar.'

'My offer is still open. Come and work here and pay it off.' Beau followed her to the door, his hands thrust deep into the pockets of his trousers. The look she directed at him should have shrivelled him to a cinder. He added insult to injury with, 'In one night—in the right dress—you'd double the takings on a single table.'

'I meant what I said. I *will* repay the money owed to you and everyone else—even if it takes me the rest of my life. You have my word.'

'The word of a Granville doesn't count much with me,' Beau retorted. 'If you didn't come here to try and persuade me not to press charges against your father, what was the reason? Is the Majestic too dull for you?'

'As it happens, I am very much at home there. I am accustomed to such surroundings,' Dominy flung back. 'I came with the foolish idea that you might help me find my father.'

'That was foolish. Perhaps you will have more luck with Austen, but I doubt it.'

'At least he will listen to the truth. Goodbye, Mr Beautrellis. I sincerely hope we do not meet again.'

The driver waiting patiently beside the carriage gave her a penetrating look as she came out of the Devil's Rest. It did not matter if he related her visit to Austen LaMotte, for she had already decided to tell him the truth about herself before she left the Majestic and found cheaper accommodation. She wanted charity from no one. As she came down the steps a boy darted from a nearby alleyway, almost colliding with a couple passing in front of her, and sprawled at her feet. Instinctively she stretched out a hand to help him up. Something was pressed into her palm, and then he was on his feet again and out of sight before she could gather her startled wits.

'Are you all right, miss? These young ruffians have no manners. Did he try to steal your purse?'

'On the contrary—he gave me something.' Dominy unfolded the crumpled paper she held. The writing was barely legible. 'It looks like an address—391 Lombard Street. Do you know it?'

'It's about two blocks from here, miss, where most of the Chinese community live.'

'Take me there, please.' Sudden hope had risen in Dominy's heart. It had to be the place where her father was living. Perhaps he had seen her too the other day. With some reluctance the driver complied with her wishes and, as she sat back in the carriage, the Devil's Rest and the odious Beau were erased from her mind.

The streets became so narrow that it was impossible for the carriage to continue further. The driver turned to her with an apologetic smile, but she heard relief in his tone that they could continue no further. She, however, was not so easily dissuaded.

'I shall walk from here. Please show me the way.' She had no intention of going alone down those dingy alleyways.

Number 391 Lombard Street was tucked between a derelict building, the doors and windows heavily boarded over, and a laundry, from which came a scorching heat that made her quicken her steps to pass it. Over the door was a sign that read 'The Floating Moon Restaurant'. She had expected a lodging house. Surely her father would not be staying here?

The interior was dimly lit. The walls were hung with Oriental paintings and some wicked-looking weapons. Wind-bells swayed beside the open windows. As she tried to accustom her eyes to the unusual gloom a woman came through the curtains in front of her. Dominy recognised her immediately as the same one who had been with her father that morning.

'Please, follow me. You are expected.'

That was the second time she had arrived somewhere and been told that, she thought as she obeyed without question. The woman's manner gave her no cause for alarm, although her surroundings were very strange. She was led down a passageway to another room. Dominy was very aware of the smoky atmosphere and the sweet odours that drifted to her. Her steps faltered as she was struck with the horrifying notion that this could be one of those awful opium dens she had been told about.

'Do not be afraid.' The woman opened a door and stood to one side, motioning Dominy to enter. 'Your father is waiting for you.'

She really had found him. Dominy could not believe how kind fate had been to her. She was shocked by his appearance, but already she was beginning to make plans in her mind. Nothing would ever part them again. Tomorrow she would find a cheap place for them to live and then tackle the harder task of finding some employment that would pay enough to support them. How tempting it was to sell her grandmother's necklace and solve the problems facing them, but she could not break her promise. If and when desperate measures ever forced her into the position where that was her sole choice. . .but that moment had not yet come.

'Don't worry, Papa. I am going to take care of you.' She tried to make her voice sound as reassuring as possible in the hope of rousing him from the lethargic state in which she had found him. He knew her—but his greeting had not been an enthusiastic one. At first she had thought it was the shock of realising she was actually in San Francisco and not still safely at the château, but as she stared at the colourless cheeks and into the blank eyes she realised it was something more than ill-health which had brought about such neglect of his appearance.

He was a broken man! His compulsion for gambling

had been his downfall in England. It was no different for him here in this new land of opportunities. She would change that. Her grandmother had been right. He was a weak man. He needed her strength and her understanding.

'Listen to me, please.' She stroked the thinning grey hair, tears springing to her eyes. 'Everything is going to be all right now. Do you remember all those plans we made before you left France?' She doubted now if he had ever intended she should join him. Knowing she would be well taken care of, he had had no need to worry about anyone but himself. 'They are all going to come true. One day we shall have a house of our own again. . .servants. . .and a carriage to ride in.'

'Dominy. . .' sudden recognition dawned upon the drawn features '. . .I have missed you, my daughter. They stole everything from me. I was winning and they stole all my money. Our money. It was for you and me. . .'

'Don't torture yourself, Papa. We are together. Nothing else matters.'

'The wheel was crooked. They let me win. . .and when I left that accursed place they followed me. . .four of them. I only went there because that's where everyone goes with money. I had so iittle, but I needed a stake. . .for us. . .'

'Where—where did you go? Can you remember?' Dominy's lips trembled as she asked the dreaded question. What was it Beau had told her in his office? 'He was gambling here the night I left for the mining camp. And winning.' But after that he had begun to lose, or so she had been led to believe.

'It is time to rest. You can talk again later.' The Chinese woman came into the room and gently took Edwin by the arm. Without protest he rose and allowed her to guide him to the single bed against the far wall. She fixed the pillow comfortably beneath his head, covered him with the only blanket there and beckoned Dominy to follow her. 'He is very tired. And we must talk.'

She wanted answers to many questions, Dominy thought as she followed her back into the main restaurant. The door was closed now. The woman indicated a table.

'Please be seated. I have taken the liberty of bringing some tea. Have you ever had Chinese tea, Miss Granville?'

Her English, although a trifle stilted, could not be faulted, and Dominy looked into the olive features curiously. She was beginning to think she could not be surprised at anything that happened to her from this moment on. She had travelled halfway across the world, only to discover that her father was on the verge of being arrested. She had been humiliated and subjected to innuendoes and suggestions not fit for the ears of a lady, including the offer of work in a notorious gambling house, and now—here—she was calmly taking tea in a Chinese restaurant with a woman who seemed at this moment to be closer to her father than she was.

'I am very confused. . . Forgive me, I don't know your name. What is my father doing here? How did he come to be in such a place?'

'He is here because he had nowhere else to go. You may call me Madam Chen. You need have no fears for his safety; he is being well cared for. And there will be no charge. I am aware of his circumstances.'

'Whatever expenses are incurred, I will pay them,' Dominy declared.

'You are very proud, Miss Granville, as he once was, but pride is not everything,' the soft voice chided her show of indignation.

How could she pay anyway? Her father's debts were already enormous, and how many people did he owe money to that she did not know of? It was a horrifying thought.

'I will make arrangements tomorrow to find other accommodation,' she said firmly. 'We cannot be in your debt, Madam Chen. If, as you say, you are aware of his circumstances, though I cannot understand how you are, then you must also know I am in no position to repay your kindness at the moment. But I will,' Dominy added quickly as a smile touched the full mouth. 'I shall pay back everyone in time.'

'I believe you will, but, for me, do not talk of repayment. I found a man bleeding in an alleyway and gave him shelter. A small thing.'

'In—an alleyway! When? Where? He told me he was robbed. . .'

'That is so. He was unconscious, badly beaten. It was several days before he could even remember his name. If you find him a trifle. . .forgetful. . .it is the medication I have been giving him. . .to ease the pain. A few more days and he will be himself again.'

'He will never be the man he was,' Dominy whispered bitterly. 'I saw it in his eyes. He has suffered so much in the past. If only I had come with him and not stayed behind. . .I could have prevented this.'

'A man bent on his own destruction will listen to no one—even his loved ones,' came the quiet answer. 'It is possible to destroy the spirit, but not the soul. Give him time. But be firm with him. Guide him, but do not let him use you as a crutch. He has to return to the world of the living on his own.'

'He is a sick man, madam; how can you say that?'

'It is a sickness of the mind which can be cured. . .and the cure is in his own hands. Not yours. You have your own life to lead. Go back where you belong.'

'My place is with my father. You speak as if you think you have more right to be with him than I do,' Dominy said with a frown of annoyance. 'I am grateful for all you have done, madam, but as soon as I have found other lodgings for us both I shall come back for him.'

'Your father's life belongs to me, Miss Granville. I will not allow him to throw it away. I shall give him back strength and self-esteem. He does not need you. You may see him again for a moment before you leave.'

Before Dominy could utter a word she had risen from the table and left the room. Did not need her—his own daughter! She spoke as if her father were *her* property! And that Dominy no longer existed in his life. The relief she had felt at finding him was suddenly replaced by a feeling of apprehension so strong that she began to tremble.

She hurried back to the small room and found her father still on the bed, his eyes tightly closed. She whispered his name, but he did not move. He was asleep. She bent to kiss a pale cheek and then gathered up her purse and gloves from the table. How she wished it were possible to take him with her at this very moment. Madam Chen, far from being the friend she had appeared at first, now appeared very sinister—and rather menacing. Her father's life belonged to no one but himself, Dominy thought as she stepped out of the gloom into the busy alleyway again.

'If you hadn't come out in two minutes I was going for the police,' the anxious-faced driver declared as he moved protectively to her side. 'Mr LaMotte would not like you wandering about this kind of place, miss.'

'I have found what I was looking for,' Dominy returned. She would have to tell Austen the whole truth—he deserved it for all the kindness he had shown her. But, between her father's fall from grace and his mother's high standards, even friendship between them had become impossible. Perhaps it was for the best. She could no longer move among his circle of friends, any more than she could work at the Devil's Rest.

Her bitterness grew on the way back to the Majestic. Her father had been robbed, beaten and left to die in an alleyway after gambling in that place. Whether Beau had been there or not when it had happened, he was responsible. His men had perpetrated the cowardly act of attacking an old man. Four of them against one! She was learning quickly about the standards of the Barbary Coast!

Back in her suite of rooms, she discovered that the remainder of her luggage—three large trunks and two hat boxes—had been delivered from the river-boat. Had the situation not been so serious she could have laughed as she stared at them. Dear, dear grandmother, insisting she always dress like a lady. She had enough clothes there to fill two large closets, and nowhere to go to wear any of them. And no possibility of it in the future either. The day dresses and a few other items she could make use of—would have to in her circumstances—but the magnificent Paris-created ballgowns and satin slippers, a pair to match almost every gown, she remembered—what use were they to her now?

She could sell them; that would replenish her dwindling resources a little. Carefully she undid the necklace around her neck—she had thought it the safest place to keep it, well hidden beneath the collar of her dress—and replaced it in the leather pouch in her purse. Her eyes widened in disbelief as she saw nothing else in her purse but an embroidered linen handkerchief and a few loose coins. In a feverish haste she pulled out the handkerchief, and as she did so two crumpled notes fell to the floor. She scooped them up in horror. Where was the wad of notes she had placed there before she had gone out that morning? It had been stolen—but how? When?

At the Devil's Rest her purse had been on the table in front of her, always in view. In the restaurant of Madam Chen she had definitely had it while with her father. She caught her breath, remembering the boy who had cannoned into her and pressed the note into her hands. He was the thief! The wretched little creature had stolen almost all her money! She sank down into a chair, her hands over her face. What was she to do now? She had only enough money to pay for lodgings for a short time, and she doubted if she could obtain a room without some payment in advance.

Her head fell against the back of the chair and her eyes closed tiredly. Everything seemed to be against her. Her hopes had been raised with the finding of her father, only to be dashed with this new crisis. She had no one to turn to offering help or guidance. She was totally alone. Alone and rather frightened as the shadows lengthened around the room and the nightmare slipped away from her. . .

She started up in the chair, awakened by a thought that had invaded her mind as she had slept and would not leave. If the boy had been the thief he would have snatched the whole wad of notes, not left a few behind. The thief had unfolded them, perhaps counted them and returned two to her purse. A compassionate thief! An icy hand clutched at her heart.

She had left her purse on the table while she had gone into the other room with the Chinese woman. *She* could not have taken the money—that only left her father! He had stolen from his own daughter. He could not have known that it was all she had in the world, but it did not make his action any the less reprehensible. How could he have done this to her? Had he sunk so low?

It was several minutes before she became aware of the insistent knocking on the door. The last thing she wanted was a visitor, but the manager had seen her come in. Austen LaMotte looked past her into the darkened room with surprise as she opened the door, and Dominy realised she had slept for several hours.

'I'm sorry. . .I fell asleep.' Self-consciously she brushed back strands of loose hair and smoothed down her skirts as he entered and immediately lighted one of the oil lamps in the centre of the room.

'My guest is being sadly neglected. I shall have a word downstairs. This is not the kind of service the Majestic usually provides.'

'I am not the usual kind of guest, am I, Mr LaMotte?' she said quietly. 'I know why you have come. I shall leave first thing in the morning. I shall not embarrass you.'

'Embarrass me! Good heavens, what are you talking about?' Austen declared, frowning at her. 'Something is troubling you, I can see it. Please tell me.'

'You know everything there is to know, Mr LaMotte, about my father. Mr Beautrellis made that quite clear to me this afternoon. You have been very kind to me and I shall never forget it, but I cannot remain here and jeopardise your good name. I know only too well how mud clings.'

Austen's frown grew at the bitterness in her voice.

'Are you responsible for his actions? His gambling?' he demanded.

'No, but——'

'Then there is no reason for you not to remain here as long as it pleases you. Nor to refuse my invitation to dine with me. I shall be proud to take you out to dinner this evening, Miss Granville.'

Dominy was not sure she had heard him correctly. When the news of her father's disinheritance and loss of all monies had broken in the Berkshire countryside where they had had their home she had been appalled at the swiftness with which they had been deserted by their friends. Invitations refused on the flimsiest of excuses, pointedly being cut in the street, ignored as if they did not exist. Made to feel like lepers.

'And be the talk of the restaurant? I could not do that to you. I do not know if I have the courage to show myself in public. . .' Her lips trembled. She turned away from him to regain her composure. 'Please go and let me leave tomorrow. It is for the best.'

'That would be the most dishonourable thing I could ever do in my life. I would like to be your friend.' Austen turned her to face him again, no reproach in his tone and a warmth in his voice that made it difficult to reject what he was offering. She needed a shoulder to lean on—just for a little while. . . 'I think you need one, Dominy. I want you to trust me, confide in me. Let me help you.'

'Will you let me tell you about my father? He is not the kind of man you all believe him to be. Such terrible things have happened to him,' she said.

'Over dinner? Candlelight and champagne and honesty. What more could I ask?' He lifted her hands to his lips. They were cold and were quickly withdrawn. If she had gone to see Beau no wonder she was in such a state. He was the last person to turn to, the way he felt about Edwin Granville.

'I shall be a while. . .to change. . .' If he was told of the circumstances which had brought about her father's present dire straits perhaps he could use his influence to hold back charges being brought against him until she could find some way of repaying the money he owed.

'I shall come back for you in an hour.'

Dominy chose her gown with great care, aware that she would be under scrutiny from the moment they set foot in the restaurant. She had not intended to open any of the trunks delivered, but the occasion warranted it. She was not going to be intimidated by looks or whispers. *She* had done nothing wrong. She was torn between two gowns. One the most seductive shade of burnt orange, which had been made for her before she had left France and had not yet been worn, and the other pale grey, trimmed with pink ribbons and satin bows. The latter, she decided, was more suitable and tasteful for an evening in a restaurant. The orange would be for a festive occasion.

'I suspect you have left many broken hearts behind you in England—and France,' Austen murmured as he helped her to alight before the restaurant he had chosen. The admiration in his voice bolstered Dominy's confidence as she took his arm and allowed him to escort her inside. 'And, unless I am very much mistaken, within a few minutes every young buck in this place is going to want to know who you are.'

And when they knew they would retreat as if she carried the plague, Dominy thought as they crossed the crowded floor. Their table was in the middle of the room. She took her seat, pretending not to notice the looks which had followed them since the moment they had stepped through the door or the whispered comments of curiosity she knew were being passed to and fro behind her back. Austen LaMotte was a prominent figure and his choice of female companions was sure to be of interest to everyone, especially as his mother's ideas on the perfect companion were certain knowledge to all she came into contact with.

'Tonight, it seems, everyone who counts is here,' Austen murmured, handing her a gold-embossed menu. He ordered champagne and then sat back, regarding her with amused eyes. 'Don't look so worried, my dear. One smile and they will be at your feet. Who—and what—your father is will not matter to them. It does not matter to me. And my mother has no say in the matter,' he added. 'She never has had in the past. I only allow her to think so. When I find the woman I want for my wife nothing on God's earth will stop me from having her. . .'

Dominy concentrated on the menu, not sure what his words were meant to indicate. Was he hinting that he might be thinking of her as more than a friend?

The champagne arrived, followed by a superb meal which was so perfect that Dominy found herself not only relaxing, but enjoying herself—and his company. He made it so easy for her to talk about the past, her father's gambling excesses, the disruption of their lives it caused day after day, the growing antagonism between Edwin Granville and his father that had resulted in his being disinherited and, upon the death of the latter, deprived of all money and properties, which had been considerable. Edwin and his wife and daughter had been left paupers, dependent on the charity of his own brother.

Dominy's mother had not survived that last harsh winter in England. After her death Edwin had sought solace in drink and more gambling. Huge bills had accumulated until the threat of the debtor's prison and an ultimatum from the new successor that, if he did not leave England and make a new life for himself somewhere where he could not be an embarrassment to the family, he would languish in gaol and she—Dominy—would be sent packing from her own home, had brought him to his senses.

Dominy knew she would never forget the bitter reproaches which had fallen from her father's lips. Even she had never thought they would be abandoned—like strangers! They had been provided with sufficient money for passage to America and with enough left out of that to purchase a small house in which to live, on condition that Edwin never returned to England. Even the cruelty of that penalty had not broken him. He had rallied as they had travelled to France to spend some time with the Comtesse before the long final parting and spoken of a new land where no one knew them, of his ambitions to rebuild all he had been deprived of. Dominy had listened in a patient silence, loving him for his courage, but doubting if they would ever again know the luxury they had been accustomed to.

In France at the château it had been too easy to settle back into the old way of life—money, servants, every wish gratified. They had stayed longer than they had intended, and then Dominy's grandmother had begged her to stay another month, then two, and her father had agreed that it would be better if he went on alone, to prepare the way and find a home for them both for her to go to. Reluctantly she had agreed. In the beginning the months had sped by and letters had come frequently. At first she had not wondered at the way he travelled so extensively. . .after all, he was looking for the best place for them to settle, and the extra money given to him by the Comtesse made it possible for him to be more selective.

And then the letters had ceased for over three months and she had grown frantic with worry. When one had arrived it had come from a place she had never heard of. Later she was to discover it was a mining camp in Nevada where a silver strike had brought men pouring to the diggings, breaking their backs day and night to wrench the precious ore from the ground. Her father would never stoop to such menial work. Her fears that he had begun to gamble had again intensified when she had received a brief letter in which he said he looked forward to seeing her again when he returned to France. He had not expected her to follow him—or had he not wanted it? He had never given her an address where she could contact him for any long period. She suspected the last letter she had written before leaving France had never reached him. He had not known she was coming to join him. From the reception she had received, she knew he had not wanted her to come, to see what he had become.

'Are you not enjoying the liqueur, Dominy?' Austen was looking across the table at her quizzically. She had talked herself dry and then drifted back to that world where she sought sanctuary whenever she felt afraid—the château and the peace there which always calmed her troubled mind.

'Forgive me, I was far away. Do you understand, Austen?' How easily she had begun to be familiar with his name. She needed a friend, but nothing more, although she could wish for no one better as a husband than the man who sat across from her and had patiently listened to her without interruption. 'I cannot abandon my father. I cannot think ill of him as others do. Life has not been kind to him.'

'Nor will it be to you if you allow him to rule your own life. He has made his choice. He is the way he is and you cannot change him,' Austen said in quiet, firm tones. 'That may sound harsh to you, but you must think of yourself. This is a new life for you too. Do not allow him to spoil it for you. Give yourself a chance.'

'You are asking me to turn my back on him,' Dominy said in horror. 'I cannot.'

'Then society will turn its back on you. These people here tonight will not think badly of you if you have nothing more to do with him. His debts are not yours. I shall see to it that you are received in all the best houses in San Francisco—and at my mother's parties. She will open any door you wish.'

'At a price I am not willing to pay,' Dominy replied, the smile fading from her face. The enjoyment of the evening had been shattered. 'Will you please take me back to the hotel?'

'The night is still young. I thought perhaps somewhere else. . . Believe me, I do understand the suffering he has caused you. You smile, but those lovely eyes are empty. They should shine.'

'No, you do not understand,' Dominy answered. 'How can you? With a snap of your fingers you can have anything you need. Don't you think I want that kind of life again for us both? To live in a fine house with servants to wait on us? A maid to help me dress——?'

'Nothing need change. . .' Austen broke off as she looked at him sharply.

'Are you sure it is friendship you are offering?'

'Nothing more—unless it is what you want. I am a very patient man.'

'Rich enough to buy what he wants and accustomed to having his own way. I cannot be bought.'

'At least you might allow me the chance to try,' Austen replied with a good-humoured grimace, then, seeing his attempt at humour was not appreciated, added quickly, 'I am serious, Dominy. I will help you any way I can.'

'But not my father?'

'No. He is living with a Chinese woman! Heaven only knows to what depths he has sunk. You cannot associate yourself with them—with that community.'

'Mr Beautrellis has a Chinese servant. He calls him a friend. He owns a gambling house and moves in all the circles you say would ignore me,' Dominy retorted, beginning to be angered by his attitude.

'He is a man! Are you so naïve, my dear?'

'I see. If he kills someone in a duel he is a man of honour. His lifestyle, his background are not important because he has money and apparently influence. I have learned a great deal about values since we lost all we had and there are times when I hate my own kind. The shallowness of their lives. Madam Chen showed my father more kindness than his own brother.'

'The circumstances were far different.'

'I was brought up to believe the family was everything. Nothing was more important than our name, our position. What mockery was made of that! My father became an embarrassment. Instead of help they turned their backs on him as if he did not exist. I will not do that. Ever!'

'Perhaps after a good night's rest you will want to reconsider your position,' Austen said gravely. 'I will take you back to the hotel. Whatever you decide—and I hope you will not continue along this hopeless road—you are welcome to remain there as long as you wish.'

'You have made it impossible for me.'

'Nothing could be further from my mind.'

'But you will only be my friend on your terms?'

'You are the most exasperating, stubborn young woman I have ever known. Are all the English like you?' Austen demanded as he escorted her towards the foyer. Dominy felt as if every eye in the place turned to watch them leave. She wished he had not held so possessively to her arm.

'True-blue blood, with a heavy dose of French aristocracy thrown in to add a little temperament,' she said, a brief smile lighting up her face.

'Why, Austen, what a surprise. And you told me you were busy tonight. Shame on you.' The remark came from a woman who had just come downstairs from the upper floor of the restaurant. Dominy stiffened at the sight of the tall dark-haired man at her side, instantly on her guard.

'Good evening, Austen. Miss Granville.' Beau nodded in her direction. 'How is your father this evening?'

'My. . .' Dominy fumbled for words. He knew she had seen him! But how?

'Are you going to tell me you did not give him money? He tried to gamble again at the Devil's Rest tonight. Weng has just brought me the news, but he ran off again before my men could detain him. I don't like people who make empty promises. You had your chance—now I'll get my money back my way.'

'You are mistaken. It could not possibly have been my father,' Dominy said coldly, aware of the other woman's curious expression. Austen did not look at all pleased at the news. Dominy had not confided to him about the missing money, too ashamed to admit that her own father had stolen from her. 'Besides, he is too ill to get about.'

Instantly she realised she had betrayed herself. Contemptuously Beau flung back, 'Birds of a feather. I was right after all. I think we should get together tomorrow, Austen. You owe me a stallion. The bet was too easy.'

'What did he mean—a bet?' Dominy turned to Austen in the carriage, glad of the shadows that hid her burning cheeks. Instinctively she sensed the remark had concerned her.

'Forgive me. . .forgive us both, please! We did not mean any harm. At the time it was a harmless moment of fun. Beau and I are always making wagers.'

Austen, who was never troubled with rhetoric, especially in the company of a beautiful woman, was horrified to find himself fumbling for words that would not make the whole incident seem more hideous than it was.

'What did you wager?' Dominy asked coldly.

'Beau—suspicious fellow that he is. . .you really must not blame him too much. . . I did agree—thought that—that you. . .and your father. . . How stupid the idea is. And was then. . .'

'But you could not resist it. Obviously it concerned my father and myself. Birds of a feather—isn't that the charming term Mr Beautrellis used?'

'He mistakenly believes that you and your father are. . .partners in crime, if you understand me?'

'Only too well,' Dominy gasped. 'You speak of helping me, yet you allow that vile man to humiliate me!'

'Your father did that to you, not Beau, Dominy. I warned you how it would be. Surely this must help you to make up your mind? You must cut all ties with him.' The complacency in Austen's tone stung her. He sounded as if he were trying to soothe a child.

Or with you, Dominy thought to herself, knowing it was useless to argue with him further. She suddenly felt exhausted. In the space of one short day too much had happened to her for her mind to comprehend it all. Tomorrow, after she had slept, she would be able to think clearly again and she would decide what had to be done. In her heart she already knew. . .

CHAPTER FOUR

FOR a few minutes when Dominy awoke the following morning she thought she was back in the château. A maid was drawing back the curtains, flooding the room with early-morning sunshine. The warmth of it on Dominy's cheeks made her even less inclined to leave the comfortable bed and return to the problems which beset her.

The two trunks which had arrived were open and some of the contents spread over chairs and the long sofa at the foot of the bed. Suddenly realising where she was, she sat bolt upright, demanding of the girl who turned to her, 'Who gave you permission to unpack for me?'

'Madam, such beautiful clothes cannot be left like that! They need to be hung. And pressed before you can wear them again. And one pair of your shoes had a stain on them. I took the liberty of sending them to be cleaned,' the girl replied with a polite smile. Rather a reserved smile, Dominy noticed, but at least there was no hostility in her manner such as she had been subjected to the day before. 'I have breakfast for you in the sitting-room. Or perhaps you would like it in here?'

'No, I shall get up.'

Instantly the maid had snatched up the robe and slippers she had laid out, and Dominy slipped into them, wondering when she was going to wake up. What had happened to change her status here? Whatever it was, she was grateful for the brief interlude of peace as she sat down to enjoy the food provided. The coffee was piping hot and very strong. There was a jug of fresh cream and bitter fruit preserve to accompany the buttered toast. Also a jug of orange juice.

'Would madam like me to prepare her bath?' The hovering maid seemed determined that she should want for nothing.

'Yes. I shall be going out directly.' Dominy threw her a curious look. 'Are you employed by the hotel?'

'No, madam. Mr LaMotte engaged me to look after you until you have time to find a suitable maid yourself. Sometimes I help out at the big house when there are extra guests. I have been well trained by Mrs LaMotte herself. I am sure I shall give you no cause for complaint.'

'I am sure you will not.' Austen's mother would employ only the most capable people. Of one thing she was certain, Dominy thought as she finished her coffee to the sound of hot water being splashed into the porcelain bath in the surprisingly modern bathroom: his mother knew nothing of this! It was his way of reminding Dominy of the luxury she had once enjoyed and could again—if she renounced her father. She could not imagine anything which could make her do that.

She lingered longer than she intended in the scented water. What she had once taken for granted was now, indeed, a luxury. In comparison her father was enduring a miserable existence.

She intended to go back to the Floating Moon and confront him about the money, and then put the incident behind them forever. If the woman who called herself Madam Chen really cared what happened to him—and Dominy was inclined to believe she had been sincere—then she must surely help in getting him out of that environment, to clean lodgings where he could grow stronger, and in time perhaps find some kind of work too.

As she crossed the foyer on her way out the manager left his desk and hurried after her to the door.

'I hope everything is to your satisfaction, Miss Granville?' The whining tone set Dominy's teeth on edge. Austen must have heard more of the conversation from the linen closet than she had realised, her heart warming towards him.

From beneath the brim of the ribbon-trimmed hat set on top of the mass of curls the maid had arranged so competently on the crown of her head, Dominy's green eyes challenged him with a haughty look.

'Don't you mean to the satisfaction of Mr LaMotte? I have no complaints—for the moment. Should I have any I shall notify you at once, be assured of that.' She hoped the words made him feel as uncomfortable as he had made her feel the day before.

Picking up her skirts, she swept through the open door and down to the waiting carriage. She had considered saving her precious money and trying to find Lombard Street again on foot, but after consideration she realised she would probably get lost, and that thought sent chills down her spine. The driver made her repeat the address twice, and gave her a strange look before they moved off. And no wonder, she thought. It was not often someone from the grand Majestic wanted to go to that part of the city.

The Floating Moon appeared just as unfriendly as it had on her first visit. As before, the driver was unable to bring her all the way. She had told him to await her return and hurried on, her heart in her mouth as she was jostled by men whose slanted eyes challenged her presence in their territory. Dominy felt as if a hundred eyes watched her knock on the door, which appeared to be locked. Several passers-by paused to watch her knock again, more insistently this time, only moving on when the well-worn door, with its peeling pale green paint, was opened the merest fraction—and she found herself face to face with a stranger.

'I wish to see my father.' A blank look and a slow shake of the head. She suspected he did not understand a word she had spoken, but the name of Madam Chen should be familiar to him. 'Then tell Madam Chen I am here.'

The door began to close before the words were out of her mouth. With all her might she pushed it open and stepped quickly inside. The little man, who barely came up to her shoulder, grabbed at her sleeve, gesticulating wildly with his hands that she should leave. She shook him off, more annoyed than afraid at the reception. Just who did these people think they were to deny her access to her own father?

'Madam Chen,' she repeated, heading determinedly across the floor towards the curtain.

'Yes, Miss Granville. I am here.'

Where she had come from Dominy did not know, but suddenly she was coming towards her, moving with the same uncanny stealth as Weng had in Beau's office the day before. She wore a tight-fitting dress of jade green, fastened high at the neck, a shapely calf revealed beneath the slit skirt. The sleek black hair was swept back from the impassive features into a large coil at the nape of her neck and adorned with a tortoiseshell comb, which was a work of art in itself. She looked so elegant and composed compared to the woman she had first seen that Dominy was momentarily taken aback.

'And why do you find it necessary to visit me a second time and disrupt the peace of my establishment? I thought I had made it clear you are not welcome here.' The effrontery of her words brought fierce colour to Dominy's cheeks.

'I want to see my father. I demand to see him.'

'He is not here.'

'I do not believe you. He was at the Devil's Rest last night. Where else could he find shelter but here? If you do not let me go to him I shall go for the assistance of a policeman.'

'The police have no jurisdiction here.' Madam Chen's full lips deepened into a smile. 'They will not set foot here. They know we have our own way of life, our own laws, and we deal with our own when it becomes necessary.'

'My father is not one of you,' Dominy retorted, her tone rising as she fought to control anger and, now, a growing fear rising inside her. This could not be happening to her!

'He is now. By his own choice. And he does not want to see you again.'

Nothing, Dominy had promised herself, would part her from her father's side ever again. That he would reject not only the help she was offering, but also her was inconceivable.

'You are lying.'

Madam Chen's eyes narrowed to sharp slits. They were as black as jet. Dominy had the feeling those long red talons that slipped from the wide sleeves of her dress would like to have scratched her eyes out for such rudeness.

'So be it. It will be better to hear it from his own lips.'

She was led down the same corridor as the day before. The sweet odour she had noticed the first time was more pungent today, causing her to wonder what went on behind those other doors she had passed. She had once heard her father remarking to a friend on the pitiful conditions of the people who frequented the opium dens in the poorer parts of London, mostly around the dock areas. How they smoked themselves into insensibility with aromatic herbs lavishly mixed with powders that both stimulated the mind and drove them crazy. How continued use of these Oriental drugs brought about a dependency that ruled their lives until the day they died. A shudder ran through her. It did not go unnoticed.

'There is no need to be afraid. You are under the protection of someone whom I do not wish to offend, even though your interference is of great annoyance to me.'

Dominy stepped through the door Madam Chen opened for her, expecting to find her father in much the same condition as she had left him the day before. Instead she found herself standing in what appeared to be a large store-room. On all sides were large packing cases and boxes. There were sacks of flour and huge canisters which might have contained oil or water. Several Chinese men were unpacking a crate. Madam Chen clapped her hands, and without a word they filed out of the room—except for one man.

Dominy caught her breath as the stooping figure straightened and she found herself looking into her father's face. But the difference in him! His beard and moustache were neatly trimmed. He was still very pale and the dark shadows beneath his eyes told her how exhausted he still was, but he appeared to be more in control of himself, and even smiled as she hugged and kissed him.

'Papa, you are looking so much better.'

'Madam Chen is to thank for that, my child.' His speech was still hesitant, as if it was necessary to think of each word before it left his mouth. 'I did not expect to see you again.'

'But of course you did. I told you I would come back today. I am going to find us a place to stay—somewhere that we can be together and I can take care of you,' Dominy said enthusiastically. She did not have the heart to remonstrate with him over the stolen money. She was too pleased to see the change in him. 'You are not to worry about anything. Anything at all, do you hear? I am going to take care of everything—for us both.'

'No.'

Dominy could not believe her ears. Was he refusing to go with her? What kind of influence did the woman possess over him? Did he owe her money too? Perhaps she was threatening him in some way?

'I don't understand. I want to take you away from this horrible place. I want us to be together—as we planned at the château,' she protested.

'We are not at the château now, child. Those were dreams, not plans, and we both know they will never come true. I shall stay here. Madam Chen has shown me the road to inner peace and tranquillity of the soul. It is better I stay with her—better for us both.'

'I think she has given you something to dull your mind,' Dominy returned, taking one of his hands in hers. For a moment his fingers curled about hers as if seeking reassurance, then were quickly withdrawn.

'I have made my decision, Dominy. Please go now and leave us alone. It will be better if you do not return here. You have a different life waiting for you. I have heard a certain influential young gentleman has taken quite a fancy to you.'

'If you are referring to Austen LaMotte he has shown

me great kindness since I arrived. But for him I would have had nowhere to stay, would I, Papa, because you had squandered all the money given to you by Grandmère?' Dominy regretted the words the moment they were out of her mouth, but she was feeling hurt and confused at his rejection of her. How could it have all been for nothing? There was no warmth in his eyes, or in his voice. She could tell herself he was ill, but deep in her heart she knew he meant what he said. He did not want to be with her! What had brought about this total lack of affection when once they had been so close? Since the death of her mother he had depended on her for comfort, consolation when despair overcame him, hope when pondering on the future. How could he discard her as if she were no more than a stranger?

'As you say, I squandered all our money. I am not worthy of your love or your pity any more. I want to be left alone, here, with people who understand my weaknesses.'

'Understand?' Dominy fought back the bright tears that glistened in the depths of her eyes. 'How can you say I do not understand you? Have I not stood by you in all this ghastly mess? Am I not here so that we can start afresh where no one knows what has happened to us in the past?'

'I have made that impossible—and that is the cross I must bear for the rest of my days,' Edwin returned gravely. He drew a sharp breath as if in pain, but when Dominy stretched out a hand towards him he stepped back out of reach. Madam Chen came to his side. He did not shrug off the hand she slipped beneath his elbow as support and Dominy felt the tears blind her. This woman, as impossible as it seemed, had taken her place in his affections. It was her he turned to, not his own daughter! 'Go away, please. Go back to where you belong——'

'I don't know where I belong any more, Papa. That's the irony of all this. I don't seem to fit into either world,' Dominy said through trembling lips. This was surely nothing more than a nightmare. She would awake at any moment and find herself in bed at the Majestic.

'Then find the one where you do belong. It's among people who share the same things as you, Dominy—a love of beauty, of music, of the good life. Your mother and I raised you to make some man a fine wife. Find that man—let him take care of you.'

'Marry——' Dominy choked on the word. She could have done that in France more than a dozen times had her grandmother had her way.

'People will soon forget your association with me. You can have anything you want just for the asking, believe me.'

'I do, Papa. I do.' But the price was far too high. Austen was willing to help her on his terms, and those were the total rejection of her father, to disassociate herself with him as he had with her. It should have been easy after the hurtful words he had spoken, but in her heart she knew it was impossible. He did not want her, but she would never stop being his daughter—and proud to bear his name. No one was going to take that away from her. Pride in herself was all she had left and it was the same pride that had sustained her all these months that now refused to allow him to know how deeply he had wounded her. 'It is worth thinking about, is it not? A fine house again, and a carriage? And a man rich enough to take care of my every need.'

'I must return to my work. The unpacking must be finished before the restaurant opens.' Edwin turned away from her and reached for another carton in the crate.

Dominy stepped forward, a last plea springing to her lips, but Madam Chen stepped between them.

'For his sake—and your own—do not come back, Miss Granville.'

'Is that a threat, madam?' Dominy had the most unladylike urge to slap her hard across the face. *She* was behind it all, but what motive did she have for parting a father and daughter? It was beyond her comprehension. She felt sure everything her father had said had been rehearsed beforehand and that she had put the words into his mouth. Yesterday he had been almost incoherent!

'A friendly warning.'

Dominy backed away, hating her, her vision blurred by the tears that could be held back no longer. Somehow she found her way to the front door and out into brilliant sunshine—and then, blindly, she began to run. . .

'Are you satisfied?' Madam Chen demanded of the tall man who stepped into view from behind a stack of boxes, where he had been standing, unseen, unheard, throughout the whole conversation. 'She will not come back now.'

'If she does you will send word to me immediately.' Beau produced a cigar from an inside pocket and lighted it, his eyes cold as he stared at Edwin. 'He is to have nothing more to do with her. I want that plainly understood.'

'I realise what is at stake, you inhuman monster.' Edwin spat the words at him and then sank back against the packing case, suddenly exhausted.

'If it weren't for Madam Chen you would be in a gaol cell now, so count yourself lucky. You will do exactly as she tells you. If you don't I'll see everyone you owe money to knows where you are—and when they come to get you I'll be the first in line. You have ruined enough lives, Granville.'

'He will behave himself,' Madam Chen said reassuringly. 'Our agreement still stands?'

'Dammit! The man isn't worth it,' he ejaculated fiercely. 'Why this man?'

'There is gentleness in him—and great sorrow. He has suffered. Most of it he brought on himself, but this he now accepts. When he accepts what he has become, then he will have cured himself. It is a pity he does not have the courage of his daughter.'

'Courage is the last thing she is going to need,' Beau replied with a bitter laugh. 'I have a friend who is very capable when it comes to helping young ladies forget their problems. Within a week I guarantee he will have set her up in a house somewhere. You heard her say it is what she wants.'

'Perhaps the gods have other plans for her.'

'Then they had better work fast. Austen does not allow the grass to grow under his feet when he's out to get something he wants.'

'You are like her father—blind. Come, we shall take tea before you leave and discuss our agreement in more detail.'

'It stands only so long as you keep Miss Granville away from her father. Remember that. That way I shall discover once and for all what manner of woman she is.'

The carriage was not where she had left it, and Dominy had paid the driver the return fare when he had appeared nervous about remaining. She looked about her in panic. She did not know the way back to the hotel! All the streets looked the same and every face she looked into was inscrutable and blank. She had no choice other than to try to find her own way back. . .

The hand laid upon her arm was as light as a feather and instantly withdrawn as she turned. Weng stood at her side. As she stared in disbelief he said, 'I shall direct you back to the hotel. Please to follow me, Miss Granville.' He walked away, giving her no chance to argue. It was not difficult to keep up with him, for he took such small steps, head downbent, hands thrust inside the sleeves of his jacket.

Not once did he look back. Only when they came in sight of the Majestic did he stop and turn to her.

'You are quite safe now.'

'Thank—thank you, Weng.' Dominy began to search through her purse for a coin. 'I do not know what I would have done if you had not found me. . .'

'It is not wise to walk the streets alone. Very dangerous for pretty girls.' He bowed respectfully before her; the brown eyes held an almost amused expression. 'No payment is necessary. It was an honour to be of service.'

How had he found her? Dominy wondered as she entered the hotel and went upstairs. It was too much of a coincidence to believe he had just happened to have seen her in the street. And why should he have been helpful at all? Could he have some connection with Madam Chen? Was that how her father's hiding-place had been discovered by Beau? And, knowing where he was, why had Beau not confronted him for his money—or, worse, informed the authorities and had him arrested? As much as she detested the idea, she needed to have the answers to her questions, and that meant another visit to the Devil's Rest.

In her sitting-room she found Austen lounging in an easy-chair, a glass of wine at his fingertips. She was not sure she liked him invading her privacy without notice, but she was hardly in a position to protest, with him not only owning the hotel, but paying her bill there too. That she must remedy immediately.

'Dominy, where have you been? My dear, you look as if you have been running,' Austen declared, staring at her flushed cheeks. He took both her hands and drew her down into the chair beside him. 'Bring Miss Granville something cool,' he ordered the maid who appeared from the bedroom.

'I am a little warm,' Dominy confessed, grateful to sink into something soft. She waited until the maid had retired discreetly into the other room again before continuing. 'I went to see my father. . .'

'I was afraid that was the case. I came to apologise for my boorish behaviour last night. I should not have left you alone. I suppose your head is now filled with fresh ideas how to make a new life for you both. . .if that is so then my coming here has been a waste of time. You know I will do anything I can to help you, Dominy, but not that worthless. . .parasite,' Austen said gravely. 'What is it? Have you been crying? What has that man done to you now?'

Dominy searched frantically in her purse for a handkerchief as fresh tears sprang to her eyes. Austen supplied a large one of white linen and pressed it into her hand, his expression softening as he slipped an arm around her shoulders. He sensed she was more vulnerable at this moment than she had been since she had discovered her father's dilemma—and if he could turn it to his advantage he was going to do so.

The words were halting at first as she told him of her visit to the Floating Moon and the terrible, crushing rejection she had suffered at the hands of the person who was more important to her than anyone else in the world. And then they flowed like a torrent. Bitter recriminations against her own helplessness. . .the friends who had deserted them. . .the loss of her beloved mother. . .the father whom she still loved, despite his weaknesses, his betrayal of family and honour. When at last she fell silent Austen fully understood for the first time since meeting her the anguish and heartache she had carried with her for so long, locked away behind that polite smile, and his determination to make her his multiplied a hundredfold.

'I am so sorry. . .' Dominy withdrew from his embrace as if only just aware of the comforting arm about her. She dabbed the last of the wetness from her eyes and stood up. 'I must look a mess. Please excuse me for a moment.'

'Go and put on that pretty hat you were wearing when you came in and I'll take you out to lunch,' Austen said with a smile. 'No argument. You need cheering up. I promise we will not discuss your father—only you. It is you I am interested in,' he added candidly.

'I wish you were not. I—I think of you as a friend. . .but. . .'

'Friendship is the beginning of most worthwhile relationships. Besides, I have something to tell you which I think you will be interested in now. Lunch first, then we shall talk about the future—your future.'

Her future? Dominy was sure that he intended to be part of that, whatever she said to the contrary. She found it impossible to even consider the future without including her father, but he had decreed that was how it must be. She was alone now. . .and yet not alone. Not if Austen LaMotte had his way.

Austen took her to a quiet little restaurant in a side-road near Market Street, owned by a jovial tubby Italian who bowed them to a corner booth and sent the waiter across with a bottle of wine before they had time to glance at the menus.

'At night couples queue all evening to get a table in here,' he told her, noticing how she relaxed visibly in the friendly atmosphere. 'Renaldo is a Count, or so he tells everyone. He was forced to flee from Italy after killing a man in a duel. He struck it rich and went home to claim the hand of the woman he loved, only to discover she had married another man, twice her age and richer than Renaldo was. In disgust he came back to San Francisco and opened this place. Look over there. Today you are dining in the presence of a Count and an Emperor.'

'An Emperor!' Dominy exclaimed in disbelief. 'Here?'

Of the ten or so people in the room, she could see no one who would fit that description. Austen motioned discreetly to a booth opposite, where a waiter was hovering over a middle-aged man in a blue military uniform with somewhat tarnished gold epaulettes. Beside him lay a beaver hat sporting a long feather and some kind of rosette. A cane and an umbrella rested near his feet.

'Emperor Norton.' Austen's voice was lowered so that it did not carry beyond their table. 'His real name is Joshua A. Norton. He came to San Francisco around '49 with forty thousand dollars, or so the story goes, and in ten years he had increased that amount to almost three hundred thousand. But a disastrous financial investment caused him to lose everything. It turned his mind, poor man. He believes the California Legislature has elected him Emperor of the United States. . .'

'And. . .and people allow him to believe it is true?' Dominy whispered, not knowing whether or not to believe such a fantastic tale.

'He is harmless. . .and well liked, for all his strange notions. He can dine at any restaurant, drink in any saloon and never pay a cent. Occasionally he will write a personal cheque for the staggering sum of fifty cents and someone will honour it—a tradesman or even a banker. I don't think anyone who had known him can imagine not seeing him striding down the street, greeting his subjects with great dignity. It's a ritual we have all grown accustomed to over the years.'

'A very romantic story, or a complete fabrication,' Dominy said, her lips twitching in a smile she could not suppress. 'Thank you for trying to cheer me up.'

'What do you intend to do now? You must start to make some definite plans, you know.'

'I intend to find work of some kind,' Dominy replied without hesitation, and Austen's eyes registered shock at the suggestion. Quickly she added, 'What little money my grandmother gave me is now gone because of my father. I must find something, but. . .' It was a terrible thing she was about to admit. After all the careful schooling, the years of being raised as a lady, she was fit for one thing only—marriage! 'I am not trained for anything.'

'There is no reason for you to consider employment. I don't see why things cannot continue as they are. You have given yourself no time to accept what has happened to you.'

'That is impossible. I must be independent—I need to be.'

'I have tried to understand this very unnatural streak in you, but it is difficult. Wait a moment. . .' his brows creased into a thoughtful frown '. . .I have just remembered something. You are fluent in French, and I heard the other night of a family who require a tutor for their two daughters. It would be an ideal position for you, in a pleasant house with people of good background. And near to me,' he added meaningly. 'I shall arrange an introduction if you think it would suit you. But promise me you will do nothing until I have.'

'Very well.' Dominy's hopes soared unexpectedly at the news. She suspected he had not just remembered it, but that this had been the reason he had brought her out to lunch. 'It would be wonderful—if you really think they would like me?'

'My dear Dominy, you underestimate yourself. I am sure you will not only be able to teach those two monsters to master the French language, but will instil in them some refinement. I shall call on Mrs Buchanan this afternoon, and let you know later this evening the day and time she can see you. Now let us forget the daunting prospect of you shut away all day, labouring to teach two horrors the finer points of life, and enjoy our meal.'

By the time Dominy returned to the Majestic she had grown quite excited at the prospect. The position would pay well, Austen had assured her, and she would live in at the house, which was scarcely a stone's throw from his own residence. That meant she could save most of the money, she realised, for she would need little for herself and, with the clothes she already possessed, she would not feel out of place within the Buchanan household.

Before she went to bed that night she took out the necklace of rubies and diamonds and laid it around her neck, a smile lighting up her features as she regarded her reflection. Now she would not have to even consider selling it to survive. She touched the cold stones to her cheek, the smile deepening as she imagined herself clad in some magnificent white creation of lace and satin, kneeling at the steps of the altar in the tiny chapel which adjoined the château. A dream—only a dream. . .but, while the necklace was still in her possession, dreams were still possible.

For the next three days she allowed herself the indulgence of accepting Austen's offers to lunch and dinner whenever he was free, and on the third evening he took her to the opera. She sat beside him in a box, now accustomed to the attention that was always paid to her whenever she was in his company. Many times her thoughts strayed as she listened to the beautiful rendition of a Verdi opera, performed by a visiting Italian company. Tomorrow afternoon Austen had arranged for her to have an interview with Mrs Buchanan. She had been pointed out as being present that evening in his mother's private box, directly opposite them.

Curious eyes and eager ears had watched and listened to the encounter in the foyer when Elizabeth LaMotte, glittering from head to the hem of her Parisian gown with jewels, had greeted her son's companion with a smile and said once again that she hoped Miss Granville would soon pay her a visit. Dominy was quite taken aback by her friendliness and she wondered why Austen had whisked her away before anything else could be said.

Mrs Buchanan had taken a long, scrutinising look at the slender girl wearing a deep violet silk gown, the brown hair swept back from the finely boned features and adorned not with combs or jewels, but a single white gardenia, and then she, too, smiled before moving on. Dominy prayed she had liked what she had seen and that the smile had indicated approval of Austen's selection. Tomorrow she would know. She sensed, although he said not a word, that Austen had been pleased with the encounter and the way she had been greeted. Again Dominy found herself wondering why everyone considered his mother such an ogre. She seemed a very nice person and was, after all, concerned for her only son.

As the carriage turned into the driveway just before three in the afternoon Dominy glimpsed Austen's house off to the left. It was easy to pin-point because of the towering poplars on both sides and the tall chimney turrets that dominated the skyline.

The Buchanan house was situated at the top of a steep incline and was one of the earliest places to be built in this area, constructed mainly of seasoned timber brought in from the enormous redwood forests outside San Francisco. The family had come originally from Scotland when the discovery of gold had brought a feverish influx of thousands, flocking from all over the world into a small, hitherto uninteresting part of the country, and their present considerable fortune had begun to amass with three simple wagons hauling supplies to the diggings of the miners. Over the years the mud-sodden streets of flourishing San Francisco had become paved with gold, and Buchanan Enterprises, which dealt with everything from hardware to haulage, was expanding to other parts of the country.

After all Austen had told her, Dominy felt as if she

had known them for years. Certainly she had no apprehensions about facing Mrs Buchanan. As she alighted from the carriage and smoothed down her skirt the front door opened and a smartly clad Negro manservant came down the steps to meet her. A flicker of surprise registered in the black eyes as if he had not been expecting anyone so elegant and composed.

'Miss Granville?'

'Yes. Mrs Buchanan is expecting me.'

'I have been instructed by the mistress to tell you the position has been filled, miss, and therefore the appointment has been cancelled.'

'But. . .I do not understand. . .' How could it have been filled? Austen would not have sent his carriage to collect her well before time if he had been aware of this. She stood on the steps, wishing that the ground would open up beneath her feet and swallow her—so great was her embarrassment.

'I have conveyed the message given to me by Mrs Buchanan not ten minutes ago, miss.'

The man turned back into the house. The door closed, leaving her silently fighting with a conflict of emotions. Turned away as if she were a nobody! The Buchanans might be wealthy, but they had no manners! Not even an apology for her wasted journey. Anger engulfed her at such outrageous treatment. Combined with this was the shattering of her high expectations which threatened to once more plunge her into confusion. Would her future never be secure again?

'What do you wish to do now, miss?' Austen's coachman asked as she slowly turned back to the carriage. She resumed her seat, opened her parasol and stared down at him, her eyes hard with suspicion. He would not look at her! Had he known what was awaiting her? Had Austen known? What cruel trick had been played on her? She took a deep breath, choking back any kind of recrimination. He was only a servant and did what he was ordered.

'Take me back to the hotel. I shall not need you after that,' she said coldly, and settled back in her seat. Whoever had devised this little charade, the coachman would not be reporting back to them that she had in any way been affected by the episode.

Some sixth sense made her feel she was under observation. Altering the angle of the parasol, she swept her eyes upwards to the upper floors of the house as the carriage moved off. There, framed in one of the windows, was Mrs Buchanan and another woman—Elizabeth LaMotte.

Dominy's breath caught in her throat. Now it was clear to her why she had not been snubbed last night at the opera. Austen's mother had arranged this humiliating moment. She had warned Dominy, as she had doubtless warned other women in her son's life, to depart from it as soon as possible—or face the consequences. If she continued to accept Austen's friendship Dominy knew her life would be made unbearable. How dared she try to dictate to her?

'Beneath the carefully cultivated young lady. . .there is a devil waiting to be unleashed. . .' Her grandmother's words returned to her as the carriage turned into Market Street. She felt it rising in her now, daring her to fight back and lead her own life. If she continued to be seen with Austen his mother would waste no time spreading the news of Dominy's father, if she had not already. And the fact that the girl her son chose to escort had no money of her own. Overnight Dominy would be branded a scarlet woman, her reputation ruined. It was a prospect she could not face, but one day, she promised herself, Elizabeth LaMotte would be forced to accept her as an equal.

'What do you mean—filled?' Austen ejaculated, tossing the flowers he had brought with him carelessly into a chair. 'Out. Leave us alone,' he wheeled on the maid waiting to take his hat and gloves, and she scuttled into the bedroom without them. 'I am waiting for an answer, Dominy. What happened this afternoon?'

Dominy finished pouring him a brandy. She added a little water and handed it to him with a shrug of her shoulders. She did not look angry, or sad, or even puzzled by the cancellation of the interview, but in the depths of her eyes Austen glimpsed a flicker of something he did not understand. Why was she so calm when it had been so important to her to find a position?

'I suggest you ask your mother for an answer. I do not have one,' she answered coolly, sinking down into a chair by the window. 'She was at the house when. . .when Mrs Buchanan's message was delivered to me on the front steps—as if she were giving instructions to some tradesman! I shall not forget the insult. Ever!'

'Nor shall I. This is the last time she interferes in my affairs. My dear, I cannot apologise enough. I was so sure the Buchanans would like you.'

'Obviously Mrs Buchanan is more interested in keeping your mother's friendship. It is regrettable that she is unable to make up her own mind.'

'I shall speak with her this evening.' Austen could see the plans he had been making rapidly slipping away from him. Damn his mother! As if she had any right to pass judgement on others!

'No.' The sharpness of Dominy's tone arrested him in mid-speech. 'I do not want your charity or hers, Austen. I shall find work on my own.'

'There is no need—if you will consider a proposition of mine.' He came to sit beside her and leaned across to pat the hands folded loosely in her lap. For a moment he hesitated, then said decidedly, 'Hear me out before you give me an answer. In no way are my words intended to hurt or insult you, but I must say them for your own good. This afternoon may be a blessing in disguise. How my mother got wind of it I don't know, but I promise you I will find out and she will regret the pain she has brought you. I think you have taken it rather well, but I know you feel slighted and you have every right.'

'Austen, what are you trying to say? I would rather be alone this evening, if you don't mind. I have so much to think about.' Dominy did not want to hurt his feelings, but she had made up her mind, and she was afraid that if he lingered her resolve would weaken.

'Very well, I shall come straight to the point. I do not

want you to stay here at the Majestic any longer. Your position—not mine—will become intolerable if you do. Tomorrow I shall find a comfortable little house somewhere for you. Leave everything to me,' he added quickly as Dominy stiffened in her chair. 'I shall engage servants to run it for you. You shall have your own carriage and I shall open accounts for you at any place here that you wish.'

'And you will visit me when your other family duties do not require you to be elsewhere. Just what will my duties be, Mr LaMotte?' She sprang to her feet, incensed by the suggestion. 'To provide companionship? What else, I wonder? If this had been tossed at me by Mr Beautrellis I could have understood it. . .but you!'

'Listen to me, you proud little fool.' Austen did not mean to snap at her, but her reaction was not what he had expected. A certain caution perhaps, but not an outright refusal. If she did not accept it, what would she do? 'You have nothing here in San Francisco. Nowhere to go. I want to take care of you. Why is that so terrible? You will be independent.'

'I shall be a kept woman.' As she was now, with him paying her hotel bills. It suddenly dawned on her that her reputation had been in shreds since the first moment she had stepped inside the Majestic. He was right in his assumption that she could not remain, but she would not sell herself for money! 'You are right—I am proud. It is all I have left. No one, not you or your mother or the people of this hateful place, is going to take it away from me. Please go now, Austen. Go back and tell your mother she has won—for the moment.'

'Everyone has their price, Dominy.' He knew the words were the worst he could ever have uttered as a fierce light blazed in her eyes. The coldness which settled across her face chilled him and made her more inaccessible than she had been before. 'Think about my offer tonight. We shall have lunch together tomorrow and you can give me your answer then. I will not accept a refusal now.' He gave a rueful smile at the flowers crushed beneath his cane and hat. 'There are more important things than flowers—more important than pride. I hope by tomorrow you will have realised that. Goodnight, my dear.'

'Goodbye, Austen.'

She stepped back as he took her hand, and she thought he intended to kiss her. He let go of it and turned to the door, pausing on the threshold to look back at her and remember what he was leaving behind. Why had he not brought some expensive jewel instead of stupid flowers? He had blundered badly, but then, he had never been affected in this strange manner by any woman before.

'I shall never say goodbye to you, my dear Dominy. I am as obstinate as a long-eared mule and I always get what I want. I want you, whatever it takes to have you.'

Dominy stood for a long while, staring after him, as if in a trance. He had offered her all she had ever had in her life before and she had refused it. A home again, servants—and money not only for herself, but to pay off her father's debts. He would never know what she did with it. And in return. . .how difficult would it have been to be his mistress, for she had no doubt that was in his mind? He was attractive, good company and, she believed, he did care for her in a selfish way. But to lie beside him in his arms and allow him to make love to her, knowing that only her submission to his demands kept a roof over her head. . . Even the decision she had made before he had arrived must be better than that!

She went into the bedroom and changed into a black and white checkered dress with a figure-hugging matching jacket. The maid looked startled when she instructed her to repack the trunks with all her clothes.

'Madam is planning to leave?'

Dominy did not know if she had overheard Austen's proposal. It did not matter either way. If she had she would think it had been accepted, and by the time the mistake was discovered Dominy would have left the Majestic without hindrance.

As she pulled on her gloves it felt as if the floor moved beneath her feet. The girl gave a cry as the windows began to rattle and the mirror on the wall tilted at a precarious angle. Dominy tottered backwards and grabbed at the bedpost to steady herself. Was she going mad? Everything was moving. . .

'What is happening. . .?' She heard something crash to the floor in the other room, and then all was still again. She laid a hand against her heart and found it racing wildly.

'An earth tremor, madam. They happen sometimes. . .especially in the bay area. No one knows why. We just thank God when it's over. This was a mild one.' She looked startled when Dominy bent to retrieve her fallen gloves and purse. 'You are not going out? It might not be safe.'

Safer out there on the streets than inside the Majestic, Dominy thought, reassuring the maid that she was only going down to the restaurant. People crowding in the doorway stepped back to allow her to pass through, wondering at her determination to go out when others were not daring to venture a foot. Dominy felt a strange atmosphere surrounding everything as she started off in the direction of the Devil's Rest. It would be dark soon and she wanted to reach it before then. Passers-by jostled her, staring up at the buildings flanking them as if expecting one to topple on them without warning. Mothers carried their children or held tightly to their hands so that they could not stray. Street vendors had abandoned their carts leaving their wares unattended. Panic was written on every face that passed her, making her grow more apprehensive as each moment went by. But if she had waited. . .if Austen had returned. . . Desperation spurred her on when her steps began to falter. She paused to get her bearings. As she turned a corner and saw the scarlet-painted sign ahead she breathed a sigh of relief. What lay ahead for her was more alarming than any earth tremor could be. Ahead was the detestable Mr Beautrellis, of whom she must ask a favour. The words would choke her. She remembered the last time she had tried to approach him. But circumstances decreed she could not turn back this time.

She was only a few steps from the awning when the

ground began to shake beneath her feet. More violently than in those few minutes in the hotel, which had been alarming enough. She was flung against the side of a building, and watched in horror as further down the street a wrought-iron balcony gave way and plunged on to the pavement, followed by shattered glass and the remains of a window-frame.

People came flooding out of their houses in various states of undress. The air was full of screaming and shouting, voices so filled with terror that she was momentarily frozen against the wall, not knowing what to do. A wagon careered down the street, no driver at the reins, as she began to run in the direction most people seemed to be going, which was towards the open square ahead. There was so much noise that she did not hear the warning shout from behind, running blindly like everyone else, seeking an escape from whatever horror was about to descend on them.

A man came leaping down the steps to one side of her. A scream was torn from her lips as she was bodily thrown to the ground, a fraction of a second before the wagon ploughed into the men and women at the end of the street, scattering them in all directions, leaving behind it dead and injured as it continued on its trail of destruction. Strong arms lifted Dominy into a sitting position. She searched frantically for her purse and the handkerchief it contained to wipe the dust from her face and inside her mouth. She felt as if every bone in her body had been broken but knew, had she not been thrown to one side, she would have been beneath those death-dealing wheels. She ran a hand over her eyes to clear them so that she could see the face of the man who had saved her and thank him.

'Are you hurt?' Beau ran impersonal fingers over her arms and legs, and tilted back her head. 'A grazed cheek. You were lucky. You choose the damnedest times to come visiting, milady.'

'You!'

'I know you would have preferred to be in Austen's arms, but he seems to be otherwise occupied at the moment or he would not have allowed you to wander around this district alone. Can you walk? We have to get out of here; this isn't over yet. . .'

His voice was drowned by a thunderous roar that seemed to come from directly overhead. He was on his feet in an instant, pulling her up after him. She stumbled and fell against him as something heavy hit her from behind. Pain tore through her as Beau attempted to lift her. Her last recollections were of the look of horror on his dark face, the smell of tobacco on the shirt beneath her cheek, and then it was as if the whole world just collapsed upon them. . .

CHAPTER FIVE

DOMINY was not in her room at the Majestic. The walls were panelled in wood and there were louvred shutters across the windows instead of curtains. By the light of the oil lamp burning on the bedside table she could see the furniture was large, again of oak, and a heavy brass-bound chest stood against the far wall, with some clothes tossed carelessly on top of it.

Dominy was suddenly wide awake. Her clothes! She was not. . . Her fingers encountered only bare skin beneath the sheet that covered her. Someone had undressed her. Dear heaven—not him! She tried to sit up, but as a knife-like pain seared her back she sank on to the pillows again with a moan.

'So you are back in the world of the living again.' Beau stood in the open doorway directly in her line of vision, rubbing his hair with a towel. Water still glistened on his naked shoulders and chest. She looked away, hating how the sight of him returned another memory to her mind—one she had tried very hard, and unsuccessfully, to erase. 'I've had you looked over by a doctor. He assures me you will be fine in a day or two. A few bruises, but you were lucky. That careering wagon killed a mother and her two children and put four more people in hospital. A good thing it was only a minor quake.'

'A minor. . .' Dominy could not believe he talked of what had taken place so calmly. She had been terrified out of her wits and so had everyone else she had seen. 'It was awful. The worst experience of my life. I never want to go through it again,' she said weakly.

'Then I suggest you leave San Francisco on the first available boat. The doctor left some sleeping powders. I think you should take one and get some rest,' he added casually.

'Stay—here? Overnight?' Dominy stared at him as if he had taken leave of his senses.

'I am not allowing you to wander the streets alone, and I am needed elsewhere at the moment, so just be a good girl and do as you are told.' As he turned back into the other room Dominy was seized with the idea of wrapping herself in the sheet and grabbing up her clothes, but even as her fingers curled about it a blonde-haired girl came into the bedroom carrying a tray. As she set it down Dominy recognised her from the downstairs bar-room—and recalled Weng had addressed her as Maisie. She stared dubiously at the glass of milk held out to her. She knew she was in no condition to go anywhere tonight, she could hardly move, but pride forbade her to acknowledge the fact in front of the man who reappeared, fastening the front of a dark blue shirt.

'I have to talk to you—now. It cannot wait. And alone.'

Maisie threw Beau an amused look. 'She thinks she's still at the Majestic, giving orders to the hired help.' She banged the glass down on the tray so violently that some of the milk spilled out on to the polished surface of the table. 'Serve yourself, spoilt little rich girl. I have better things to do than wait on the likes of you. Some of us have to work for a living.'

She flounced out of the room, slamming the door after her. Beau came to the end of the bed and regarded Dominy, his hands on his hips, his eyes narrowed to sharp angry slits at her high-handed manner.

'Around here we take time out for a "please" and "thank you" when someone does us a favour. Maisie isn't a servant. She was just trying to be kind. What is so important that it cannot wait until morning? After one of these quakes there are always people needing help, and their problems are going to be far more unpleasant than anything you have to worry about.'

'I—I have to find some kind of work. . .and new lodgings. I cannot afford the Majestic.' Dominy knew that if she paused to think of what she was going to ask of him her courage would disappear. As it was, she could not look into those glittering pale eyes.

'I can offer you both, you know that. Although I am surprised Austen has not suggested something which would be of satisfaction to you both. Or perhaps his offer did not come up to your expectations,' he added as the colour rose in Dominy's cheeks until they were a fiery red.

As clear as that night was still in Dominy's mind, so was it in his—the warmth of her skin as he had crushed her against his chest, the perfume of her hair, the mounting realisation, as he had plied lips that had at first resisted him then been almost child-like in their response, with burning kisses, that she was by no means the experienced woman of the world he had at first believed her to be.

'My friendship with Austen is none of your business,' she returned coldly.

'He must have said something to bring you here in such a hurry. Or maybe it was someone else. . .' Beau said and knew by the tightening of the soft mouth that his assumption was correct. 'The dragon lady has been at work again. I hoped he would stand against her this time. Perhaps you are not his ideal woman after all.'

'I hate you,' Dominy said in a low, fierce whisper.

'I can live with that. We will talk in the morning. I have to go out now; people are waiting for me.'

'I cannot stay here. I won't—unless you say you will help me find work. It is to your own advantage, after all,' she added as he turned from the door with a frown. 'My father has no money, so if your IOUs are to be repaid the money will have to come from me.'

'I might just pull you from that bed and put you over my knee,' Beau threatened, stepping away from the door. 'And then have Weng take you straight back to the Majestic. It would be worth losing the money just to hear you beg. You don't give orders here, milady, you take them, like everyone else does—or you get out. If you want me to help you, say "please, Mr Beautrellis".'

'Don't call me by that hateful name. . .' Dominy cried angrily. 'If I were a man I would call you out. . .'

'Let me make it easy on you.' His hand reached for something tucked in the back of his trouser waistband. She gasped as he tossed a long-barrelled pistol on to the bed, within reaching distance. 'Go ahead, pick it up. Use it. I am sure a jury of twelve men will not convict you of cold-blooded murder if you shed a few tears and tell them what a blackguard I was to you. How you came to me, desperate for my help, and I refused you because you were too ill-mannered to ask—instead of ordering.'

Dominy shrank back from the evil-looking object. She had never touched such a thing in her life, let alone fired one with intent to take a human life.

'So you are a coward too—I suspected as much. You can stay here tonight; I wouldn't turn a dog out on the streets to fend for itself, let alone a useless object like you. Weng will take you back in the morning.'

'No!' If he heard the sudden panic in her voice it did not reach his stony heart, and as the door closed after him Dominy sank back in the bed, shivering.

After a moment the tremors stopped, and she reached for the glass of milk, hesitating only briefly before consuming all of it. If she could sleep for a few hours. . . But as she began to drift away Beau's derogatory words came flooding back into her mind. A useless object was all he thought she was. She did not know how as she turned on her side and pulled the covers around her bare shoulders, but somehow she would prove otherwise to him.

When she awoke the next morning it was impossible to believe that the nightmare of a few hours ago had really happened. The shutters had been opened, and sunshine streamed through the windows on to the polished floor. Her clothes, washed and pressed, were laid over a chair. Beside these was a silk wrap and slippers in the most vivid shade of pink Dominy had ever seen. Cheap and tasteless, was her first thought as she tentatively climbed out of bed and, finding that, although a little stiff, she could once more stand without pain, she wrapped it around her and thrust her feet into the fluffy slippers. That was just the kind of remark Beau would be expecting her to make, and if she was foolish enough to do so she knew he would send her packing without hesitation.

Outside the window she could still see some devastation remaining from the two tremors, which, although they had lasted only agonising minutes, had caused the collapse of a house immediately opposite the Devil's Rest. Men were still searching through the rubble for survivors, faces wet with sweat as they laboured with bare hands over the last remaining mound of bricks and broken furniture. Silent women stood watching not far away, some weeping, others dry-eyed, as they waited and prayed for some miracle to return a missing loved one to them.

Dominy's gaze wandered down the street. The building beside which she had stood, petrified with fear, when the ground had first begun to shake was also an empty shell. Nothing remained except two tall pillars, towering over chaos and perhaps death lying beneath them. Had Beau not appeared when he did. . . No matter how detestable he was, she could not ignore the fact that he had saved her life. She had been only seconds away from being crushed when the front walls had begun to disintegrate and crash down on to unfortunate passers-by, perhaps some, like herself, too terrified to have moved and saved themselves.

'Miss Granville. Breakfast is prepared for you in the sitting-room. Please forgive me, I did not mean to startle you.' Weng gave an apologetic smile as she caught her breath sharply, startled by the unexpected voice. 'When you are ready I will take you back to your hotel.'

'I shall not be returning there,' Dominy answered, following him into the adjoining room. 'I must speak to Mr Beautrellis. . .'

Beau folded the paper he had been reading and regarded her across the table. If he made some comment about her appearance she would hit him, she thought as she seated herself in the chair Weng pulled out for her.

'How do you like your coffee, Miss Granville?' Weng hovered by her elbow, waiting to serve her.

'I would prefer tea. . .if it is not too much trouble. With lemon.'

'It is no trouble. It will only take a moment to prepare.'

'Did you sleep well?' Beau enquired, helping himself to more coffee from the pot beside him.

'Yes, thank you. Mr Beautrellis——' she forced the words out through stiff lips '—we have never liked each other. . .surely you must realise how difficult it was for me to come here and ask for your help?'

'There you go again. . .assuming I must either like or be interested in you. My only interest is in the return of my money and, despite what you said last night, I can see little hope of you repaying it.'

'I will do any work that helps me wipe clean my father's debts.'

'I've told you how you can repay those,' Beau answered with a shrug of his shoulders. 'Work for me.'

'I would rather. . .'

'What?' He stared at her challengingly. 'Sell yourself on the streets? Offer your body in a Chinese crib?'

'You are disgusting to suggest such a thing to me,' Dominy gasped, horrified at the suggestion of such immorality.

'No, just realistic. Tell me, what can you do? Do you sing? Can you dance? There are plenty of jobs about for girls who can. I suppose you could work as a waitress, or in a kitchen. I don't suppose you can cook, but if you find yourself a sympathetic boss and are nice to him. . .' Weng brought Dominy's lemon tea and, as if understanding the personal nature of the conversation, retired immediately, leaving them alone. 'Well, milady, what are you capable of doing. . .if anything?'

Dominy was silent. She had no skills.

'My music teacher told me I have a passable singing voice—and I do play the piano very well,' she said defensively.

'But not the kind of music we are accustomed to

hearing on the Barbary Coast. Help yourself.' Beau motioned to the toast and butter in front of her, but she shook her head. 'Very well, then, go and get dressed. I'm going to take you on a tour of the coast. We will visit every saloon and dance hall where you could find work—if you are willing to accept the terms offered. Perhaps by this afternoon you will realise the only place for you is right here. And I can think of a couple of restaurants, a hotel and several coffee shops. Who knows? You could get lucky.'

'Anything would be better than working here,' Dominy said, rising. She lifted a hand to her loose hair. 'I shall be a while. . .'

'Leave it as it is. Believe me, that is the last thing anyone is going to look at,' Beau replied with a deep chuckle. 'Half an hour. We have a lot of ground to cover.'

And somewhere along the way she would find respectable employment, Dominy told herself resolutely.

'Have you seen enough?' Beau asked, drawing deeply on the cigar he had just lighted.

The carriage was halted on the rise of a hill. Dominy had been silent for over five minutes, staring at the array of broken-down shacks all around them. This was the notorious Telegraph Hill. The tumbledown houses were places of pleasure, he had told her, which in the early days of the city had been occupied by Chilean girls, who had plied their trade here and along the waterfront. With the growth of the city, much of the trade had moved to Portsmouth Square—he had shown her that place too on his guided tour—and the red-light district, where many blocks contained nothing but saloons, gambling halls and places of prostitution. Dominy had turned her face away from the sight of young girls, many no older than she was, lingering in the alleyways, trying to attract customers.

He had taken her to the Cobweb Palace, the strangest place she had ever seen. She had sipped a hot toddy of whisky and cloves—but had not finished it, remembering in time that she had not eaten anything—beneath a mass of cobwebs which festooned the interior. Around the walls were cages of every size and description, full of chattering monkeys and parrots. She had been stared at here as rudely as elsewhere they had been, but no man had accosted her. Only because of her companion, she suspected, who seemed to be known no matter where they went.

He had taken her to the Bella Union, a popular resort on Washington Street. Here floor shows were performed throughout the day, and it proved to be a favourite haunt of the town youngbloods. Dominy had felt herself grow quite hot when Beau had introduced her to the owner, a woman, and explained her desire to find work—and the first request she had made was for her to raise her skirts so that she could see her legs.

She had lost count of the places he had taken her to after that. Always it was the same. More was required of her than she was willing to agree to. Even the hotel owner had suggested that as well as the reception duties offered she would be expected to, as he had put it, 'accommodate' gentlemen in their rooms. She had fled from him, near to tears.

'You have proved your point, Mr Beautrellis,' she said bitterly. 'I am a useless object. Are you satisfied now?'

'I shall be satisfied when you agree to work for me, not before.' Beau ordered the driver to return to the Devil's Rest. 'You were never meant to wash dishes, or be someone else's servant.'

'Will it be any different working for you?' she challenged. 'I will not do anything dishonest—or wrong.' He had never said what he intended for her, and she was too frightened to ask after what she had seen this morning.

'You won't be asked to. My plans involve something rather special, and you are going to be the main attraction.'

'Am I allowed to know what they are?' She did not like the sound of that one little bit! She suddenly had a vision of herself looking like Maisie, in a low-cut scarlet dress, her long stockinged legs barely concealed by the short flounced skirt. Would she be expected to entertain his customers the way she supposed the other girls did? Drink with them, let them lay their hands on her? He would not—could not—ask that of her!

'All in good time, milady. Most of the girls lodge with Mrs Griffiths in the next street, but you'll be more comfortable if you stay where you are. I'll have Weng find some more feminine pieces of furniture to pretty the room up for you.'

'If that is to be the case then I would like a key for the door. I noticed it does not have one,' Dominy said firmly, and a wicked gleam sprang to Beau's eyes.

'You won't need that kind of protection in the Rest. No one will intrude on your privacy, including me—after working hours, that is. And if I did find you interesting—which I don't—a locked door would not keep me from you. You have a high opinion of yourself, don't you? I can see this is going to be the start of a beautiful friendship.'

'One I shall do everything in my power to end as soon as possible,' she retorted. She had made her decision; there was no going back now. As the carriage came to a halt before the Devil's Rest she saw a smile curve around Beau's mouth. Her uneasiness grew. If he would not supply a key then she would put a chair against the door tonight and every night she remained beneath his roof. He had given her good reason *not* to trust him.

'Weng, bring a bottle of champagne to my study,' Beau instructed with a broad smile as he came to greet them in the foyer.

'A celebration, Mr Beautrellis?' One of Weng's smooth eyebrows rose just a fraction.

'Of sorts. Miss Granville is coming to work for me. I shall want to talk to you later about some alterations to her room.'

'Mr LaMotte is waiting for you upstairs. Shall I bring the bottle up now?'

'Why not? I have never known him to refuse a drink

at any hour.' For a moment Dominy thought he was not pleased by the news of his friend's arrival.

As she followed him up the stairs she herself began to wish she did not have to see him again. Still smarting from his offer, she suspected another confrontation would only alienate her still further from the friendship they had shared so far.

'Beau, thank heavens, you've come back. Dominy is missing. . .she left the hotel yesterday just after the first. . .' Austen's voice trailed off in sheer disbelief as Dominy came through the door after Beau. 'I can see there is no need to be concerned; you are being well taken care of.' His tone became sarcastic as Weng entered directly after them with a tray holding the bottle of champagne and three glasses.

'It was important that I saw Mr Beautrellis,' Dominy replied, not knowing quite why she found it necessary to defend her actions. She had made her position quite clear to him and he had refused to accept the need for her to become independent.

She had wounded his manly pride, she realised, but he had shattered hers with his suggestion that she should become his mistress.

'Unfortunately she was caught in the next tremor, but there was no harm done, apart from a few bruises. We have had a very interesting morning,' Beau said cheerfully, reaching for the champagne as Weng melted away without a word. 'We visited most of your favourite haunts—drinking ones, that is.'

'I hardly think a tour of the Barbary Coast would be interesting for a lady of Dominy's background,' Austen replied. He had been wandering the streets for the past two hours, his fears for her safety growing. Her bed had not been slept in and her trunks were packed as if she was leaving—and she had vanished without a trace. He had subjected the poor maid to such withering reproaches that she had been reduced to tears. Likewise the manager had felt the sharp edge of his tongue, although he suspected the man's skin was too thick for his anger to have penetrated.

'The idea was my own,' Dominy said. She refused the glass Beau held out to her. Austen did also, then relented and accepted it. 'I wanted to find out for myself the kind of work I would be expected to do if I went looking for a job. The prospects were not very appealing.'

'Thank goodness you did nothing foolish,' Austen said, a relieved look crossing his face. 'I shall take you back to the Majestic and we can talk later this evening. We did not finish our discussion, if you remember?'

'But we did, Austen.' Dominy ignored Beau's enquiring glance. 'I gave you my answer. And I have found work. Here, at the Devil's Rest. Mr Beautrellis offered me a position and I have accepted it.'

'Preposterous. I will not allow it——!'

'Come now, Austen, she's over eighteen and quite capable of making up her own mind,' Beau interrupted, relaxing in the nearest chair. 'Why do I get the impression you have other plans, which she does not approve of? I am intrigued.'

'Please excuse me, I think I shall go and change,' Dominy said, moving towards the door which led to her room. Only as she began to open it did she realise she had no other clothes to change into, but that did not stop her. She had no wish to remain and listen to the two of them arguing over something which she had no intention of altering. Austen's motives for wanting her were as selfish as those of Beau. Each, in his own way, sought to use her. Had money been her prime concern Austen was offering her an easy way out of her problems. He called her name, but she ignored him and went into the bedroom and closed the door behind her.

'Leave her,' Beau said as his companion started in that direction, and something in his tone arrested Austen in mid-stride. 'She has made up her mind and you will not change it. Believe me.'

'Suddenly you are an expert on what she wants and does not want,' came the suspicious reply. 'Is our bet so important to you?'

'That has nothing to do with it.'

'From time to time you and I have been in competition

over a woman, but it's never been anything serious enough to affect the very strong friendship we have shared for years. So why are you trying to steal this one from under my very nose?' Austen demanded, swallowing his champagne without appreciation. Beau's nonchalant attitude both puzzled and annoyed him. One day he would learn to assess what went on behind that half-smile.

'Are you telling me you are serious about her? Ye gods! Have another drink and think what that would entail. . .going against your mother, for one. I believe she has already rendered a warning of her displeasure.'

'So you heard about that—I'm not surprised, I suppose. You seem to hear most things almost as soon as they happen, whether they are on the other side of San Francisco or not. Damn it, do you have a network of spies?'

'Something like that,' Beau grinned. 'You did not answer my question.'

'I have certain plans, as you correctly surmised. This is not the place for her, we both know that.'

'She obviously does not think what you have in mind will suit her either. What is it? A nice little place somewhere out of sight of Mother and friends?'

'That's being unfair. I don't intend to rush her into anything. I just want her to stop this stupid idea of finding work and repaying her father's debts. She will never do that.'

'She wants to try and she has the right to do so,' Beau returned with a shrug.

'If she were the gold digger you believe her to be she would have jumped at my offer,' Austen said pointedly.

'She still can, although I have my reasons for believing she could be holding out for something more. . .permanent.' Beau's thoughts flew back to the room at the Floating Moon and the conversation he had overheard between Dominy and her father. 'So long as I am repaid what is owed to me, I don't care what she does or who she is with.'

'I hear you have been buying up her father's IOUs. How many do you hold now? And why?'

'All of them. It is my way of ensuring repayment. If she defaults I go to the police.'

'I don't believe I am hearing this! You can afford the loss.'

'So can you—if you really like the girl. That was quite a neat little fiasco your mother arranged. She has not lost her touch. Be careful, my friend, she seems to be more than usually annoyed with you over this one.'

'She will discover—as you will—that when I find what I want I do not let go,' came the determined answer, which brought a sharp furrowing of Beau's dark brows. He would go to hell on a sleigh if Austen was not serious! 'I'm not going to pester her now, Beau, but I give you fair warning. . .I shall be back.'

'Any time. The doors of this place are rarely closed.'

'I don't mean to gamble. I shall see Dominy when I please.'

'If she wishes to see you.' Beau rose, stretching lazily, and divested himself of his restricting coat and cravat. 'I have work to do or I would invite you to stay. Why don't we get together Wednesday evening. . .just the two of us? It's been a while since you have sampled the delights of my cellar with me.'

'You wouldn't last the night,' Austen said, forcing a smile. Strange as it was, nothing could strain their friendship to the point where he no longer wanted the company of this man. Not even his determination to win over Dominy—and Beau's disregard for his intentions—seemed that important as he gazed into the dark features and saw the devil's own mockery gleaming in those pale glittering blue eyes. 'Wednesday—just the two of us—and, if I'm standing by dawn and you are not, I get that mare anyway.'

'I was thinking the same thing. Seven sharp. I'll have Weng line up a few bottles to start.'

Dominy sat on the edge of the bed and stared disbelievingly at her trunks. All her luggage had been brought from the Majestic while she and Beau had been out that morning. He had anticipated she would accept his offer! The voices continued in the other room for some while and, tempting though it was, she did not try to listen and hear what was being said. Should she unpack? She was staying, after all, but how could she wear the contents of the trunks in this place?

'You will be needing help to unpack, Miss Granville. May I suggest the assistance of my sister, Su Lin?'

When Weng brought her a lunch tray some while later she was still in a quandary what to do. She had not thought beyond finding work; now she was beginning to regret allowing herself to be talked into remaining here. She shook her head with a smile.

'I must begin to do things for myself now, but thank you for the kind thought, Weng.'

'I am sure Mr Beautrellis will not want you bothering yourself with such trifles. You will be far too busy.'

'Will I?' Dominy looked at him curiously. Doing what?

'I shall speak with him as soon as he is free. He thought you would prefer to eat in here while he is occupied, but he hopes that you will dine with him this evening. In the meantime I will send word to my sister that she is required.'

She was being treated with as much politeness and consideration as at the Majestic, Dominy thought as she sat down to eat, but, as she began to enjoy the light meal provided and relax after a frustrating morning spent in Beau's company, she gave up trying to fathom his reasons for providing such comforts for her. And yet it was to his advantage to ensure she did not want to leave. If she did he would never get his money back, and that was all he cared about.

Su Lin arrived in the early afternoon, a petite girl of about seventeen, with two long jet-black braids hanging down over her embroidered blouse. Weng apologised for the fact she could speak no more than a few words in English, as she had been in the country only a few months, but said that he had explained her duties.

When Maisie poked her blonde head around the door

an hour later she gave a low whistle of astonishment at the array of dresses and undergarments spread everywhere. Dominy, kneeling beside the chest of drawers, waited for a sarcastic comment as she sauntered in, skirt bouncing around her legs, and picked up a petticoat heavily embroidered with lace frills.

'Now what wouldn't I give for one of these. It would drive some of those boys from Nob Hill crazy.'

'Take it. It's yours. I have others,' Dominy said, and at once there was hostility on the painted face. Maisie would have been pretty without all the rouge and thick lipstick, she thought, determined not to be baited into an exchange of heated words. She would gain nothing by aggravating the people who worked here, whether she liked them or not.

'I don't need your charity! I may only come from a family of dirt farmers, but that doesn't make me any the less proud. I ain't got money, but I ain't in debt either, and my old man never owed anyone a cent.'

'I am going to repay Mr Beautrellis everything my father owes him,' Dominy said firmly. 'I have never owed anything to anyone before either, and I do not like it. If you cannot accept that and the fact I would prefer us to be friends rather than enemies then please go away.'

'Friends! You and me? You wouldn't be seen dead on the streets in my company,' Maisie scoffed, although she looked taken aback by the offer of friendship.

'Why not? We both work here now, do we not?' Dominy's gaze challenged the rebuff.

'Is that what you think—that Beau is going to put you to work here?' A broad smile spread across Maisie's face. 'He's a dark horse not telling you what is going on. And I owe you an apology. I thought you were—well, you know—just being kind to one of the lower classes.'

'You really are being most unfair to me,' Dominy protested. 'It is not my fault my parents were wealthy—or my grandmother. Look where I have ended up anyway—in a gambling house!'

'Not just any gambling house! One of the élite in San

Francisco, and you would never have a better boss. If you are in trouble Beau will always help you out.'

'Are we talking about the same man? Help is not exactly what he has offered me. More an ultimatum.'

'That's because you got on the wrong side of him to start with—or rather your father did. Beau has a heart of gold, but if anyone deliberately tries to cheat him then watch out. Sparks fly. He's a pretty dangerous character when the chips are down.'

'I am hardly a threat to his reputation,' Dominy returned with a shrug of her shoulders. 'I shall never change my mind about him. Not after what he has put me through. I loathe him.'

'Women either hate him or love him, usually the latter,' Maisie laughed, relaxing on the bed. It was obvious she no longer considered Dominy an outcast among them. Su Lin, who had been watching them carefully and, although unable to understand what was being said, had sensed the hostility in the atmosphere, now relaxed and continued to put Dominy's clothes away in the wall-length cupboard with a smile on her face.

Had she been sent as a maid or a watchdog? Dominy wondered.

'Tell me about this paragon of virtue,' she said, sitting back on her heels.

'Paragon of what? Oh, you mean Beau. I can only tell it as it is. Since I've been here—that's almost two years now—I've never had reason to want to leave. I won't until I have enough money to pay off the mortgage on my parents' place and take my mom away from that kind of life. It killed my pa last summer, and now it's killing her too. I reckon in another six months I shall have enough to go back to Wet Gulch and open the little dress shop I always promised her she would have. You've never seen stitching like hers. We'll never be rich, but we won't starve either, and that's all I care about. I know what it's like to go without food because rain has washed out the spring crops, or early snow has killed everything that should have been put away to tide us over the winter. Never again! I guess we are alike, you and I.

Both of us stubborn females when it comes to getting what we want.'

'You were going to tell me about Mr Beautrellis,' Dominy said, pleased to have someone to talk to. Although at the back of her mind there lurked a suspicion that all this attention was meant to lead somewhere. Was she expected to pour out her heart to Maisie, who would in turn report back to Beau everything that had been said? The more he knew about her, the easier it would be for him to manipulate her.

'Oh—yes, Beau. Well, as I said, I've never known him turn away anyone in trouble. Not in real trouble, I mean. When he first took over this place it was as crooked as the louse who had owned it before—Philippe Gascoigne. He cheated everyone. Beau cleared the place of all his hangers-on, closed up for a week, and when he reopened every table had been stripped and inspected. This is the cleanest place around, and everyone who comes here knows they will get a fair deal.'

'An honest gambler. That is something new.' Dominy was not convinced.

'Take what he has done for the people around here, then. He's always loaning money to different people. Ah Fong, to open his laundry. Mrs Potts to keep her boarding house going when her old man poisoned himself on wood alcohol. And Weng, to get his sister into this country. There's not a soul hereabouts who will have a bad word to say against him.'

'I have never seen that side of him,' Dominy admitted. It was so hard to accept that beneath that black exterior there beat a heart of gold. Stone perhaps.

'You ask your old man next time you see him about Madam Chen and what Beau has done for her. This last quake all but wrecked the Floating Moon—it was a bit of a dump anyway—and she wants to find new premises. I overheard them talking a little while ago. She's found two houses which need renovating, and Beau is going to lend her enough to turn one into a restaurant and the other a boarding house.'

Beau knew Madam Chen—that meant he had known

where her father was all along, and he had kept silent! Maisie mistook her silence to be astonishment at the news she had just delivered.

'See what I mean about him? But then, he and Madam Chen go back a long way. She first came to San Francisco with two sisters. They thought they were to stay with a relative, but the man sold them to the owner of a crib. You know—those places down near Fisherman's Wharf. I reckon that's where I could have ended up if Beau hadn't kept me on the straight and narrow. But that's another saga. . .I guess I'm boring you to death.'

'On the contrary, I find this insight into his character fascinating.'

'My, you do use fancy words, don't you? Where was I? Madam Chen. . .she was found in an alley by Weng about six years ago now. He brought her here and Beau gave her a job—and sorted out the men waving knives who came to take her back to the crib. Her sisters were dead and she just didn't care what happened to her any more. He soon put her straight. After a couple of months here she opened the Floating Moon, married a rich old man and paid him back every cent. After he died his sons made sure she didn't get any of his money, but she still had the restaurant. Until the other night. . . Boy, and I think I've had a rough life.'

And now Beau was going to lend her money again, knowing she was sheltering Dominy's father. It did not make sense. Why had he not gone to the police the moment he had discovered where he was hiding? He had made it quite clear that the return of his money was all that mattered to him, yet he did nothing about it when the opportunity arose. She would have it out with him that evening.

'I am going to put my feet up for a couple of hours.' Maisie yawned and stretched her arms above her head. 'Saturday nights are always the busiest. Don't worry if the noise keeps you awake—you'll get used to it in time.'

'I shall plug up my ears and make sure there is a chair against the door,' Dominy answered, and the other girl laughed aloud at the gravity of her expression.

'You need not worry about anyone bothering you. Beau wouldn't allow it. You are going to make him a lot of money. He will take care of you. Why don't you come down later on—before things get too hectic, I mean—and see how the other half lives?'

'I may just do that.'

What was going on? Dominy wondered as she continued to put away her clothes. Beau had promised she would be forced to do nothing illegal or wrong. Whatever he had in mind, she suspected she was the only one who did not know what it was.

When Su Lin left late that afternoon the bedroom was as tidy as a new pin. Most of Dominy's clothes had been pressed and hung in the cupboards, undergarments folded with loving care and placed carefully in one of the chests of drawers. There was nothing the girl was not prepared to do. Dominy felt so ashamed that she could not thank her in her own language. But later, when Weng came to light the lamps and close the shutters, he assured her his sister had been pleased to be of service and that no payment was required—or even considered. Nevertheless, Dominy decided that somehow she would find a way to repay the kindness shown to her, no matter how small the gesture.

'Does Mr Beautrellis have many people working for him here—besides the girls downstairs?' she asked curiously as the man turned to leave. The door to the sitting-room beyond was open, and she saw the table had been laid for dinner—gleaming silverware, crystal glasses and a spotless white tablecloth. And only two places. Obviously Beau did not expect a refusal to his invitation. Not that she could afford to antagonise him; there were too many questions to be answered.

'Apart from the young women who have employment in the downstairs bar and the gambling-room, there is myself, Su Lin and, of course, the restaurant staff. Six in all.'

'Restaurant? Where? I have not seen one.'

'I use the term broadly, Miss Granville. Mr Beautrellis is of the impression, and rightfully so, that a man who is in pleasant surroundings with excellent wines at his fingertips and the smell of succulent steaks in his nostrils will relax and not think twice about parting with his money.'

'Mr Beautrellis is quite a businessman.'

'This is not one of those places you will find on Montgomery Street. This is a respectable house and caters for only the best clientele. Mr Beautrellis *is* a gentleman.' Weng's tone was slightly reproving, making her realise he would having nothing said against the man he worked for. He obviously adored him. 'You are extremely fortunate to have his protection, Miss Granville. There were others—not as forgiving as Mr Beautrellis—who wanted to have your father thrown into prison should he not be able to repay the money he took from them. Which, as you are well aware, he cannot. Had my employer not taken it upon himself to reimburse them out of his own pocket that would have happened.'

Dominy's eyes widened as she considered the full implication behind his words. Beau had bought up all her father's IOUs. She was totally beholden to him and only him!

'Dinner will be served in one hour. Please be punctual. Mr Beautrellis does not like to be kept waiting, Miss Granville.'

A few minutes before seven o'clock Deminy opened the communicating door and entered the other room. She discovered that the sweet, pungent perfume which hung in the room came from a small pot containing what appeared to her to be no more than grey ashes, set in an alcove in one wall. Beside it sat a stoic-faced green jade idol. How she wished it could talk to tell her more about the increasingly confusing man with whom she had become involved.

She seated herself at the table, casting an experienced eye over everything laid out before her. The preparation could not be faulted. Whatever he was now, she could not ignore the fact that in the past Beau had experienced all the good things of life—and had not forgotten them.

He was not trying to impress her—he had no need; she was totally in his power. That was a daunting thought! She must not allow herself to relax for one moment in his company, for if she did she knew her thoughts would stray back to his kiss—and how pleasant she had found it to be.

Her eyes fell upon an envelope propped against one of the glasses beside the empty chair opposite her. It was addressed to a Mr Lance Beautrellis of the Devil's Rest, San Francisco. So now she knew his given name. She was seized with a sudden urge to reach out and see if there was a return address on the back, but even as she decided upon it the door opened and Beau came in.

'You look very elegant tonight, milady.' He smiled at her across the table as he sat down, as if they were old friends.

Elegant was exactly what she had wanted to look and was pleased she had achieved her aim. She had chosen a dark grey dress, cut low across the shoulders and quite plain. Her hair was swept back from her face and piled in a mass of curls on the crown of her head. A long grey ribbon held them in place, the ends trailing down to her bare shoulders. She wore no jewellery. She had known none was needed as she had gazed at her reflection. Poise and breeding she already possessed, and that was what really mattered.

A faint touch of mockery crept into her eyes as she replied coolly, 'I was raised a lady, Mr Beautrellis. My circumstances may have changed, but I have not. Do you always entertain your employees in such style, or am I to hear something unpleasant concerning the terms of my work here?'

'Have you considered I might be attempting to—shall we say—put our relationship on a better footing?' Beau's gaze rested momentarily on the slender hands on the linen cloth. He had noticed them before and thought how delicate they were. The fingers were long, the nails perfectly shaped. Tonight they were ringless. Deliberately, he suspected, and considered them a moment longer, graced with expensive rings, a bracelet of rubies—real, not imitation—around one creamy wrist.

'I am here because I have no other choice, and that is all there is to it. We share nothing other than your desire to have your money back. Mine is to have my father's IOUs returned to me—including all those you have bought from other people. Then I shall leave here as quickly as possible and forget you ever existed.'

'Straight back into Austen's loving arms?' Beau's brows rose quizzically. 'Somehow I cannot imagine him being faithful to those few short days you spent together. Unless you and he. . .' He paused meaningfully and watched Dominy's lips tighten.

'I am very fond of Austen, but that is all. . .there is nothing between us—such as you are suggesting.'

'Most girls would settle for less. If you are holding out for the gold band you are wasting your time. I've seen a variety of women come and go in Austen's life. Never once has he considered marrying any of them.'

And she was not interested in marrying Austen LaMotte, Dominy thought, but she knew she would not be believed if she said so. And Beau's continued invasion into her private life annoyed her. A smile touched her lips as Weng began to serve them with the soup.

'That was before he met me,' she murmured. 'Never underestimate a determined woman, Mr Beautrellis. And if he does offer me a wedding band I promise you will be the first to know. Now, do you not think we should discuss business?' Let him think what he liked!

'Why don't we enjoy our dinner first and then I'll tell you what is required of you? In fact I'll show you.'

He saw Dominy's poise momentarily falter at his words. He did not elaborate further and knew that throughout the meal she would be wondering what on earth he intended. It served her right for being too sure of herself.

'When did this arrive?' His sharp tone arrested Weng in the middle of pouring Dominy a glass of wine. It was the first time Beau had seen the letter. His attention until that moment had been centred on his companion.

'While you were dressing, Mr Beautrellis. It was delivered by hand—by a Mr David Lessington. He said you knew each other in Savannah.'

Beau nodded, frowning as he reached for the envelope. Dominy found herself holding her breath as she waited for him to open it. The perfume that wafted beneath her nose did not come from the incense burning behind her. Only a woman would use scented notepaper. To her disappointment Beau stowed it away inside his jacket and continued with his soup. At least she had discovered two more things about him: his name was Lance and he came from Savannah. But the enigma of the man behind the mocking façade still remained, although for a moment she was sure she had glimpsed pain in the depths of his eyes at the sight of the letter. She recalled that on the *Enchantress* river-boat he had told her he had killed a man in a duel over the favours of a woman, which was why he had been forced to leave his home. Was it the same one? Was she writing to plead with him to return to her?

Angrily Dominy thrust such thoughts from her mind and tried to concentrate on the meal. Lance Beautrellis meant nothing to her! His kisses had meant nothing! Why was it so difficult for her to dismiss him not only from her thoughts, but her dreams at night?

CHAPTER SIX

'WHERE are we going?' Dominy asked as Beau helped her into the carriage, which had arrived outside the Devil's Rest exactly on the stroke of nine. The dinner had been pleasant and unhurried and she had enoyed it immensely, although she would never have told him that. It would never do for him to begin believing she might like his company. And she did. It was no use denying it any longer.

'Are young ladies not raised to contain their curiosity?' he replied, settling down into the seat opposite.

'I am not a child, Mr Beautrellis. Please do not treat me like one.'

'Indeed you are not.' The pale eyes rested on her indignant features with an intensity that made her inwardly quiver. 'But if I was to treat you like a woman—now that might cause a few problems. You see, I have not forgotten how sweet and tempting those lips tasted that night we—I kissed you. And, if I remember correctly, you did not find it so distasteful an experience.'

'On the contrary, I found it very distasteful,' Dominy protested, stiffening as he leaned past her to tap the driver on the back with his cane and his arm briefly touched hers. 'You still have not said where we are going.'

'Of course, a romantic after-dinner drive with me is not as attractive as it would be with Austen. I must be losing my touch,' Beau mocked in a soft drawling tone. 'I really do think we should at least try to be civil to each other—as it is to your advantage.'

'And not to yours?'

'But of course, also to mine.' He leaned back in his seat and reached into his tailored jacket for his cheroots. His fingers touched the envelope nestled deep inside a pocket and immediately his eyes grew thoughtful.

Dominy's curiosity was killing her, he mused as he lighted a long black cheroot. His own was none the less intense. What would he find in the unexpected communication? He had recognised Julia's neat handwriting immediately and his first thought had been bad news—his father! Yet would he—could he—go back even if he was ill—or dying? Too much had been said between them—bitter, searing reproaches had widened the gulf which had existed between them since he was a boy. They had never been close. They never would be now. What might have been was a disillusioned dream. He himself had snuffed out the only spark of hope for them as he had poured out years of suppressed anger and discontent on the head of the man who had sired him and then given all his love to his younger son—his damning condemnation of the man whose love he had fought so hard to earn had struck his father dumb. Beau knew he would never forget the stunned look on the leathered features as he had turned on his heel and strode from the room—as if he had only then become aware of his neglect, his lack of understanding, his failure. . .

That afternoon, one short hour after the quarrel which had sent servants scurrying to hide, Lance Beautrellis had turned his back on the home he loved, the family he had sought to protect with no thought of the consequences to his own reputation—now in ruins—and the father he secretly worshipped. He had never looked back as he had ridden off down the tree-lined driveway. He had never known if his father had watched him go and perhaps wished him to return. He could have called out. . .he had not!

'Are we here?' The carriage had stopped and Dominy was looking around her in puzzlement. It had come to a halt in the dock area, a few yards away from where the *Enchantress* was moored. The whole place was ablaze with hanging lanterns, swinging in a strong breeze from roughly erected scaffolding placed about the landing area, to combat the swiftly gathering dusk. Workmen swarmed everywhere with pots of paint, timber, tables, chairs, all kinds of objects. 'What is going on?'

'Welcome to your place of employment, milady. You are going to run the *Enchantress* for me when she is refitted, which should be in another week or so. I hope to have the grand opening—and it will be grand—on the fourth of July. I thought it rather appropriate.'

Beau watched the disbelief mounting on her face as he helped her to alight.

'Here! I am to work—— You cannot be serious. I know nothing about gambling. And I loathe everything associated with it. How can you ask it of me?'

'Is it not preferable to keeping my customers company at the Rest?'

Dominy nodded. Anything was better than that!

'Good. Let's take a look around,' Beau said cheerfully, starting towards the gangplank.

Loud whistles exploded from a group of workmen unloading a wagonload of timber as Dominy picked up her skirts and followed him.

'This a new girl, Mr Beautrellis? I'll be a customer if she is. What a looker!' someone commented, and a dozen pairs of eyes swept Dominy from head to toe with such intense scrutiny that she wished the ground would open up and swallow her. She was glad of the shadows that concealed her scarlet cheeks.

'You can't afford her, my friend,' Beau chuckled, pausing to allow Dominy to hurry past him. A flurry of skirts, which revealed trim stockinged ankles, brought more whistles after them.

'Have you no control over the men who work for you?' she demanded as they reached the deck and he ushered her through an open door.

'It is not a crime to admire a pretty woman, is it? And I'm sure you don't really mind being looked at. Most women worry when they are not attractive to men. I'd be a fool to believe that you are not aware how easily you can turn a man's head, milady. Maybe I shall have some handbills made up for the opening. Something to catch the eye of potential customers. . .let me see. . ."Lose your heart aboard the *Enchantress*—your money to milady——"'

'Was she an enchantress? Is that why you called it that?' Dominy interrupted stiffly, and Beau's eyes narrowed as they turned in her direction.

'She?'

'The woman whose husband you killed. . .isn't she the one who has written to you?' she flung back, not knowing why the knowledge of another woman should cause her such chagrin. She had seen him in the company of numerous women over the days since she had arrived, but she had never believed him capable of harbouring any kind of deep feelings for one in particular.

'In the Middle Ages a woman who asked too many questions often had her tongue cut out,' he replied. 'Personally I think the practice should never have been stopped. Now, if you can get your mind off my private life, perhaps we can discuss a few things. Maybe you can remember this as the dining-room—where you and I and Austen spent such an enjoyable evening together,' he added.

'And you won your bet,' Dominy replied. 'I do not think I will ever understand what makes a man so eager to part with his money.'

'Why not ask your father? He seems to know the answer,' came the cruel retort, which brought a quiver to her lips.

Quickly turning away so that Beau would not see how his words had upset her, she took a long look around the room. It was far longer than before, and then she realised it had been extended at least another thirty feet. At the far end, where there had been a door leading towards the cabins on the lower deck, there was now a large empty space, and instead of a small narrow flight of steps there now stood resplendent in that place a wide carpeted flight of stairs with ornate carved handrails. These were in the process of being stained and polished. Above, a crystal chandelier dominated the new entrance.

'The restaurant will be here, where we are standing,' Beau said, moving to her side. 'I thought the bar could go at the far end. New kitchens have been fitted out directly below us. We shall be able to cater for almost a hundred people at a time. The bar area will be more of a lounge where the customers can go after they have eaten—and before they go upstairs to part with their money.'

'Feeling full and satisfied,' Dominy said, remembering Weng's words. 'Another comfortable trap to entice people to lose their money.'

'A trap which, hopefully, will bring in a great deal of money—for us both. Let's take a look upstairs; the furnishings arrived today.'

Dominy wondered what she would find next as she followed him. Despite the lateness of the hour, there were still men labouring at a variety of jobs. Most greeted Beau with a casual wave or a friendly greeting. Was she the only one not to like the man? she wondered. Although even she now found her original feelings towards him suspect. How could she like him after the insults he had thrown at her? The way he was forcing her to work for him? She, who had been raised a lady, reduced to running a gambling establishment. Yet at least it was work and it would earn her money. How much, she supposed, would depend on how successful she was with the customers.

It would be nothing like the Devil's Rest, she told herself determinedly. If she was to be in charge—sole charge—then it would be a respectable place and cater for only the best. And the best, after all, was where the money was. Now she was thinking like Beau!

'What do you think?' Beau motioned to the plush-covered chairs and sofas being arranged in the long, low room which had been tastefully decorated in pastel shades of grey and gold. The ceiling was pale green and very restful to the eyes, she noted. Not that many men would be gazing upwards; they would be too busy concentrating on the cards in their hands.

'The tables and chairs should not be dotted about so untidily,' she commented, and could have bitten off her tongue for such thoughtless words as he turned to her with a broad smile, demanding,

'Well—how would you have them?' He had her

attention at last. He could feel it as well as see it in her eyes. He had thrown down a challenge and she had been unable to refuse it. Perhaps she had more courage than he had given her credit for—or was the natural womanly craving for money at last beginning to show itself? She would meet a lot of influential people across the tables, people who could help her mount the ladder of success and give her entrance to many fine houses on Nob Hill, even if it was through the back door at first. Why should he feel annoyed that the traits with which he had endowed her when they had first met were surfacing?

Dominy advanced to the middle of the room and took her time before answering. She remembered how some of the rooms had been arranged at home in England and at her grandmother's château—comfortable, elegant, but above all with a feeling that people could retire to different parts of the same room and sit or talk, or do whatever they wanted, without feeling intruded upon by the other occupants.

She considered the green baize tables and matching chairs spaced out around her and against the walls.

'Everything to do with gambling should be arranged in the centre of the room,' she said slowly and waited for a reaction from Beau. None came. He produced a second cheroot and lighted it. She drew a deep breath and continued. 'No one will want onlookers breathing down their necks. I want no hint of anyone cheating, nor the suggestion being made that they can. The players should be isolated from those who simply want to sit and watch—or enjoy the company of the hostesses. And that is all they will be, Mr Beautrellis, or I will not set foot on your boat.' There was still no reaction from her companion, who blew a cloud of grey smoke towards the ceiling, sat down in a chair and waited for her to go on. The pale blue eyes had grown very thoughtful as they considered her, but Dominy did not notice, seized with a sudden excitement she did not understand, but could not control as she said, 'The sofas and some chairs should all be placed against the walls, with some smaller tables in front of them. The walls should have concealed lighting. . .'

'They will have. . .' Beau murmured.

'Good. But over the tables there should be good light—suspended lamps perhaps. As for the hostesses—no more than six, and well dressed. Not like your scarlet hussies at the Rest.'

'Scarlet hussies!' Several workmen looked up from their work and grinned as Beau threw back his head and laughed aloud. 'Maisie would be most offended to hear herself called that. For your information, my girls don't slip their customers knock-out drops and relieve them of their wallets when they are unconscious, and I don't have bouncers who throw the unfortunates into back alleys afterwards either. . .despite what you may have been told happened to your father. It's not my way. I face people I don't like,' came the sharp comment when she opened her mouth to speak, that exact incident springing to her mind with his words. 'Neither do they pick their pockets or take them outside for some private transaction. I lay down certain ground rules—as I shall lay them down for you. I expect them to be obeyed.'

'I—I did not mean to imply. . .' Dominy faltered beneath the narrowed gaze.

'Oh, but you did. I intend only the best for the *Enchantress*, and so tomorrow you can start hiring girls that you consider suitable. And then you can put your back into getting these alterations and any other changes you want made finished by the required time.'

'Me! But I know nothing about that kind of thing. . .' He was being impossible, and did he not care that their conversation was being overheard by the men working near by? Did he have no regard for her feelings at all? No, he did not, she decided. He wanted her to make a fool of herself. Either she refused to work for him, in which case her father would go to prison, or she tried to do all the impossible things he required of her—and when she failed the result would be the same. She was beginning to wonder if he cared about the return of his money after all. Perhaps it was more important to him to have revenge on the man who had deprived him of it. Perhaps she would have had more success if she had thrown herself at his feet and begged his mercy, Dominy thought, her full mouth tightening determinedly.

Well, she was not going to fail.

'You are about to learn. I've told you—you are going to run the *Enchantress* for me. And before we open I am going to make you the best attraction in San Francisco.'

'That is impossible.' He was pushing her too far!

'Think of the money pouring across those tables. You will pay off your father's debt in no time and still have some left over to give you a stake somewhere. If you want to, that is. Who knows? You may grow to like the life. Is it a deal?'

Beau held out his hand, but she ignored it. She had never liked anything less in her life, but she would do it and she would wipe that smug smile from his face. And when she was free of debt and could hold her head high again she would show the Nob Hill society—and Austen's mother in particular—what she was made of. No one would ever tell her what to do again, or bar her from their homes as if she were a nobody!

'Yes, Mr Beautrellis—we shall have a deal when you have told me exactly what I shall get out of all this,' she said in a businesslike tone. 'And I should prefer the remainder of our conversation to be conducted in a more private place.'

'Milady has only to ask.' Beau uncoiled himself from the chair. She did not miss the wink in the direction of the workmen or the smothered laughter which followed them from the room. She would not allow herself to be intimidated by his manner, she thought as she followed him along the deck. When she no longer retaliated to his taunts he would soon tire of trying to make her angry. She paused as he opened another door, puzzling over where they were. The whole structure of the boat had been so altered that she was completely lost. 'This used to be the main cabin area. I've had them knocked into two large state-rooms, with adjoining bathrooms. I thought I would leave the choice of décor to you.'

Dominy stepped into the large room, feeling as if she were in a dream. The cabin she had occupied before had vanished completely. The vast space around her cried out for soft colour and a woman's touch to soften its starkness. Apart from a few pieces of furniture, it was untouched. She lifted suspicious eyes to Beau's face.

'Two large state-rooms?' she queried. For her—and him!

'I intend to open the *Enchantress* at weekends only in the beginning, unless the life appeals to you so much that you think you can stand a few days in the week,' she was told. 'Believe me, after a night here you will want to retire somewhere quiet—and if you stay aboard then you are on hand to deal with any emergencies. I will use my rooms very rarely. You will be the boss. *You* will be the *Enchantress*. Make it work for you.'

'Don't you mean for us both?' Dominy's head began to reel with the enormity of the challenge she was taking on.

'For us both, then. After all, the more money we make, the quicker you will be out of my hair,' Beau replied with a shrug.

'I am surprised you are not afraid I shall run off with all your precious money,' she said without thinking, and the pale eyes that came to dwell on her face harboured a dangerous glint.

'I will warn you now how dangerous that would be for you—and your father. He would end up in prison and I would do more with you than put you over my knee. . .'

'Thank you for reminding me why I am here,' she said coldly. For a moment she had felt as if she was under some kind of spell; now they were back to reality and the enormous task ahead of her, which she knew she had no way of completing successfully alone. But who could she turn to? 'Now—about my wages. . .'

'Wages?' Beau looked at her as if she had taken leave of her senses. 'Do you expect me to pay you? It's the other way around, my dear girl. Everything you take aboard the *Enchantress* will come to me and I shall check your figures most carefully, so be sure they always tally.

If I gave you any money you would take off at the first opportunity, taking your father with you. I'd probably find you in the next boom town fleecing unsuspecting miners of their gold or silver.'

'And how do you propose I live?' Dominy gritted her teeth, her temper rising.

'You will have everything you need here—or at the Rest. A roof over your head, good food. You can purchase necessities, of course, and charge them to me, as you will do with anything needed for the *Enchantress*, but excesses will be added to what is already owed. Do I make myself clear?'

'Very clear.' Dominy's anger subsided. She even managed a faint smile into the enquiring features. He was not being as clever as he thought, but she was not going to allow him to guess what she had in mind. 'What you are offering me is little different from Austen's proposal,' she added. 'In fact, his sounds far more attractive to me now.'

'There is one very big difference,' she was reminded with a smile that set her pulse racing faster. 'Of course, you may no longer consider it as important as you did when you refused his offer. In that case we can look forward to some interesting evenings together. You could make these rooms most appealing. . .'

'And myself. . .available. . .?' Dominy stepped back from him, paling at the implication behind his words. The wall halted her. Panic rose inside her as a familiar glitter stole into Beau's eyes. Firm hands on her shoulders held her immobile. He moved closer until his body touched hers and the weight of it pressed her back against the unpainted wall. 'Let me go or I shall scream!'

'You threatened that the last time. Your show of indignation was the performance of a lifetime, but I no more believe it now than I did then. Why do you pretend that you don't enjoy my touch? My kisses?'

Beau trailed his fingers over the softness of one cheek, down over a bare shoulder to the rise of her breasts. They came to rest against the fabric of her gown over her heart.

'It beats like a frightened captured bird. Are you afraid of me, Dominy? Or of what you feel?' The dark face bent closer to hers, the glittering eyes searching her tortured face. 'You act like a spoiled brat, but you have the emotions of a woman. Hunger. . .isn't that what you are experiencing now? The need to be held, comforted, loved?'

'Not by you,' she gasped. Her voice was barely audible. Her lips quivered. Beau's mouth closed over them, held her silent for a long moment.

'Close your eyes, then, and pretend I am Austen,' he mocked. 'After all, if you think about it I am offering more than he did. He would not lift a finger to help your father. I am. . .and I'm giving you a chance to get back at those snobs who thought you were not good enough to sit at their tables. Think of all those faces you are going to see aboard the *Enchantress*, milady. . .all those fine gentlemen who are going to come to you for credit. You will refuse them, of course. A firm, polite refusal. You will enjoy it.'

He was right, she realised, but at this moment the knowledge brought her no satisfaction. She could think of nothing but the warmth of Beau's breath against the nape of her neck, the burning sensation of his fingers as they explored her body. The weakening of her knees—her resolve to keep him at arm's length. Unless she did that she was lost. If she once allowed him to believe she was in love with him. . .

The clarity of her feelings struck her so suddenly that she sagged in his embrace, her mind reeling. As he felt the change in her Beau's lips sought hers again and found no resistance. Taken aback, he allowed himself the pleasure of her surrender, aware of a growing fire within him that cast aside all caution.

Love! She loved him! Dominy fought to retain some semblance of reason, difficult though it was with the fierce pressure of his mouth on hers, the expertise of hands that scorched her skin, enticing her to surrender all. If he discovered it it would be another weapon to hold over her head like the sword of Damocles. He must never know!

'I can give you more than Austen. Much more,' Beau whispered, gently sliding the gown from one shoulder. She quivered as his mouth was laid against the fullness of her breast where the fabric had slipped away. 'Anything you want. . .'

She did not know if they were just words to him, she knew she would never have the courage to ask, but they gave her a straw to clutch at.

'Anything?' At the harshness of her voice, he lifted his head slowly and stared into her face. How strange she looked—almost contemptuous of his offer. Had he really promised her that? 'A house on Nob Hill—bigger and better than that of Austen's mother. Clothes from Paris. Jewellery—not imitation. *You* cannot afford me, Mr Beautrellis, but perhaps, across one of your tables, I shall find a man who can.'

The cruel words tore at her heart, but she knew they had to be said. Knew by the way Beau's expression changed, his hands fell away from her and he stepped back, that she had achieved her aim.

'But I can, milady.' The derision on his face made her inwardly wince in pain. 'You shall have anything you want—I am a man of my word—and when you have your heart's desire then I shall extract my pound of flesh. And you had better be prepared to pay up—or God help you!'

He spun around on his heel and strode from the room, not waiting to hear an answer. She did not have one. She had made him think the worst of her and he would make sure she paid in full for anything he gave her. His pound of flesh. She knew only too well what that meant. And there was nothing she could say now to alter the situation. She was his property—as surely as if he had bought and paid for her. His property! The thought made her shiver—not as she had shivered a few moments ago in his arms, thrilling to his kisses, but with fear such as she had never known before. . .

At last she realised he would be waiting for her to join

him to return to the Rest. She found her purse, which had fallen to the floor, and miserably left the state-room without a backward glance. At the top of the gangplank she paused, took a deep breath of tangy sea air and started down towards the carriage where a stony-faced man awaited her, her shoulders squared, her head held proud, her heart in pieces.

'What's this I hear about you running the *Enchantress*? I knew Beau had something in mind, but you in charge. . .' Maisie came upon Dominy the next morning as she pondered the enormous list which had been presented to her by Beau—through Weng—as she was eating breakfast. There was no sign of Beau and she thought twice about asking where he was.

'Have you eaten?' Dominy looked up, her mouth full of buttered toast. Her figure would be ruined if she continued to allow Weng to force such large breakfasts on her. 'Help yourself. Isn't it a little early for you to be here?' she added as the girl reached enthusiastically for the toast and preserves.

'I've been dying of curiosity ever since Beau told us what he intends to do.' Dominy watched rich, sweet apricot preserve being lavishly spread over two pieces of buttered toast. 'Is it true?'

'That is what he told me last night.' She squashed the other memories that came flooding into her mind to distract her again and frowned at the paper she held. 'I—am in trouble! I don't know where to start. I am supposed to supervise the decorating, as well as put my head on the block by choosing a colour scheme for the state-rooms. Then I have to engage waiters and kitchen staff and girls for the gambling-room. Oh, Maisie—he has given me an impossible task.'

'He doesn't think so, or he would have done it himself. Strange, that. . .' Maisie chewed thoughtfully on her toast, her head tilted to one side as she pondered Dominy's face. 'He usually doesn't give jobs to other people—not important jobs anyway. He really must have some faith in you.'

'He's using me. . .what I am. . .I mean, was. . .to attract publicity. Bringing me down to his own level to get back at my father,' Dominy said bitterly. 'But he's not going to get the better of me. I will run his precious boat and I will make it the most sought-after place in San Francisco. . .but first I have to hire these people, and then I want to look for a dressmaker. A really good dressmaker.'

'If Beau is buying you a new wardrobe try and fit in a few bits and pieces for me. I'd give my soul to dress the way you do,' Maisie said with a sigh. Weng appeared to enquire if Dominy had finished. Maisie reached for another tempting piece of toast, changed her mind and nodded.

'I think that can be arranged,' Dominy said, beckoning her companion to follow her into the bedroom. 'If you will help me then you shall have any dress you want—made just how you want it.'

Maisie needed no further encouragement. Pulling up a chair, she took the paper from Dominy and began to reel off a list of names.

'There you are, no problem. I can give you at least two people for every one of these jobs. You'll have to see them yourself, of course. Tell me when and I'll have them lining up in droves.'

'You make it sound very easy.' Dominy was not convinced that her troubles were over—in fact, she suspected they were only just beginning—but Maisie's light-hearted chatter was easing the load a little. 'Let us say the day after tomorrow—on the *Enchantress*, at eleven in the morning for the waiters and kitchen staff, and one o'clock for the hostesses. I would like you to be there too. I am not sure I can handle it by myself.'

'Rot! Be yourself. They'll be falling over themselves to work for a real lady like you. I suppose I could ask Beau for a couple of hours off. I'm sure he won't mind. These hostesses. . .' She paused, two spots of colour beginning to rise in her cheeks, brighter than the rouge she wore. 'I don't. . .no, you wouldn't want a low-life like me around.'

'Why not? I cannot think of anyone better qualified to not only help me pick the right girls, but keep them in order when they are working. I will not have any. . .how can I put it. . .?'

'Monkey business?' Maisie laughed. 'You want honest girls—with a bit of class. Well, that does let me out, but if you're willing to take a chance on me. . .I won't let you down. I promise. I guess it will be all right with Beau.'

'I shall tell him. Besides, for the moment we shall be opening only at weekends. That will give you a chance to see how you like it.'

'Like it! In a fancy dress with all those nobs? I shall love it!' Maisie cried, and the aroma of cheap perfume invaded Dominy's nostrils as she threw her arms around the other girl and hugged her. 'If you need a real classy dressmaker there's one who runs a place on Dempsey Street. Boasts she used to make clothes for some of the French aristocracy. Mrs LaMotte herself goes there.'

'Does she, now?' Dominy rose to her feet and threw open the closet doors. 'Come and find yourself something suitable, Maisie. You and I are going visiting.'

'This corset is killing me,' Maisie groaned, shifting awkwardly in her chair. 'Cutting me in half, it is. Do all ladies wear them this tight?'

'If you wish to have a small waist it is essential.' Dominy gave her an encouraging smile. They had been seated in the establishment of Madame Charlotte d'Aubigny for almost half an hour, during which time they had been approached by one attendant only, who had enquired what they wanted. When Dominy had requested to see the proprietress she had been told *madame* would join her after she had finished a fitting. Dominy's patience had begun to wane after the first fifteen minutes; now she was certain the long wait was deliberate.

She understood why when a woman emerged from one of the dressing-rooms, followed by a tall, thin woman in black who was obviously Madame d'Aubigny. She heard Maisie catch her breath as she, too, recognised the woman heading towards the door and heard the remark, made in loud tones and intended to be overheard by all in the room, 'I do hope you are not catering for another class of person, *madame*. I would be appalled to see a creation you had made for me being worn by some dance-hall girl on the Barbary Coast.'

Madame d'Aubigny visibly shrank beneath the withering gaze of the most important woman to grace her premises.

'Rest assured, Mrs LaMotte, I would never accept custom from that kind of woman.'

'I am glad to hear it. Send the gown to the house no later than tomorrow evening. I require it for a very special occasion.'

'Did you hear what the old cow said?' Maisie whispered vehemently. 'I was wrong to bring you here. Let's find somewhere else.'

'On the contrary, *madame* is exactly what I need.' Dominy rose, smoothing down the skirts of her dress, aware of the woman's eyes scrutinising her. To an experienced eye such as hers it was obvious that the material was very expensive and the cutting of the fabric had been done with great professionalism. The dressmaker had spent some embarrassing minutes listening to her most important customer telling her about this woman who had had the nerve to set her sights on one of the most eligible bachelors in San Francisco. And, having failed to catch him, had taken herself off to live with a gambler.

Dominy walked slowly to the full-length mirror in the middle of the room and examined her appearance for a long moment, then swung around on Madame d'Aubigny with a disarming smile.

'I have come to you, *madame*, because I have been told you are the best dressmaker in San Francisco. I intend to discover that for myself. It would be such a relief to find someone who can design clothes for me the way my dear old Laurencin did,' she said in French, and the woman gaped.

'Laurencin. . .of Paris. . .Claude Laurencin?' The name was said with great reverence.

'But of course. My grandmother would never use anyone else. I never found anyone like him in England, which is why I had all my clothes made in Paris,' Dominy said, as if it were the most natural thing in the world. The two women who had been examining bolts of cloth behind her and taking more interest in Maisie than the cloth were now exchanging puzzled looks. They had been waiting for her to be shown the door, Dominy thought, beginning to enjoy the confusion she was causing. 'Of course, if you are too busy to undertake the creation of a new wardrobe for me. . .and additional evening gowns—at least a dozen—which I shall require for my staff. . .'

'Staff?' Madame d'Aubigny echoed weakly, the warning of Mrs LaMotte fading rapidly into the background. A whole wardrobe—*and* a dozen gowns! Whoever this woman was, she was certainly not from the lower classes. Only the aristocracy could afford Claude Laurencin! Mrs LaMotte was a difficult woman who ordered new gowns when the fancy took her, quibbled over the design and the price until she drove everyone mad and then on several occasions had cancelled the order with the work still in progress.

'I am in the process of opening a new restaurant, which I shall be surpervising personally. I shall therefore need clothes for myself and for the young ladies I shall be engaging. I require a high standard of workmanship, *madame*, so if you do not think you and your staff are adequately competent I shall quite understand.'

'There is no question that I can provide you with whatever you want. . .' *Madame* paused, realising how eager she sounded.

'Good. Then perhaps you have some designs you can show me. I shall need at least half a dozen gowns by the end of next week. . .and one for myself, of course.' Dominy gave her no chance to change her mind.

'The—the end of next week!' As Dominy's slender eyebrows rose questioningly she nodded. She would have to take on extra seamstresses and watch them night and day or they would ruin her precious fabrics with their clumsy stitching, but the rewards would be great. 'Yes, that will be in order. You require something for. . .that person too?' She indicated Maisie, trying not to fidget in the velvet-covered chair. That awful dyed hair. She could never look a lady, even though the blue dress she wore gave her some semblance of respectability. The look Dominy directed at her made her wish she had not asked such a foolish question. 'Please come this way—both of you. Perhaps you would care for some iced tea. . .?'

'Beau sure is popular these days,' Maisie remarked as the two young women crossed towards the front door. It was the day of the all-important interviews, and Dominy wanted to make an early start. After selecting designs and materials the day before, she had spent the remainder of the afternoon and most of the evening aboard the *Enchantress*, supervising the completion of the gambling-room. 'That's the second letter he has received this week. And you should smell the perfume on those envelopes. Does our illustrious boss have a woman hidden away somewhere?'

Beau was leaning against the bar reading the letter which had just been presented to him by Weng. At the sound of Maisie's voice he looked up, inclined his head in their direction, acknowledging their presence, and returned his full attention to his correspondence.

'At a guess, I would say we hold no attraction for him at this moment,' Maisie giggled, following Dominy out to the waiting carriage.

'The attention of Mr Lance Beautrellis is the last thing I want,' came the sharp reply. 'I detest the man. I am working for him under duress and I do not care who knows it. The methods he employs to have his own way are quite unscrupulous.'

'Boy, you have got it bad.' Maisie regarded the pale face turned in her direction with sympathy in her large brown eyes. 'Beau has that effect on some women. . .'

'If you are insinuating. . .' Dominy began indignantly, horrified that her dreaded secret could become common knowledge.

'You can't hide that kind of thing from another woman,' she was told quietly. 'You can tell me you can't stand him until you're blue in the face, but I can feel what's inside you. . .pain! He's not a good guy to fall in love with. I guess because someone hurt him he's given up trusting his heart to anyone.'

'Do you know that is what happened? There was someone he cared for in his past?' Dominy asked, hating herself for needing to know the answer.

'Beau's not the kind of man to open up with just anyone. I guess he kind of trusts me. There have been nights when he's gotten lonely. . .we've sat together after the place has closed up—drunk too much, I can tell you. . .and he hasn't, well. . .let his hair down exactly, but a couple of times he's spoken of his home. . .a grand old place, from his description. . .and his brother. Never his father, though. I don't think they got along.' Maisie raised long painted nails to ease away a lock of hair from her cheek, her smile almost wistful. 'One of those nights I was feeling pretty homesick. Would you believe, *I* made a pass at him? Guess what? He patted me on the shoulder as if I were his kid sister and told me it was time to go to bed. I did—alone. He's a strange guy—but I'd do anything for him.'

'You make him sound like your guardian angel. He certainly is not mine,' Dominy declared. And he had not treated *her* like a sister. More like a piece of property with which he could do what he liked.

He had seen her come in the night before, but had made no attempt to speak to her. For almost two days all communication had come through the stoic-faced Weng. She had gradually accepted that he intended to keep his word. He would return to her all that she had been deprived of since the loss of her father's fortune and status, and in return he would extract his pound of flesh.

'Will you look at that?' Maisie ejaculated. The carriage

was having a hard time making progress through the people lining the dock in front of the *Enchantress*. 'When I put the word out that there was work to be had here I didn't expect any of this. I reckon you ought to have some of Weng's relatives down here to keep things in order. I'm surprised Beau's letting you cope with this by yourself.'

'I'm not,' Dominy said bitterly as she climbed down and pushed towards the gangplank. As her way was deliberately barred a heavy giant of a man came thrusting his way through the crowd, dragged away the men attempting to detain her and cleared enough room for her to hurry through. When she reached the deck, Maisie still complaining about the individual who had ripped her skirt, in vivid language that made Dominy wince, he was still behind her.

'Paddy O'Neill, miss. At your service.' The craggy features split into a broad smile and her apprehension disappeared. 'Best barman this side of Limerick. And I'm good at knocking a few heads together too, so if you'd like me to stick close by to take care of these roughnecks. . .?'

'Mr O'Neill, your presence would be appreciated,' Dominy returned, and the quiet, cultured tones brought a touch of awe to the man's eyes. At once the cap was snatched from his head.

'Beggin' your pardon, ma'am. I didn't know you was a lady. . .I mean. . .' Words failed him as he looked about him.

'Meaning, a lady is not usually found in such circumstances. I assure you, Mr O'Neill, I am quite capable and so, it would appear, are you. If you will follow me?'

She had arranged to have a table and chairs set up in a corner of one state-room so that she could conduct the interviews in peace and comparative quiet. Even so, the sound of banging and sawing invaded the room. It was going to be a long day, she decided. It was barely ten o'clock, and she had not intended to see anyone before eleven, but by then, she suspected, the waiting people would be getting irate and out of hand. Better to get it all over with as soon as possible.

'You are a barman, Mr O'Neill. . .a good one?'

'I can mix any drink you care to name,' came the proud boast.

Dominy thought twice about asking for a demonstration. Her own experience on the subject was far too limited. It was something else she would have to learn very quickly.

'That is all that will be required of you. Do you understand? No adding any ingredients of your own—for any reason.'

'Dear lady, you would not be suggesting. . .?' The man looked offended, then that same warm, friendly grin spread across his face and she knew they understood each other. It was a hopeful beginning. 'Sure, now, it would be fun to add a livener to my concoctions and watch a few of those fine ladies let their hair down. . .but no. . .not if I came to work for you. This place will be a gold mine, and I'll be in on it from the start. You'll have no trouble with Paddy O'Neill, ma'am. Nor anyone else, that I promise you. . .not while I'm here. Sure, I think someone who looks as good as you will be needing a little protection.'

'Then I shall not have far to look, Mr O'Neill. Consider yourself hired. We can go into terms of your contract later on. Right now I would like you to look over those men waiting outside, question them as to their abilities, and bring in one by one those you consider might be suitable. I require waiters, five or six. They must be quick on their feet and with some experience, although I am prepared to teach those who are willing to learn quickly. Maisie, would you show him the list of people we need and go with him? When you have found some likely candidates, call me, I shall be somewhere around.'

Two and a half hours later, her head throbbing from asking questions of the continuous faces who had passed in front of the table, Dominy sat back in her chair and reached for a now cold cup of coffee. She grimaced after the first mouthful and pushed it away.

'How about if I fix you a Paddy O'Neill special. . .something to pick you up? You look fair worn out,' the Irishman said, remembering the bar he had seen being installed earlier. And the abundance of full bottles standing by waiting to be put away on the shelves. 'You have finished?'

'I think I have enough staff now. Those girls, Maisie. . .what did they expect?' She inwardly shuddered, remembering some of the comments which had come in answer to her terms of work. They had expected to be able to do all the things that went on in other places. . .stealing, drugging their customers, taking them somewhere quiet. Out of over three dozen assorted young women she had had great difficulty in finding five, and had at last settled for one short. When the others discovered how pleasant it was to work aboard the *Enchantress* without having to do anything underhand she should have no trouble finding the sixth. But without the presence—the very daunting presence—of Paddy O'Neill by her side Dominy knew she would have been subject to far more abuse, and worse, when she rejected anyone. She must pull herself together, for she had hardly begun to do what was required of her. She could not afford to feel tired—or despondent. Perhaps a refreshing drink would help—and some fresh air.

'Yes, Mr O'Neill, why not? We have done well, all of us. I shall leave the choice up to you. I shall be on deck.'

It was after dark before Dominy returned to her room at the Devil's Rest. The potion Paddy had poured into their glasses had contained some magic ingredient, she thought, for less than an hour had passed before all the problems still before her began to seem less important and troublesome, and she had lingered behind after he and Maisie had left to make the final decisions on the colour schemes for the two state-rooms.

As usual Weng appeared the moment she set foot over the threshold, to enquire if there was anything she required. For once she was glad of his thoughtfulness. She was tired and longing to relax in a soft bed.

'A bath, Weng, please, with lots of hot water.'

'I shall have Su Lin prepare it for you at once. And perhaps some jasmine tea, Miss Granville. You look quite exhausted. Have you eaten at all today?'

'I am too tired to eat and it is too hot. I will be up directly. Where is Mr Beautrellis?'

'In the card-room. He was wondering where you were too.'

Wondering how his money was being spent, Dominy mused as she turned towards the room behind the velvet drapes. Most of the afternoon customers had drifted away, and it was too early for the rich young men who frequented the place and rarely put in an appearance before ten o'clock. Several men, whose faces had become familiar to her since her arrival, were grouped around a table playing poker. A few feet away, seated at a table alone, except for a bottle of bourbon in front of him, was Beau. So absorbed was he in the cards he held that he was unaware of her presence in the room.

As she began to cross the floor towards him a man stepped away from the bar, blocking her path. She found herself confronted by a swarthy-faced man, who was vaguely familiar to her, although she could not determine where they had met before.

'Philippe Gascoigne at your service, *mademoiselle*.' The name was supplied with a flourishing bow and a broad smile. 'May I be permitted to buy you a drink, and then perhaps you will sit at my table and bring me luck?'

Gascoigne! Of course, now she knew who he was. The very first day she came to the Rest he and Beau had been fighting, and he had landed in an unconscious heap at her feet. She was aware of Beau's interest suddenly turned in their direction, his cards forgotten.

'Thank you, no. Not tonight.'

'Another evening, then. Perhaps supper too.'

'Perhaps. Excuse me.' Dominy found herself growing quite warm beneath the boldness of his gaze, but she managed a polite smile and quickly hurried around him to Beau's table. He hooked out a chair with a booted foot, beckoned to the bartender, and said as she sat down, 'Be careful of Gascoigne, he's a notorious womaniser. If he has invited you to dine with him, refuse him. Sam, something long and cool for milady. You look as if you have had a long, hard day.'

Dominy was sure he was not in the least interested in how her day had been. As Philippe Gascoigne turned back to the bar his attention returned to the cards he was dealing himself, confirming her suspicion.

'Are you telling me not to accept the invitation?'

'You should know what you are getting into. It's his habit to change the rendezvous at the last moment. You would probably have a cosy little supper—a late-night supper, I might add—at his house on Walnut Avenue. The food would be excellent and he would behave like a perfect gentleman. You would drink a great deal of wine, probably because he made you feel relaxed, cosseted—he has a charming way about him when he's out to get something he wants——'

'Rather like Austen—and you,' Dominy interrupted with iced sweetness.

Beau ignored the gibe, but for a brief instant there was a glitter in the depths of the pale blue eyes.

'When you were feeling more mellow,' he continued, gathering up the cards and reshuffling them, 'then the game would be over. Most of the women he entertains find themselves in his bed before they realise what is happening. More than one unfaithful wife carries a memory with her that she is terrified will be revealed to her husband. Those who don't return of their own free will are. . .persuaded—shall we say?—by a gentle hint that their secret will not be safe unless they do.'

'Do you mean he is a blackmailer too? Why is he not in gaol?' she asked in a low tone.

'Can you imagine any woman confessing how indiscreet she has been just to put him behind bars? He lives well on the money they provide to keep his mouth shut. You are never to allow him aboard the *Enchantress*. If he gives you trouble I'll have some of Weng's relatives take care of him. I'm thinking of putting some aboard anyway as protection.'

Dominy watched the lean hands begin to deal the cards face upwards on the table before him. As he saw her lips tighten he asked, 'Do you have some objection to my protecting what is mine—the *Enchantress*, I mean?'

'No. But I do object to being a figurehead for your vanity.'

'Vanity.' Beau's face went blank with amazement. 'What on earth are you talking about?'

'If I am to run the *Enchantress* I intend to be capable of doing my job properly. I do not want to have to rely on others. It takes experience to know when someone is cheating at cards—as you are now, dealing from the bottom of the pack.' The movement had been so swift, so expertly manoeuvred, that she had not been sure if her eyes had deceived her, but as a smile spread slowly across the handsome face she knew she had been correct. 'Are you just keeping your hand in—or practising for your next victim?'

'You have a keen eye—I shall have to remember that. And a very foolish tongue. I am good! I have no need to cheat. I was taught by the most experienced man on the Mississippi.'

'Then teach me.' She had stood in the gambling-room aboard the *Enchantress* and suddenly wanted to be more than an elegant bystander, in charge, and yet not in control.

'Why? What are you intending to do, rip off my customers and line your own pockets? Or those of your father?' The suggestion was too ridiculous to consider. Who had put such an idea into her head? She was more capable than he had given her credit for, but to become a dealer. . .!

'If I thought that were possible, that I could be so deceitful. . .yes, I would. Anything to get away from here as soon as I can.'

'Without paying your dues. I knew you would welsh on the deal. Cowards always do,' Beau said contemptuously, refilling the empty glass at his fingertips. His cold gaze contemplated her over the rim, daring her to continue.

'I will not. . .welsh, as you call it,' she retorted, cheeks flaming. 'Because, even though I admit you could afford me, Mr Beautrellis, you have neither the style nor the breeding to be of interest to someone like me. I tolerate you because I have to. No amount of clothes or jewellery would be enough——'

'What about the house on Nob Hill?' His words stopped her in mid-speech, froze her in her chair. 'You and your father looking down your noses at all those people who have turned their backs on you?' Was he mad? He had deliberately kept them apart, and now he was offering her what she really wanted. Julia's letters had affected him more than he cared to admit. He was beginning to think of things which could never become reality—not the way he wanted them.

'My—my father,' Dominy stammered.

'If I have what I want. . .' He shrugged. 'He is of no importance to me. If you want him with you and if Madam Chen will let him go. . .'

'He is just another pawn in one of your games, isn't he? Like me?'

'The cards are stacked against you. They always were. But with me dealing them. . .' Beau added meaningly.

Respectability for them both! The restoration of the kind of life they had once lived. And in return. . . Once she had considered the payment demanded too high, but she had not been in love with Austen. Could she—for her father? For herself—and the love she knew she could never reveal? No decision had ever torn her apart as this one did. She had been raised to respect the bonds of marriage, a faithful marriage. A home, family. Here she was being presented with the outrageous suggestion that she allowed herself to be installed in an expensive house, the kept mistress of Lance Beautrellis.

Austen, perhaps, she could have held at arm's length, but not this man! Once she had agreed. . .if she agreed. Why did she not think it totally abhorrent? How could love have changed her way of thinking so drastically? She was ashamed to realise that she was even considering the idea.

'Sleep on it,' Beau murmured. 'There's no hurry.'

Five minutes after Dominy had left Beau rose and returned his pack of cards behind the bar. He would bathe and change and spend the evening down here, he decided. He needed a diversion to keep his mind off the events of the past week or so and the disastrous path he was cutting towards Dominy's door. It would be disastrous for them both. Some small spark of conscience which still remained in his embittered body warned him he could only hurt her. Yet what had started out as a challenge had now become an obsession to make her belong to him. He did not understand what drove him, and could not control it.

'She's a skittish little filly, isn't she?' Gascoigne remarked as he turned to leave. 'Not so much with you, though. You must have a velvet glove, Beautrellis.'

'Stay away from her.' The man behind the long bar, as if recognising a certain tone, moved closer to the Frenchman, but Beau waved him aside with a humourless smile. 'It's all right, Sam, he's just leaving. You seem to have forgotten you are not welcome here any more, Gascoigne.'

'Are the rumours that I heard true, then, *monsieur*? She is your property? I saw no brand, and the young lady gave me no indication that she did not welcome attention from another source.'

'What she does or does not want is immaterial. You will not bother her again, or I shall kill you sooner than I intended,' Beau drawled.

'Empty threats do not frighten me, *Mr* Beautrellis,' Gascoigne said, brushing an imaginary speck of dust from his jacket. There were too many witnesses present for him to use the small derringer nestled beneath his armpit. But later. . . He always worked better in the dark. . .

Beau, however, safe on his own ground, had no hesitation in backing up his words. The features of the man facing him became quite sallow with fear as he found himself staring at a thin-bladed stiletto which suddenly appeared from the sleeve of Beau's shirt. The blade gleamed in the candlelight—bright, deadly. . .as deadly as the man who carried it.

'I could take your worthless life now and have you dumped in some alley, as you did Edwin Granville. I still owe you for that, among other things. No one would mourn your passing. I could even get a medal for taking you off this earth, although some people might object if I left such filth to rot beneath their windows. The stench would pollute the whole area.'

'You and I will settle old scores very soon. . .'

'Any time. Anywhere. I'm not an old man you can beat into the ground, or a naïve young girl. I am dangerous, Gascoigne, and I look forward to the day I can show you just how dangerouus. . .'

CHAPTER SEVEN

'DON'T you dare tell me I have come to the wrong place,' Dominy said in a fierce tone to the Oriental who blocked her path. 'I have come to see my father and I am not leaving until I do. Now, do you fetch him, or do I go and get the aid of a policeman? In this neighbourhood he will be more willing to help me.'

The address which Maisie had supplied to her was in a far better part of the town than Madam Chen's last establishment, and was in the process of being renovated. Gleaming red tilework and well-washed brick stood out against the drabness of its neighbours. A new awning with Chinese letters painted on it shaded the bright yellow door. A sign erected alongside this place proclaimed that soon the adjoining building would be opening as a hotel. Expansion on a grand scale, thanks to Beau's money! But where did her father fit into the scheme of things?

'There will be no need for hysterics, Miss Granville. I want no problems before I have even opened my doors.' Madam Chen appeared behind the servant, motioned him to one side and stepped into the sunlight, as cool and distant as on the other occasions Dominy had encountered her.

'I am not given to hysteria, madam. Where is my father?'

'Working. The change in his lifestyle becomes him. His soul is at peace.' The woman's eyes, as black as jet, swept over the young woman demanding entrance. As if sensing something different in her attitude, she stepped back, and Dominy followed her into the cool interior. It was only ten o'clock in the morning, but already the heat was becoming unbearable. It would be a relief to go aboard the *Enchantress* and perhaps have the chance of a pleasant sea breeze to cool her. But before that she had a fitting at the dressmaker. She was not looking forward to several hours of being closeted with Madame d'Aubigny in those tiny stuffy rooms. 'I believe you, also, have found a new vocation in life?'

'I have work, madam. Someone has to pay off my father's debts,' Dominy returned icily. She was not surprised the woman knew. Weng was a fountain of knowledge on almost every subject, despite his apparent loss of memory when it had come to supplying the present address of Madam Chen. Had it not been for Maisie she might never have discovered it. The thought of returning to the old restaurant and trying to trace them from there had been positively terrifying.

'An admirable achievement on your part. In China the young always shoulder the responsibilities of their parents and the aged ones of their family. It is as it should be. Unfortunately in this part of the world the old are left to care for themselves. It is not our way. Not our way at all.'

'Is it your way to take a father from the daughter who loves him?' Dominy demanded with sudden boldness. 'What hold do you have over him, madam, that he chooses to remain with you, rather than with me?'

'Hold?' Madam Chen's face broke into a smile. There was no mockery in it, no reproval at the suggestion. Perhaps a touch of sadness, which Dominy could not understand. 'He is free to stay or go with you. It is his choice. Ask him if you do not believe me. Hear from his own lips the decision only he can make. Will you please wait in here and I will tell him of your arrival? Perhaps you would care for some refreshment? I believe you have become partial to jasmine tea?'

'No, nothing. Just my father.' Dominy stared in disbelief as the curtains fell in place behind her. How had she known that? It was true. Since Su Lin had first brought her the jasmine tea she had become accustomed to partaking of it as soon as she returned to the Devil's Rest. She found it soothed an aching head, restored life to tired limbs and on some occasions had even, she suspected, helped her to have a night of untroubled sleep.

Weng! Who else? Of course he had known the address. Most likely Beau had warned him against giving it to her. Yet why, when he had already said he did not care any longer if her father returned to live with her? There was something going on she did not understand. Perhaps her father would have the answers. She had no doubt he would be willing to leave Madam Chen now. There was no reason to stay now that Dominy could support him. And if she accepted Beau's offer of the house on Nob Hill. . . She closed her mind against the pictures that inviting suggestion brought into her mind. If she could find another way. . .

'Dominy! My dear child, how well you look. I saw you the other day down on the dock with all those people. You are becoming quite a personality in San Francisco these days.'

In the time since she had last seen him her father had filled out considerably, and there was strength in the arms that hugged her, a new confidence in his voice. Tears filled Dominy's eyes as she held him at arm's length. He had on a new suit. Not expensive, but well cut. It suited him better than Chinese clothes and returned to him his identity.

'There is an old Chinese legend that parents never tell their children how pretty they are for fear they offend the gods. In that case I must say you are the ugliest daughter any father could have,' Edwin added.

'I did not know you were interested in Chinese philosophy, Papa?' Dominy said with a feeling of disquiet stirring inside her. He was pleased to see her, she was sure of that, yet she felt as if he was distant from her. Why could he not have said she just looked pretty as he would have once?

'I have become interested in many things since I met Madam Chen,' came the answer, which brought a furrowing of her slender brows. 'She is a remarkable woman.'

'So was Mama,' Dominy returned defensively as he

seated himself beside her on a cane couch. Chinese lanterns, hanging from the ceiling, gave out a muted glow of light that softened the angry surge of colour to her cheeks. 'And she did more for you—for me—than this woman could ever do.'

'Don't misunderstand me, child.' Edwin reached for his daughter's hand. It lay stiffly in his grasp without responding to the warmth of his touch, the need in him to touch her again, to stop her from slipping away from him forever. 'I shall carry the memory of your dear mother with me as long as I live. And the terrible things I did to her in my craving for gambling. Madam Chen is a totally different person. You can guess the pitiful condition I was in when she found me—you saw me not long afterwards. I cared for nothing. No one. Not even if I died. There were times when I was so ashamed of what I had become that I wanted to. She restored my will to live. She told me that to have the respect of others I must first respect myself. Look.' He extended both his hands. They were the hands of a man accustomed to manual labour, clean, but calloused—and, Dominy saw, without the tremor induced by an abundance of drink. She could have helped him to achieve the same recovery, she thought, had she been allowed to do so.

She knew it would have been charitable to feel gratitude for all Madam Chen's hard work, but all she could feel was a sense of loss and deep, burning resentment that she had been deprived of the opportunity. It was her right, after all!

'I have no excuses for what happened to me,' Edwin continued after a long moment of silence, which Dominy had not interrupted. She sensed a need to talk and unburden himself to someone he knew would understand—and forgive. She would never understand the weakness that had driven him to ruin their lives, but she could forgive, because she loved him. But his rejection of her. . .that was another matter—and she did not believe he was to blame for that. 'When I left France with the money your grandmother had given me I hoped. . .' his voice faltered and broke; Dominy's fingers curled around his, giving him the reassurance to go on '. . .that she would persuade you to remain with her. She could have given you everything you wanted. Perhaps you would have met some fine young man and married.'

'I wanted to be with you,' she whispered, allowing her head to rest on his shoulder. Once she had shared moments like this at Granville Manor. Her mother on one side, she in the middle and her father on the other. How wonderful those idyllic days had been. She so rarely allowed herself to dwell on them now. She had been cosseted, often spoiled—and secure. 'Nothing could have kept me from following you.'

'Not even my letter?'

'What letter? I had not heard from you in months when I left. And then you were in some place called Virginia City. I went there first and they said you might have gone on to the gold fields around Santa Rosa or some place called Eureka, where a new strike had been made.'

'You did not go to that God-forsaken place?' Edwin asked in disbelief. 'It was a hell-hole.'

'I did. . .only to learn you had left in rather a hurry—some problem over you claiming the same piece of ground as some other man. . .and then losing what did not belong to you to someone else in a card game. That was some while before I had arrived, so that when I landed here in San Francisco you had already made yourself known. Had you not?'

'Dominy. . .Dominy, can you ever forget the nightmare of those first few days? Madam Chen has told me how you were subjected to gossip and rudeness. . .and heaven knows what else.'

'Has she, now? Weng told her, I suppose?' It was only a guess, and she caught her breath as her father nodded.

'But of course. She is some kind of distant relative. Everyone I have met around here seems to be a relative of someone else. They call on each other whenever they need help or advice. The family ties here are so close. Almost frightening. If one of their own is threatened there is nothing they will not do to protect him—or her. But you know all this by now, working for that man. . .'

'Do you mean Beau—Mr Beautrellis? Weng is his right hand. Is there something else I should know, Papa?'

'I cannot imagine you—working in a place like that! I thought you had rather a rich young man dancing attendance on you. . .LaMotte?'

'I am sure Madam Chen has supplied you with information about that too. I am sorry, Papa. I did not mean to snap, but I feel as if our lives are somehow being manipulated for us. I did not mean any of this to happen—with Beau, I mean. I was going to find a job and earn enough money to keep us both, then you said you did not want to live with me, that I should do better for myself. . .with someone like Austen LaMotte.

'Do you know what he suggested, this fine gentleman? It seems to be common practice in San Francisco. He offered to set me up in a house of my own. He would, naturally, be the only man allowed to visit me. All my bills would be paid, but I would never be able to set foot through any of the doors on Nob Hill. And that is what I want! I have done nothing wrong!'

'And you think you will be better off working for this Beautrellis man?' Her father's voice did not hold the concern Dominy had expected to hear.

'I am not a saloon girl, papa. I am to be in charge—sole charge of the *Enchantress*. We are having a grand opening on July the fourth. It has been turned into a restaurant with a gambling-room above. For the élite, of course. In a very short time I shall have paid back Mr Beautrellis and we shall be free of him.'

'You are doing it—for me! Dominy, I will not have it. You cannot tie yourself to a man like that. . .'

'The alternative is you spending a long time in prison. He was quite adamant what would happen to you if I did not repay him,' Dominy said. 'But I shall do it. I am determined on it, and you know what a stubborn little brat I used to be.'

'And when you could not have your own way you

would come to me and climb on my knee and nestle your head against my chest and say, "Please, Papa," and I would give you anything you wanted. I hope you are not going to try the same tactics with Mr Beautrellis?'

'No, Papa. I have something entirely different in mind for him. He is going to regret the day he met me.' Dominy drew back from him, a smile masking the conflict which suddenly rose up inside her as love challenged her reasoning. 'I want you to come to the opening; will you? I have brought you an invitation.' She produced a card from her purse. The name of Edwin Granville, Lord Edgemont, had been engraved on it in gold lettering. 'I want you by my side—to give me courage. Believe me, I shall need it. I want everyone to know you are my father and that I love you. Please come. Promise me you will. I shall send you clothes—everything you need.'

She had intended to tell him about Beau's offer too, making it sound as if she wanted it, enhancing the thought of them living together in style on Nob Hill, but now she thought better of it. She had to be more subtle in order to wrench him away from the invisible chains Madam Chen had woven about him. He did not want to come with her or he would surely have suggested it himself.

Once he was aboard the *Enchantress* she would ensure he was treated like royalty, while being kept discreetly away from the gambling-room, in the hope that what he saw would become too appealing to turn his back on.

'Dominy, my dear, you do not want me. . .looking like this at your side. People have to forget we are father and daughter. . .'

'I shall not let them. Nor shall I let you forget I am your daughter and I love you. Everything you need for the evening will be here days before. I shall see to it this afternoon.'

'You are so confident. . .different. . .' Edwin began, and she bent to kiss him on both cheeks before turning to the door. It had suddenly occurred to her that Madam Chen could be listening to their conversation on the other side, and she did not want any interference from that quarter. Nothing would stop her from having her father aboard on the opening night. Nothing! No one!

'And more stubborn than ever, so be warned.'

Dominy was so pleased that her father had not directly turned down her invitation that she did not mind the next few hours of endless fittings and alterations—and, as Madame d'Aubigny slipped the gown she was to wear on opening night over her head, she was even more satisfied. The hostesses would be dressed in pale blue. She had chosen midnight-blue silk. She smiled at her reflection as the dressmaker fastened the last hook and stood back admiringly.

'There are few women I know who can wear such a gown without first going through the torture of a corset, Miss Granville. How I envy you such a figure.'

'Your own is most becoming, *madame*,' Dominy returned. *Madame's* last lingering doubts about her new customer had been dispelled long ago, after they had spent an afternoon discussing Paris and places that were familiar to them both. And Dominy had had no scruples about reminding the woman of her connections with the aristocracy. *Madame* had beamed when she had said she would be mentioning her in letters to the Comtesse.

'Alas, these days men look first at my face, not my figure.'

'They will have plenty of opportunity to do both when you come to the opening of the *Enchantress*,' Dominy returned, presenting her with an engraved invitation. 'In return for all the hard work I have put you through. I hope you will be able to find the time to attend.'

'I shall be delighted. . .'

'Good. Now I must have everything ready and delivered to the boat by the first of July. If there are last-minute alterations for any reason I shall need to call on you immediately, you understand that.'

'I am here whenever you need me. . .' *Madame* dared not think of the uncomfortable time she was going to have when she tried to tell Mrs LaMotte her gown would not be ready on time. Twice the wretched woman had changed her mind about the sleeves, and had kept the seamstress waiting a whole week while she had decided yet another insignificant change. How pleasant it was to do work for someone who knew exactly what she wanted!

Dominy had dismissed the carriage before her fittings, deciding to walk back to the Devil's Rest. As she opened her parasol and stood wondering which shops looked most inviting a monogrammed carriage was pulled to a halt in front of her and she found herself staring into the daggered gaze of Elizabeth LaMotte. From the opposite seat Austen's face broke into a smile, and the hand his mother stretched out towards him was ignored as he climbed down, exclaiming, 'Dominy, it's good to see you. I was hoping to run into you tonight, but this is even better. Shall we go somewhere and have some tea?'

'Austen, have you forgotten me?' came the icy comment from behind him.

'No, mother, you would never allow me to do that,' he returned with surprising good humour in the face of such rudeness, Dominy thought as he helped Elizabeth LaMotte to alight.

'We shall be late.' She totally ignored Dominy, and that was a foolish mistake.

'Good afternoon, Mrs LaMotte. Do you have a fitting with Madame d'Aubigny? I expect you have asked for something very special to wear for my opening. She really is a treasure. Nothing is too much trouble for her, even though I have kept her working at all hours.'

'Opening.' Elizabeth repeated the word as if it were some insult. 'There will be no LaMottes present at the affair—whatever it is.'

'You know very well what it is, Mother. We received the invitations yesterday. Thank you, Dominy, we shall be there. I shall, anyway; you can count on it,' Austen said, some of the friendliness vanishing from his expression as he stared at his mother. 'You will be late for your appointment. You can take the carriage home—I won't be needing it. If you remember, I told you I shall be out all this evening, and, as I shall probably be very drunk when I get home, I suggest you go to bed. You know how you hate to see me in such a disgraceful state.'

Tucking Dominy's arm beneath his, he drew her away from the carriage. She thought he was more amused than disturbed at his mother's attitude.

'Why have you been avoiding me?' he asked in a low tone as they walked.

'Have I?' Twice he had left messages for Dominy at the Rest. She had thought it best to ignore both. 'It would not be wise for us to continue our. . .friendship, Austen; surely you can see that? Your mother made it very clear how she feels about me, and your friends will do the same when they discover where I am working. I expect most of them do already.'

'And most of them will be at the opening to stare at you all evening,' Austen returned, guiding her into a fashionable tea-shop. 'But I shall be the one monopolising you.'

'I shall be far too busy to pay attention to any one man,' she returned firmly.

'That sounds like a very polite way of telling me Beau has elbowed me out of the running.' No sooner had they sat down at an empty table than a waitress brought them a pot of tea for two and freshly baked cakes. 'This is one of my mother's favourite haunts.' He looked about him, nodding and smiling in the direction of several women a few feet away. 'If I have to pick her up after one of her afternoon charity functions she insists we come in here; then she spends the next hour deciding if there are any eligible young ladies in here who would make me a suitable wife. And, of course, fit in with her routine.'

'What do you mean about Beau? The decision not to meet you again was totally my own idea,' Dominy said, wishing the cakes did not look so delicious. She weakened and took one, and sank her teeth into soft sponge filled with cream and strawberry jam. 'We do not want the same things from our friendship. You want so much more. I cannot give them to you, Austen. Not until I have ensured my father's peace of mind and my own. He is an embarrassment to you. I understand that, but I still love him dearly. Beau has given me the opportunity to earn real money and repay what is owed to him.'

'At the same time persuading you what a gentleman he is. Watch out for him, he's a devil when he pursues something he wants,' Austen warned, frowning at her over the rim of his teacup.

'The only thing he wants is his money.'

'And when he has it? What then? Do you have any plans? To stay on in San Francisco, I mean?'

'I really have not given the future much thought. There is very little for me here when I do think about it. I can always go back to my grandmother in France.' Dominy's eyes grew wistful as she allowed her mind to drift back to the château and the summer afternoons she had spent lazing on the lawn beneath a shady tree.

'But you have not decided on it yet?' Austen leaned across the table, reaching for her hand. Before she could draw back his fingers had closed around hers, holding them fast. She dared not pull free for fear of attracting attention. As it was, she was becoming aware of the many women glancing in their direction. Among them surely were friends of Elizabeth LaMotte. 'The offer I made to you before, Dominy. . .that clumsy way I tried to keep you close to me. I was wrong and I apologise for backing you into a corner like that. Naturally you refused me. I should not have expected you to do otherwise. My only excuse is that I was desperate not to lose you. Are we still friends?'

'Yes, of course we are.' How could she refuse the plea? She was quite touched by his concern. 'But that is all. I do not think I could ever be anything else.'

'Not now. I realise your first priority is for your father and, although I still consider you are allowing your love and loyalty to him to misguide you in this matter, I will respect your feelings. However—I am a patient man. I want us to be more than friends, Dominy, and I am prepared to wait until you can come to me with your head held high and tell me you want to be with me.'

'It would not be fair of me to ask you to wait,' she

whispered, and his fingers tightened still more around hers. 'I do not know if I could ever love you.'

Why did she not have the courage to tell him she loved his best friend? End it before he began to hope? But he was being so sweet that she could not hurt him. It was so nice to be with someone she knew was not going to pull her into his arms and subject her to the mastery of kisses which reduced her to little more than a limp rag doll, or whose conversation was underlined with innuendoes and mockery that at times made her want to throw things at him. At others, it almost reduced her to tears.

'Is there someone else?' Austen's eyes searched her face and caught a moment of indecision before she nodded.

'But I do not mean anything to him in that way.' Dominy could not bear to see the pain that appeared on his face. She realised how wrong she had been to think Austen was simply amusing himself with her. Perhaps at first he had not realised how deeply he cared, but he did now—and he did not attempt to hide it. 'I can never mean anything to him.'

'Then let me help you forget him,' Austen insisted. 'The house I have rented is still yours. Without strings. If you want it.'

'No, Austen, I do not.' Dominy looked down at the tiny gold fob watch pinned to her bodice. 'It is getting late. I think I should go before your mother appears.'

'Don't you understand what I have been trying to tell you?' Austen said, reluctantly allowing her to pull her hand free of his. 'I cannot get you out of my thoughts. I'm not a young man in the throes of first love. I know that what I feel now is what I have been searching for all my life with a variety of women. None of them has affected me as you have. Come to me on your terms, Dominy—and to hell with the rest of the world. I know what I want now and I'm not going to let you get away from me a second time. Do what you have to and then make me the proudest man in the world by consenting to be my wife.'

His words robbed Dominy of speech. She froze in her chair, a blush of colour stealing into her cheeks. His wife! Austen rose and drew her to her feet, smiling down into her confused face. Curious eyes followed them to the door, but suddenly Dominy did not care who saw her in his company or what was said about her.

'You would have me, knowing I cared for someone else?' Bright tears pricked her eyelids as they came out into the sunlight, and she quickly searched for a handkerchief, pretending it had dazzled her.

'On your terms, remember only that,' Austen murmured and, in full view of the crowded thoroughfare, bent and kissed her full on the lips.

'I think I am taking root in this chair,' Austen declared, unfastening another button of his shirt. He had discarded his jacket and cravat ten minutes after following Beau down to the cellar and partaking of the first bottle of excellent claret, which accompanied thick, juicy steaks, cooked to perfection as usual by Weng himself. On these occasions, when the two of them were closeted together for the evening, no one was allowed to disturb them for any reason whatsoever.

There were several rooms and passages which ran the length and breadth of the area beneath the Devil's Rest, filled mostly with furniture and oddments. The largest room contained racks of wines and spirits: aged French brandy, mellowing in bottles dusty with age; full-bodied Burgundies; light, tantalising white wines. Over the years Austen had sampled them all.

From the other end of the long table that Weng had waxed and polished that afternoon, before setting out the silver candelabra and sparkling glass goblets for them to drink from, Beau refilled his glass from the bottle at his fingertips, a thoughtful look in his eyes as he considered his friend. He had seen Dominy return—and seen who had been her escort. The way they had looked at each other before she had entered the Rest. . . Was he reading something into it that was not really there?

An ugly suspicion had leapt unbidden to his mind that perhaps she was reconsidering Austen's offer in the light of the one he himself had made. Comparing them perhaps? Austen had said nothing of the encounter, although he had been in a cheerful frame of mind when they had dined early and then spent several hours at the roulette wheel in the Bella Union, and, Beau recalled, had not been over-anxious for the company of the attractive hostess who had taken a fancy to him.

'Are you asleep down there?' Austen banged his bottle on the table. 'You should be celebrating, not sleeping.'

'I was thinking. What am I supposed to be celebrating?'

'The *Enchantress*, of course. What else? That place is going to knock every other in San Francisco out of the running. What are you thinking about? All the money you are going to make?'

'You have to admit, it is a beautiful thought,' Beau answered, his lips deepening into a smile. Money could not have been further from his thoughts. Or the *Enchantress*. For the first time since he had thought of the new venture she did not occupy his mind. Another woman did that, more tantalising, more challenging than any he had met before. Annoying, confusing, frustrating him, driving him to unbelievable lengths to have her, even though he knew he would only ever possess her body, never her heart.

He had offered her what she asked for and she had run straight to Austen—why? Hoping he would improve on the offer he had once made her? She was playing a very dangerous game if she thought she could out-manoeuvre him, Beau mused, but it was her choice. Women were so devious!

'Of course, I can offer you some fine investments in my bank,' Austen chuckled. 'I enjoy the horrified looks on the faces of some of my customers when I tell them my best account was once king of the waterfront.'

'I'd almost forgotten that. How the mighty are fallen.' Beau stared into his glass, his mind wandering back to those early days when he had first arrived in San Francisco, fresh from the gold fields with enough dust to buy a piece of property. He had fallen in love with a broken-down, dilapidated river-boat and done a deal with the owner over large jugs of ale within an hour. Every dollar he had possessed had gone into the refitting and repainting of the old boat, and he had renamed her the *Enchantress*, promising himself as he had stared at the name that this would be the only female in his life. The bitterness still lingered in him and at night rose up to inflame his temper. It had been four years before he had been able to remember the past without a murderous desire for revenge welling up inside him. 'From southern gentleman to waterfront gambler.'

'I'll drink to that. This is a good wine—have you any to spare?'

'Take a couple of bottles with you. On second thoughts, it will be safer if I have Weng bring them to the house. Good heavens, man! Are you still eating? Leave some room for the wine,' Beau declared in amusement as Austen helped himself to a piece of chicken from the dish Weng had placed between them.

It had been cooked first in wine, then coated in honey and baked. It was Austen's favourite. Beau never ceased to marvel at his friend's appetite. They had eaten a substantial meal before going on to the Bella Union, yet Austen could still find room to sample the culinary delights that Weng produced on their return.

'A good appetite is the sign of a man healthy in mind and body. LaMotte's first rule of survival,' Austen joked. 'Why don't you take more time to enjoy the finer things in life? You can afford it, and this place practically runs itself.'

'I still have the *Enchantress*, remember—and I don't exactly live the life of a monk,' Beau answered.

The smell of the chicken reached him and a tiny frown furrowed his dark brows. The room suddenly darkened with shadows as his mind went spinning back into the past and the warm comfortable kitchen at home, where he would retire after dinner, relax down into the rocking-chair beside the open fire and unwind after a day's toil. Often he would miss the evening meal, especially at the height of the season when the cotton was to be picked and there were not enough hours in the day to get through all the work waiting for him. He had hired good, reliable men as overseers to work with him, men who could get the best results from the Negro workers without the use of a whip and without constant supervision.

It had not been his father's way to be close to the hired help, as Beau had been. He had liked to sit and chat with them, drink with them. He had respect for men who worked as hard as he did and knew how to enjoy themselves when there was time.

There would always be a supper for him in that kitchen, no matter how late the hour, usually one of the housekeeper's chicken stews, full of plump meat and chick-peas and swimming in a rich sauce. He had not tasted anything like them since he had left South Carolina.

Dammit! What was the matter with him, dwelling on what was no longer possible? Julia's letters had reopened the wound, and it was festering again. But there was something else churning inside him too—homesickness. Only she could have roused it in him. Hair the colour of ripe chestnuts and a face that angels must have moulded.

And then, as swiftly as her image had appeared, it was replaced by another. That of a woman with hair of as rich a brown and eyes that once—on the occasion she had dined with them aboard the *Enchantress*, he recalled—had shone with the brilliance of emeralds. He had never seen the same lustre in them again, and in that moment, perhaps because of his own nostalgia, Beau acknowledged the sadness in her which he had chosen to ignore. Had he become so callous? So indifferent, that he could only think the worst of people?

Austen, totally oblivious to his friend's deep reminiscences, was expounding on the opportunities available to him.

'You are too restricted here, as you would be aboard the *Enchantress*. Buy yourself a decent house. Think of the privacy.'

'It's funny you should mention that.' Beau took a deep swallow of wine. It had lost its taste and he rose to select a bottle of brandy, which he opened and placed on the table after filling his glass. 'The Barton mansion hasn't been sold yet, has it?'

'It goes up for auction next month if no one comes up with the asking price beforehand.' Austen's interest was diverted from the chicken. He waved a half-eaten drumstick down the table. 'Are you interested—seriously?'

'My money is the same colour as anyone else's up there, isn't it? Why not? If I can afford it?'

'There's no problem there. You have my wholehearted support. But what has brought about this surprising decision? Are you getting nostalgic about the past? I mean, the Barton place was built to the specific requirements of its last owner—a retired Southern Colonel. He had magnolia trees planted around the place to remind him of the home he lost in the war, and to look at it you would think it had been transported lock, stock and barrel from some plantation. You would surely be at home there, my friend.'

'The past has nothing to do with it.' Liar—it had everything to do with his decision. Julia was pulling him one way—Dominy the other. If he bought the Barton mansion he could have the best of both worlds. Or was he desperately clutching at straws?

'Sorry. I can hear I've touched that raw nerve again. Why don't you go home, Beau? It would be less expensive than buying a house. Exorcise the ghost—or ghosts. I did. I discovered that the father I had hated as a child, who I had been told had abandoned me, was no ogre after all. He was—is—a man of integrity, warm and caring, with a love of life that has led me to take a closer look at my own.'

'The circumstances are somewhat different,' Beau said. 'My father was—and no doubt still is. . .' despite what Julia had written, he could not imagine his father handing over the reins of power to anyone '. . .a strict, unyielding man. There was no room in his life for imperfection—and I was far from perfect. My grandfather, bless his heart, taught me what to expect from the world at the tender age of six. His philosophy was to take one day at a time, trust only yourself and expect nothing from anyone. I worked like a Trojan, as hard as any field hand, to please a man incapable of uttering one word of praise—to me. . .not my younger brother, who could do no wrong. The work I didn't mind. I loved my home. I took pride in what I did, but it was never enough. When the war came it tore me apart to leave, and there was not a day went by that I did not worry about the place, dreamed of the day I could go home. God! What a homecoming!' A bitter smile spread across Beau's features; pain seared through him as red hot as the surgeon's knife that had extracted a bullet from his shoulder on one of those days. 'The return of the elder son, covered not in glory, but in shame.'

'You never did tell me what happened.' Austen had never known his friend to be so forthcoming with his past life and he was not going to allow him to stop now.

'And tonight is not the night to bore you to death. Let's save it for another time and another bottle of brandy. The night is still young and you haven't finished Weng's chicken yet.' Beau leaned back in his chair and lighted a cigar, then pushed the silver-topped box and matches towards his companion, deciding it was time to say what was uppermost in his mind. 'Have you and Dominy found a solution to your little problem?'

'No more wagers, please,' Austen pleaded. 'I think I am too vulnerable.'

'You! Austen LaMotte, the scourge of unmarried ladies of San Francisco?' Beau chuckled. The pale blue eyes had narrowed slightly and there was no humour in them. Then a hint of laughter sprang to their depths. 'By the way you were gazing into each other's eyes this afternoon, I thought love's young dream had been reawakened.'

'Cynic. You could do worse than find yourself a wife,' Austen answered, not minding the mockery. The brandy was beginning to mellow him and he grinned, almost shyly. Dominy had not said no; therefore he could allow himself to dream a little—and plan. . .'It is important to Dominy that she clears her father's debts, but we have come to an understanding. . . She's not going to get away from me again, so if you don't have the Barton place it would do very nicely for us.'

Patience would bring its own rewards, he told himself as he watched for some reaction on Beau's face, but, apart from a narrowing of the pale eyes, there was nothing. Dominy would accept him. He had so much to offer.

'A love-nest for two. Don't fall into a ready-made trap,' Beau warned. So she had decided to play them against each other. How foolish of her. 'I still believe she's like her father. She will do anything for money and—like all women—she's as devious as hell!'

At the top of the cellar steps, Weng quietly closed the door and turned to the young woman at his side. By the sight of her ashen cheeks, he knew she, too, had overheard Beau's last caustic comment. But she neither gave way to an outburst of temper, nor a fit of weeping to hear herself maligned so unjustly, and his respect for her grew. Only her eyes, like the softest jade, in his opinion, expressed the distress she was experiencing.

'I do not think it wise to disturb Mr Beautrellis tonight. Perhaps if you leave the papers you have in the sitting-room he will look at them first thing in the morning.'

'Yes, Weng. I do not want to intrude on his evening's entertainment with business matters,' Dominy said, turning blindly away.

How dared he? Austen looked like a cat who had just stolen a jug of cream, and very drunk. But Beau—he was stone-cold sober. What had been said to provoke such a comment? Each and every word spoken by Beau had been uttered with the conviction that she was her father's daughter in every sense of the word.

She found herself standing in the midst of the sitting-room, with the heady perfume of incense surrounding her, still clutching the sheaf of bills and proposals she had drawn up for Beau's perusal. For a moment she had thought it possible she might gain some respect—or at least a pleasant working relationship with him once she had shown him how capable she was—but he had shattered that hope.

She dropped the papers on to the table and turned to go, then realised there had been something already there, propped against a small vase of flowers. She recognised the envelope immediately. Her fingers trembled as she reached for it, drew out the single piece of scented paper. There was writing on both sides, but she had no interest in it all—only in the last paragraph, and the signature.

> Please come back, I beg you. The past is behind us both now and I have so much to make up for. . .

Tears blurred Dominy's vision, and it was not possible to read the flourishing signature until she had wiped a hand across her eyes to clear them.

> My heart is with you always, Julia.

So that was the name of the woman he had left behind, who pined for him, begged him to return to her. Dominy had seen no sign that he was touched or affected in any way by the heartbreaking plea. He had abandoned her without a second thought. And now he was using Dominy, as he had no doubt used this Julia and countless women in his life, to satiate his desires without affection, consideration and certainly without love! Well, she was not going to allow him to treat *her* as he had others, especially that poor lovesick woman who had written to him and made no impression on his stony heart.

There was one escape open to her—one way in which she could free herself from him forever. A last resort that she had never allowed herself to consider until this moment. . .she must sell her grandmother's necklace!

CHAPTER EIGHT

'How do I look?' Dominy spun around in front of Su Lin and Maisie, holding her breath for their reactions. She felt as if she were about to go to her first grand ball, rather than just trying on the gown she was to wear for the opening. It was impossible to stem the excitement which was growing inside her. If the opening of the *Enchantress* was a success then it was all due to her, and no one—not even Beau—could take that from her.

Su Lin broke into a stream of rapid Chinese, nodding her head and beaming.

'She approves and so do I!' Maisie's admiration for the girl who had become a close friend over the past weeks was multiplying with each passing day. Nothing flustered her, and her quiet but firm manner with the men working on the boat had caused the wolf whistles to disappear and the suggestive comments—if anyone was foolish enough to utter them aloud—to be dealt with in the sharpest fashion by Paddy O'Neill. And that meant anything from a warning look to a bruised jaw.

'Milady' was how Dominy was known aboard the *Enchantress*. Whether Maisie had allowed the name to slip or someone had overheard Beau addressing her in that fashion she did not know, but now the derisive nickname brought her pride, and she no longer winced each time she heard it.

She was the daughter of a lord; why should she forget it?

'You look stunning, but not very enthusiastic. Getting cold feet?' Maisie added, secretly dreading the thought of the tight corset she would be imprisoned inside in order to look half as good as Dominy did.

'I am so frightened something will go wrong,' Dominy admitted. 'I think I will stay aboard tonight and take a last look around. We open in three days. . .'

Three short days. . .she could hardly believe how the time had flown by.

'I shall need all the girls aboard this afternoon, Maisie, for the final fittings of their dresses, and if you can spare the time I would like you to look over the food list with me again. I am wondering if I have ordered enough lobster.'

'Never having tasted the stuff myself, I can't tell you how much people are going to eat. Of course there will be enough. I've never heard of half of those fancy dishes, but I'm looking forward to trying a few.'

'I have arranged a special little celebration of our own when everyone has gone to thank them all for their hard work—if we can still stand, that is,' Dominy added with a smile, beckoning Su Lin to unfasten her gown. 'It is going to be a very long night. One I intend San Francisco to be talking about for a long time.'

'That's the kind of fighting talk I like to hear.'

Dominy wheeled about with a gasp, the blue silk slipping to the floor, leaving her in nothing but a thin chemise. Su Lin waved Beau back with a comment in Chinese and, when he ignored her and moved further into the room, snatched up Dominy's wrap and threw it around her. She struggled into it, hating him for spoiling what had been a very private moment.

'Did you want anything in particular, Mr Beautrellis?' she asked icily.

'You always call me that when you are annoyed with me,' Beau murmured, his eyes following the slender hands which belted the wrap and then pulled it together high about her neck. Laughter sprang to his eyes at the unnecessary gesture.

'I guess she must always be annoyed with you, Beau,' Maisie giggled, and received warning looks from both directions not to interrupt. She thought Beau looked as if he would prefer to kiss Dominy than make conversation with her. And she. . . Maisie marvelled at her will-power. She was in love with him, yet she looked at him as if he were a stranger. Given half a chance, Maisie would not have said no to such a handsome man, but

Beau had never looked at her like that. Not the way he looked at Dominy when he knew she was unaware of it. She hoped they would resolve their problems soon—she hated unhappy endings. What they needed was a push in the right direction, and perhaps she was just the person to do it. If she could bring them together. . .

Beau bent to pick up the gown Dominy had discarded, and examined it for a long moment.

'I prefer you in green. This colour does not do justice to those eyes.'

Dominy slowly lifted her eyes from the long brown fingers caressing the dark material. She felt as if they were caressing her skin.

'Is that all you came to find out?'

'I, too, like to reward those who work well,' came the reply, which brought a low whistle of approval from Maisie's lips.

'Does that include us all?'

'If the *Enchantress* does as well as I expect her to I'll stand you to a trip back home. How does that sound?'

'Too good to be true, but I'll take you up on the offer.' Home. Maisie had almost forgotten what it looked like. After living in a bustling place like San Francisco she knew it would look worse to her now than when she had left, for, with her father dead, there was no man to keep the property maintained. But her mother was there, and to be with her she could put up with anything. . .even getting up at dawn to milk the only cow, feed the chickens and collect the eggs. 'What does Dominy get?'

Beau looked at Dominy—a look so intense and penetrating that she felt a shock tingle up and down her spine. She knew exactly what he intended for her.

'I thought you knew everything, Maisie. I'll see you on board this afternoon, milady. If you have any problems we can go over them together.'

'This place is beginning to look like a florist's shop.'

Dominy was hanging away the clothes she would wear on opening night when Beau appeared in the doorway of the state-room. He had not put in an appearance by the time it grew dark, and she was about to leave to return to the Rest. Now it looked as if it would be another late night, she thought in annoyance at his lack of thought.

He strolled into the room, stepping over and around baskets of flowers, which had been arriving most of the day. She had placed as many as possible close by, but there were so many that she had decided to decorate the dining-room with the remainder. She hoped there would be no more tomorrow.

Unfastening his jacket, Beau discarded it and tossed it across a chair. From a mass of white roses he plucked a small white card, and her lips tightened as he read it aloud.

'"To the fairest flower of them all."' He grimaced at the sentiment and dropped it back amid the tall-stemmed flowers. 'Austen is acting like a lovesick boy. If he doesn't suffocate you with meaningless words he intends to do it with flowers, obviously. I hope you haven't put any in my room?'

'No, I knew they would not be appreciated,' Dominy returned, adding tartly, 'You have to be a gentleman to know how a lady likes to be treated. I think they are lovely, and I shall tell him so.'

'*Touché*. And what does milady prefer? Flowers—or something like this?'

From a pocket Beau produced a small well-worn leather box and snapped back the lid. He considered the contents with an expression of satisfaction on the sun-tanned features. Then he held it out to her. 'Someone once told me about a Jewish jeweller in town who has quite an amazing collection of jewellery. As I wanted something special, I thought I would look him up. He had, too. Do you know, I spent an hour trying to decide between a black pearl, which he swore had once been worn by Catherine the Great of Russia, or this. . .? You may or may not believe this once belonged to one of the English royal family, but I thought it rather appropriate for an English lady.'

Dominy had no idea what to expect. A bracelet, perhaps, or diamond earrings. . .certainly not the exquisite creation that he slowly lifted up before her stunned eyes. Diamonds, hundreds of them, sparkling and glittering with pure white fire in the candlelight. They had been fashioned into a collar on a spider's web of the finest gold. It was the work of a craftsman of the highest degree. A work of art. She could not believe she was looking at anything so beautiful—and that he had bought it for her. She did not want to know his reasons—she did not care. She had never owned anything like this. Not even her grandmother's necklace matched this lustre and brilliance.

'Turn around and let me put it on for you,' Beau said quietly, and she obeyed without argument, lifting the loose hair from the nape of her neck so that he could fasten it.

'What do you think?' He guided her to the wall-length mirror so that she could see her reflection. 'Of course, to be shown off to perfection they need to be against your skin.'

She flinched away as his fingers reached for the fastenings of her dress and stepped well out of his reach.

'I—I cannot take it.'

'Why? Austen seems to think you and he have some kind of understanding, but it is you and I who have that—do we not?' Beau said quietly.

'I have not committed myself to either of you,' Dominy returned defensively.

'Waiting to see which one of us comes up with the best offer? If I am prepared to meet your terms, why look elsewhere?'

'Perhaps Austen is prepared to give me something you are not—respectability. The kind of girl you believe me to be would consider that important.'

'So you mean marriage?' Beau's eyebrows winged upwards in genuine surprise. So he had been telling the truth! 'Hell will freeze over before I trust a woman enough to give her my name.'

'Or love one,' Dominy said bitterly as his words shattered all hope in her.

'I have never been loved by anyone in my life, so I

have no experience of the emotion—and am grateful not to have it complicate my life.'

What of Julia? Of the home he had been forced to leave? Had that not been in the name of love? If not love—then what? She noticed a small pulse had begun to beat at one side of his forehead as if the conversation was disturbing him. What was there in the past to do that? It had to be a woman, whether he admitted it or not.

Could she ever step into another woman's shoes? Dominy wondered as her fingers lightly caressed the stones against her skin. If she told him she loved him. . . No, he would not believe her. If she accepted his proposition perhaps in time she could make him love her. It would be a stony path upon which she trod, a precarious one, for she would never know what awaited her at the end of it. Love—or grief and pain.

'You must have bought up every can of paint in town for these rooms,' Beau remarked as he came back into the room. He had been inspecting the adjoining stateroom, which he would use when he stayed aboard, and could find no fault with the décor. In fact, although he did not say so, it came close to what he would have chosen himself. The bedspread and drapes were a mixture of autumn colours, reddish brown and yellow and russet. Carpets of burnt orange were scattered on the polished wood floors, and the furniture was of light pine.

In contrast Dominy had chosen green for her own room. Dark green and cream floral wallpaper with a matching bedspread and curtains. The paintwork was all cream. On the floor was a dark green carpet.

'Do you approve?'

'You have done for the *Enchantress* what no man could have—brought a touch of feminine elegance to her. Yes, I do approve. I looked her over when I arrived. Shall we call a truce?'

'What?' Dominy echoed, taken aback.

'We have both worked too hard to make the opening a success, so why don't we put our personal problems behind us until after then?' Beau dragged his eyes away from the huge canopied bed and the vision of Dominy there, her rich brown hair spread over the pillows like waves of fire, dreaming of Austen. . . 'Let's open a bottle—or two—of champagne and relax. I promise to keep my distance—if that is what you want.'

'You are in a suspiciously good mood to seek my company.' Dominy warily followed him to the main dining area, casting her gaze over everything while he found and opened a bottle of champagne, to ensure nothing had been left out.

It all looked so perfect. She could imagine the room filled with people, the hubbub of voices, the smell of food wafting through the boat to entice others to come and sample the delights offered. She had chosen the wines and approved the menus personally. She was beginning to feel more than just an employee aboard the *Enchantress*. She had become part of something very exciting, and as Beau pushed a tall glass filled with sparkling champagne across the polished bar towards her she decided it was time she should be proud of what she had done. It was quite an accomplishment. She could not wait to receive a reply to the letter she had written to the Comtesse telling her of the twist of fate that had altered her life.

'To the *Enchantress*. . .' Beau raised his glass, touched it against hers with a smile that softened her still further. 'May she bring us both what we want most in life.'

'That is an ambitious wish and a very strange one for someone without one iota of romance in his soul. . .'

Beau put down his glass and came around to where she stood. A flicker of alarm darted through her at the glitter which had sprung to his eyes.

'You promised to behave. . .' she began, and he chuckled deep in his throat. Her glass was plucked from her fingers, put to one side.

'Like a gentleman. . .like Austen?' He placed his hands one either side of her, trapping her between. She could feel the warmth of him, smell the sweet odour of cigar smoke on his shirt. 'Are you going to tell me you have not considered my offer? That it does not appeal to you?'

Dominy lowered her eyes so that he would not see the confusion mirrored there. She had tried to be level-headed about it for her father's sake, but, in the light of the letter Julia had written, she had decided the best thing, the only sensible thing to do would be to return to her grandmother as soon as she had sold the necklace. But there was also another alternative—to stay and fight for his love!

'I do believe milady is weakening,' Beau teased, tilting back her head so that he could look into her face again. Such indecision there. Why was it so difficult?

'Must you always make fun of me?' He temper flared at his insensitivity, and instantly the laughter faded from his expression.

'Nothing was further from my mind.'

'And Julia?'

'Has nothing to do with us. She is part of the past I consider dead and forgotten, and she is not a topic open for discussion—ever,' came the harsh reply. 'That is the second time you have mentioned her to me. Damn it, have you been prying into my personal mail?'

'Certainly not!' Dominy gasped indignantly, although she knew she had been totally in the wrong to even glance at the letter, curiosity or no. . . 'I just happened. . .I mean, it was in the sitting-room——'

'And you read it,' Beau interrupted stonily. His hands had closed over her shoulders, and for a moment she thought he was going to shake her, so furious did he look. 'Hoping to do a little blackmailing of your own, perhaps, and extricate yourself from your present position?'

'Blackmail I leave to you, Mr Beautrellis; you have had far more experience!' she flung back, eyes blazing as she stared into the dark face and love and hate merged again into one seething, destructive emotion. 'If your conscience did not bother you so much over the way you treated the poor woman you would not be so angry. At least marriage to Austen would get me out of your clutches!' She seized on Austen like a protective cloak—protection from Beau's touch and his kisses. . .and herself!

So heated was the exchange between them that neither was aware of the shadowy figures entering the room, converging on where they stood from the deck, the state-rooms, climbing the stairs from the kitchens below. Beau became conscious of their presence first as a movement drew his attention to the long mirror behind the bar. At the oath which broke from his lips, Dominy's eyes flew past his startled features to the dozen or more men, mostly dressed in seamen's clothes and wielding an assortment of unpleasant-looking weapons, who were now surrounding them.

He wheeled about, protecting her with his body as a vicious-looking club was raised in his direction. Dominy screamed as he threw up his arms to protect himself, and it was brought down on one shoulder with a sickening thud.

He dropped to his knees. . .she saw him desperately trying to free something from his boot, and caught the flash of candlelight on a polished blade as he came to his feet, knife in hand.

'Get behind the bar. Duck down. Stay there—they don't want you. . .'

She turned to obey him, was tripped by the man nearest and fell into the arms of his companion.

'This one's a real wildcat. Not very ladylike, is she?' came the comment as she struggled to free herself, heard her dress tear at the shoulder and raked with long nails at the unshaven cheeks of her tormentor. 'Maybe a ducking will quieten her down, boys.'

Dominy almost fainted with horror. Were they going to throw her into the water? She could not swim! She would drown! She twisted and turned with the litheness of a slippery eel in the man's grasp, and then brought her high-heeled shoe down on his foot with all her might. With a howl of pain and rage he let her go, but immediately she was seized by another man, and a savage blow across the face sent her reeling against the bar. As she slid, barely conscious, to the floor she saw Beau go down beneath five men who were beating him mercilessly with fists and sticks. She tried to lift herself up—somehow she had to help him. . .they were going to kill him—but someone thrust a booted foot into her back and kept her immobile. Sobbing helplessly, she was forced to lie still and listen to the terrible grunts of pain, blow after blow being delivered upon a man unable to defend himself.

And then there was laughter, accompanied by the deafening crashing of chairs being hurled against the walls, glass shattered, bottles smashed. Cowards! All those men against one, and now they were wrecking weeks of hard work, destroying the beauty that had been created aboard the *Enchantress* for the pleasure of others. These men were deriving pleasure from its destruction. They were insane. How could they hate Beau that much?

The heavy weight was removed from her back, but it was a full moment before she dared lift her head. The devastation which was spread out before her eyes was horrific. She swayed to her knees, brushing back the hair from her face which had become loose in the struggle. Her head ached. . .she must have hit it as she had fallen, although she did not remember doing so. Her vision momentarily blurred, and the inert figure of Beau was dizzily out of focus.

There was someone bending over him. He had Beau's knife in his hand! She threw herself across the floor, shielding him with her body as he had tried to protect her moments before.

'For the love of heaven, leave him alone. Haven't you done enough to him?' she cried, cradling the bruised and bloody head in her arms. He was so still. . . She lifted her head—and found herself looking into the swarthy features of the man who had tried to buy her a drink at the Devil's Rest. The previous owner, Philippe Gascoigne, the Frenchman who lived off rich women and blackmailed them for their indiscretions. 'You!'

'It would be better had you not seen me, *mademoiselle*. . .' The flat, emotionless voice chilled her to the bone. But even as he reached down to haul her away from Beau there came a warning shout from outside and he straightened with an unpleasant oath. 'You will keep. . .'

His eyes fastened on the necklace around her throat. His men were busy ransacking the boat for any valuables, but this looked worth a king's ransom. Dominy was too weak to avoid the hooked fingers which reached down and fastened in the collar, plucking it from her neck. At a high-pitched whistle from his lips his men emerged from all directions and disappeared into the darkness as silently and as swiftly as they had appeared. Dominy slid down beside Beau, faint with relief. He had intended to kill her! To kill them both! She felt her senses slipping away from her. . .

'Weng, I am perfectly all right. I fainted, that is all.'

Dominy did not realise she had fully lost consciousness until she recovered to find someone had carried her into her state-room and laid her on the bed. Weng's anxious face was hovering over her, and he was trying to trickle brandy between her clenched lips.

'Please don't fuss, and don't give me any more of that horrible stuff or I shall be sick. It is Beau you should be looking after.'

'Mr Beautrellis is on his feet, Miss Granville,' Weng assured her, and she stared up at him in open-mouthed disbelief.

'He was bleeding. And unconscious! He should see a doctor.'

'Cuts and grazes are inclined to bleed and look far worse than they really are,' came the calm reply. 'I assure you if he was in need of medical care I would be the first one to insist a doctor be called.'

'I must see him. . .' Dominy swung her legs from the bed and tried to stand. Instead, with a cry, she pitched forward into Weng's outstretched arms and was immediately deposited back amid the mound of pillows.

'It is you who must rest, Miss Granville. There is a very large bump on the back of your head and, if you remember, you have already suffered from one unpleasant blow in the earth tremor. I shall send for Su Lin to come and take care of you. Please remain where you are until I come back.'

No sooner had he left the room than Dominy again attempted to get up, with more success this time, although her legs felt like two thin twigs about to snap at any moment and pitch her to the floor. Gingerly she raised a hand to her head, and searching fingers discovered a very definite lump, which began to throb as she touched it. She still did not remember striking it against anything, but then, everything had happened so quickly. One moment she had been on the point of being kissed—and then she had been forced to watch a man being brutally beaten. If he was all right then where was he? Had Weng lied to her?

A movement from the other room drew her attention. She was walking towards the door, carefully stepping over clothes and furniture which had been hurled into the middle of the room by men who had obviously enjoyed the work they had come to do, when she froze, a hand against her mouth stifling the cry of horror which rose in her throat.

Her jewel box lay upturned on the carpet. It was empty! The contents were gone. The loss of imitation jewellery did not concern her; what brought a chill to her heart was the sight of the secret compartment in the box, also open—and empty. There was no sign of the velvet bag which contained her grandmother's necklace! The impact when it had been thrown to the floor must have triggered the mechanism to release the tiny drawer.

She reeled unsteadily into the other state-room, and caught at the door-post to support herself as a wave of giddiness swept over her.

'What the devil are you doing out of bed? Do I have to tie you down to keep you there?' In two long strides Beau had crossed the space between them and caught her up in his arms as her legs began to buckle beneath her. Depositing her on his bed, he fixed the pillows comfortably under her head and pulled the comforter over her shivering body. 'You can stay here tonight; I won't be needing it, and this room's not such an unholy mess as your own. When I get my hands on the men who did this. . .'

'It was Gascoigne,' Dominy said, her lips quivering as she stared up into the bruised face. 'He took my necklace. . .and all my jewellery. . .everything I had. . .I think he wanted to kill us. . .'

'Me, maybe, but not you. He has no reason to harm you,' Beau said, his features softening as he heard the fear in her voice. He dropped on the edge of the bed and took both her hands in his, forcing a smile to his lips even though it hurt like hell to do so. There was no doubt in his mind that Gascoigne, having him at a disadvantage—unconscious and helpless—would not have missed the opportunity to have his revenge, and if he had killed Beau he would have left no witness alive to testify against him. 'Don't worry, I'll get your jewellery back for you. Or replace it,' he added. 'Apart from one, all the pieces were worthless, were they not?'

'They are as important to me as the necklace you gave me tonight, but I would not expect you to understand that,' Dominy returned with a shrug. 'Are you going to the police?'

She watched him pull on a shirt, not missing the grimace of pain as he flexed bruised muscles. His actions were very controlled, very precise, as if he dared not allow the anger in him to be unleashed until the right moment. From the table he picked up the knife he had attempted to use earlier and returned it to his boot. Aware of her eyes following his every move, he said as casually as possible, 'You are quite safe now, so try to sleep. There will be a twenty-four-hour watch on the boat from now on. I'm a damned fool not to have had men here anyway, but the *Enchantress* is the last place I thought he would give me trouble. I didn't think he had that kind of nerve.'

'He hates you very much. He could be waiting for you out there, in one of those dark alleys. . .'

'Then that is where I will leave him.'

'Do you mean. . .do you intend to kill him?' Dominy gasped. 'But why. . .?'

The dangerous glitter that sprang to the pale blue eyes told her that was indeed what he had in mind.

'The last time someone walked on to my property and took what did not belong to them they destroyed years of hard work—and enjoyed what they did; they wore blue uniforms and it was called war. This is no different to me. The men who did this here tonight will pay as surely—as completely—as did those who rode their horses over my mother's grave that day. I protect what is mine.'

Weng met him in the dining-room and wondered at the disquiet which registered on the sun-bronzed features.

'Everything is all right, Mr Beautrellis?'

'No reason for it not to be, except—except I've just told something to that girl in there that I haven't shared with another living soul since it happened. Why her, of all people? You are the expert, Weng, so you tell me.'

'To know others, Mr Beautrellis, is wisdom. To know yourself is enlightenment. If you were to ask Miss Granville why she saved your life I do not think she would be able to give you an answer either. When I looked through the window I saw her crouched over you like a protective lioness, shielding you with her body. Mr Gascoigne had your knife and I believe would have used it had I not caused a disturbance to make him believe there were many men returning aboard. Unfortunately I could not prevent him from taking the necklace you gave to Miss Granville, but I consider a few diamonds cannot compare to the loss of two lives. Do you wish me to come with you or remain here?'

Beau ran his fingers through his thick black hair with a low expletive. What kind of hand was fate dealing out to him now? He owed Dominy his life! The blow on the head must have dazed her; she could not have known what she was doing. Come to his aid? Never! With him out of the way she would have been free to take back her father's IOUs and destroy them and then accept Austen's offer without a second thought. It just did not make sense. . .

'Stay here. I leave the *Enchantress* and Miss Granville in your capable hands, Weng, and if. . .' a humourless smile touched the swollen lips '. . .I should disappear without trace tonight you know where my papers are and who is to have them.'

'I shall also know where to look for your remains, Mr Beautrellis. That man Gascoigne has no finesse.'

'A comforting thought—I think.'

'My cousin Ah Fong is waiting for you at the corner of South Street. The Frenchman's men began celebrating when they left here, and some of them set fire to his mother's laundry. You will have as many men as you need, Mr Beautrellis.'

'I am indebted to your cousin,' Beau returned with all solemnity. Gascoigne and his men would be hunted until every last one of them had paid for their wrecking tonight. The *Enchantress* was only a small part of it now. They had gone against the Chinese community, the most closely knit people he had ever known, and that was a cardinal sin.

'Why are you not resting, Miss Granville?' Weng returned to the state-room, to find Dominy sitting on the edge of the bed, surrounded by crumpled clothes. 'Su Lin will be here soon and she will take care of all of this. Please go to bed. I have brought you some herb tea and something to help you sleep.'

Dominy put aside the dress she was holding and reached gratefully for the delicate porcelain cup decorated with a flaming red dragon which he placed beside her on a small carved table. The glass containing a milky white substance she ignored.

'Yes, you are right. Most of these things will need to be pressed again. Poor Su Lin, after all her hard work the other day. A few may be torn too. . .those *canaille*. . . Mr Beautrellis—has gone?'

'A few moments ago. Do not be alarmed, we are not

alone. He has many friends and I have more relatives than I can count. We are well protected.'

'Good, we shall need to call on some of them later on.'

'After a good night's rest it will be easier to look at things in a better light,' Weng said. No one ever disputed his authority, except Beau, and then never within the hearing of another, but he sensed it was being questioned now. He stared pointedly at the glass. Dominy followed his gaze and smiled, but made no attempt to take and drink it.

'Later, when we have done something to start getting rid of the mess everywhere. We still have an opening in three days,' she said, getting to her feet.

He watched the blood drain from her cheeks and insisted, 'You must rest. Mr Beautrellis would insist if he were here. In his place I must do so.'

'*I* want to do something useful, Weng. Too many people have worked too long and hard to have a man like Gascoigne ruin everything for them.' Dominy forced herself past the pain and dizziness in her head. 'Either you can help me, Weng, or go away.'

Had anyone else spoken to him in such a fashion Weng would have turned on his heel and left them, but the determination in the young face touched him. Both father and daughter, although complete opposites, had hidden strength of character, the potential of which had not yet been fully realised.

'I shall stay, of course.'

'Good, then let us start with the restaurant and make a list of the furniture we shall have to replace.'

Dominy lost track of all time as she worked, concentrating fiercely on making it as easy as possible to start repairs the following morning. She almost cried when Paddy O'Neill appeared, ready to help in any way required of him. The whole waterfront was talking of the attack, he told her, and, as most of them had been making a comfortable living in Beau's employment over the past weeks, they were incensed at the needless damage and eager to confront whoever had done it. On the dock he had over two dozen men.

'I understand that you would rather get your hands on the men who did this than broken furniture,' Dominy said, a faint smile lighting up her pale features, 'but you would all be of so much more use here. I have made a list of what we shall need to replace, but some of the chairs and tables are not as badly damaged as they look. If you will have your men clear out the useless bits and pieces perhaps someone could start a few repairs to them. By the time they are revarnished that will be a whole day gone. . .leaving only one,' she added meaningly.

'Anything for you, milady. There's quite a mess outside too. . .a couple of broken rails, doors smashed. Sure, now, I couldn't be that destructive if I'd been on the heavy stuff a whole week.'

'Men with a grudge seem to be able to rally great destructive power,' Dominy said with a shake of her head. 'I don't understand them. . .to enjoy it. . . Will you ask Weng about outside? I haven't had the heart to go out there yet—in here is bad enough.'

'We'll have this room organised in no time,' Paddy assured her, surveying the debris around them, tight-lipped. 'There'll be a few bodies floating out to sea for this piece of work. . .'

'Don't even think such a thing, let alone say it aloud,' Dominy replied, reminded of the cold anger which had possessed Beau before he had left. Where was he now? What danger was he facing?

'Don't worry, milady, your man's a tough nut. He knows how to deal with waterfront scum. Come on then, Weng, me old Chinese mate, let's get to it.'

For a moment the inscrutable mask almost dropped as Weng heard himself addressed in such a fashion. From Beau he expected and accepted familiarity—after all, they had shared much, and the bond between them was as binding as blood. But this common labourer. . .! That he, Weng Lo Yan, only son of Chang Si, chief magistrate of Wong Su, should be called 'mate'! It reduced him to the level of a seaman. But then, he mused, understanding that this poor man, in his ignorance, knew no better, he was a long way from China and the old way of life. With his usual polite bow to Dominy, he led the way out on deck.

It was a relief to see him go. Dominy sat down in one of the unbroken chairs and laid her aching head against the padded back. He had been one step behind her in everything she had done, those slanting eyes disapproving of her every move. But if she did not keep herself busy she would begin to wonder where Beau was. If he had found Gascoigne. . .had used that knife nestled in his boot. . . Would he—could he use it? How little she knew of the man she had come to love. . .and yet at times still hated. He brought out the worst in her—a love she could not acknowledge, which burned inside her night and day, crying out to be satiated. A desire for justice for her father, or was it really revenge she wanted on the man who had forced her to work for him so that she could pay off the debt owed to him?

Her father had been foolish, but she had been very wrong. Beau had offered her a way out in which she lost none of her own dignity. In fact, these past weeks she had begun to respect herself again, and took great pride in her achievements. He had made that possible. But to separate the love eating away at her. . .and the contempt for the way he had made her father's peace of mind possible. . .it was sometimes beyond her to do that.

How she ached. Now that she was still a moment, she realised how heavy her legs felt. Her head was throbbing maddeningly and one cheek had begun to feel very sore where she had been struck.

It was a minute or two before Dominy realised she was not alone in the room. She sat upright in her chair as Beau reached behind the bar, helped himself to a bottle and took a long, deep swallow. Weng was at his side, and both had moved so quietly that she had been unaware of their presence—as they were of hers. As she rose Beau wheeled about, his hand instinctively reaching for his hidden weapon. There was a fresh bruise just below his left eye and his shirt was torn in several places. He had found the men he had sought, she realised, smoothing back her loose hair, suddenly conscious of her dishevelled appearance. Beau took one look at her white cheeks and swung round on the Chinese man with an oath.

'I told you to look after her!' Had she not known differently Dominy would have sworn he was concerned for her.

'To do that I had to remain with her, Mr Beautrellis. The lady has a mind of her own—but then, I do not have to tell you that.'

'Did you find the men you were after?' Dominy ventured to ask.

'Most of them. Gascoigne has gone to ground, but he'll have to surface again soon and I'll be waiting for him. Perhaps it's better I didn't find him tonight. I would have killed him for sure.'

'It would not be the first time you have killed over a woman, would it? Even if this one isn't flesh and blood?' The words were out of her mouth before she had thought what she was saying.

Beau's hands tightened into fists at his sides as he stared at her. Did she really believe it had all been because of what had been done to the *Enchantress*? He wanted to grab hold of her and shake some sense into her, but then as he saw her mouth begin to tremble he wanted only to kiss her, to be gentle with her. But gentleness, kindness—they were only other words for weakness, and he had already lost too much tonight. No! He was giving away of his own free will what had become most important in his life. After tonight's events, what other choice did he have?

'If I weren't so damned tired I'd take you to task over those pretty words. Go to bed.'

'My jewellery?' Dominy was almost to the door of her state-room when she remembered that her most precious possession had been stolen.

Instantly Beau's mouth deepened into a mocking smile.

'Safe.' Reaching into his shirt, he brought out a handkerchief, securing the contents with a large knot.

'You should find it all there—they didn't have time to divide it up. If there is anything missing let me know and I'll replace it.'

'That will not be necessary,' Dominy replied stiffly, taking the bundle, which he had passed on to Weng.

She stood with her back against the closed door, her fingers fighting to undo the tight knot. It had to be there. . .the imitation jewellery, which had been passed down to her on her mother's death, spilled out on to the bed. Everything. . .but the ruby and diamond necklace. Even the beautiful creation Beau had given her that evening lay sparkling and gleaming upon the coverlet, but not her grandmother's necklace. She sank down beside the mound of bracelets and rings, her mind refusing to accept it could be gone. Its loss meant she must go on working for Beau until the debt was fully paid. . .

Once again fate had trapped her. . .

CHAPTER NINE

DOMINY awoke with the sound of hammering ringing in her ears. The whole boat vibrated with noise. From the deck above her came the heavy tread of many feet. As she slowly sat up, wondering why she felt so stiff and why her head still ached, she heard the unmistakable brogue of Paddy O'Neill shouting orders. He was in his element when given charge of men, she mused, pushing aside the covers.

Just for an instant, her mind still fogged with sleep, she stared at the disorder of the room which the night before had been full of sweet-smelling flowers and a picture of elegance. Of course. . .Gascoigne's men! That was the reason for so much activity. It sounded to her as if every available man in San Francisco had arrived to give them a hand with repairs. Beau obviously had every intention of still opening on time.

The clothes that had been scattered over the floor had been put away in the closets. The broken vases and flowers too had gone. All that remained to show of the terrifying assault was a broken chair and a smashed mirror. Not until she went to the vanity beneath one window and reached for the silver-backed brush which should have been there did she realise several other things were missing, besides the precious necklace. The brush was gone and the matching mirror, both presents from her parents on her seventeenth birthday. Also several little trinket boxes of Limoges porcelain which had once belonged to the Comtesse.

The articles were valuable and when sold would fetch a large sum of money, but to Dominy the theft of them was more devastating than any monetary loss. She felt as if she had lost part of her identity and was now left with nothing more than memories, which would grow fainter and fainter in her mind as time went by. She laid her throbbing head between her arms and tried to shut out the horrendous banging from overhead. She did not hear the knock on the door and was unaware of anyone else in the room until Maisie deposited a cup of lemon tea in front of her.

'You look awful,' she declared, taken aback by Dominy's ashen cheeks, the dark shadows beneath dull eyes. 'I intercepted Weng. I want to hear all about last night. The whole waterfront is talking about it. Did Gascoigne really come aboard and tried to set fire to the *Enchantress*?'

'I don't know about that. . .' Had Beau not told her everything? Was that the reason he had gone after the man with such fury in his heart? 'He came aboard with some men and they tried to wreck the place. . .it looked worse than it really was, I'm glad to say.' Dominy sipped the hot, sweet tea, hoping it would revive her flagging spirits.

'Beau looks as if he had a brush with runaway train—head on,' Maisie said. 'And you don't look much better. You should be in bed.'

'Not while everyone else is working,' Dominy replied adamantly. Instinctively her hand reached again for the brush and discovered it was not there. Huge tears trembled in her eyes, and Maisie slipped to her knees beside the chair, an arm around her shoulders, as they spilled down over her cheeks. 'They have stolen my grandmother's necklace. . .I was going to sell it so that I could pay back Beau and go back to France, where I belong. I hate San Francisco. I hate everything about it. I shall never be happy here. . . Now. . .I have to stay. . .with him. Oh, Maisie, I am so unhappy. . .I don't know what to do.'

'First you tell Beau about this necklace and anything else you've lost. He'll soon get it back for you—or make good the loss. You'll see,' Maisie said, hugging her. She was shivering, despite the warmth of the sun that streamed into the room.

'I should have worn it on my wedding-day. . .I promised Grandmère I would. I promised I would never sell it, too, but it was the only way open to me. And now it's gone!'

Dominy was silent for a long while, then, straightening her shoulders, she reached for a handkerchief and wiped dry her eyes.

'What is the matter with me? Acting like an idiot.'

'You've had a nasty shock. They didn't hurt you?' Maisie did not like the flush of colour which was creeping into Dominy's cheeks. She would have a word with Weng.

'They frightened me out of my wits. I hope nothing like that ever happens again.' Dominy wound her loose hair into a thick coil and secured it at the nape of her neck with comb and pins. 'There—a slight improvement.'

'I still think you should be resting,' Maisie protested as she went to the closet and pulled out some clothes.

'Rest! In this madhouse? No, I shall be better off doing something useful.' No matter how trivial the task, it would help to keep her mind off her loss—and the consequences which would result because of it.

When she came up on deck she was blinded by the strong sunlight, yet found herself shivering in the soaring temperature as it reached noon. Men had stripped off their shirts to work, and the bodies around her glistened with sweat as they laboured. As well as many faces that had grown familiar to her she saw at least two dozen nimble-footed Chinese men—and at the far end of the deck Madam Chen stood, deep in conversation with Beau.

Dominy felt a gnawing ache reawakened inside her as she stared at him. He had discarded his shirt like so many others, revealing the sunburnt chest with its matt of dark hair. His arms were loosely folded, but, even so, Dominy could see the sinewy muscles which flexed with the tiniest movement, reminding her of the strength hidden behind that relaxed stance. He lifted his head and saw her, and even at a distance she felt the intensity of his gaze, was drawn to where he stood. He said something to Madam Chen and immediately the woman turned and acknowledged Dominy's presence with a polite smile.

'Good morning, Miss Granville. I have just been hearing about your unfortunate experience of last night. I trust you are fully recovered?'

'She would be if she stayed in bed long enough,' Beau said with a frown.

'I am perfectly well, madam, thank you.' Dominy chose to ignore the remark.

'I am so pleased to hear that. I have brought a gift from your father for the opening of the new venture. He hopes it will bring you pleasure—as I do. I have given it to Weng.'

'That is most kind of you. Will you thank my father for me? And tell him I look forward to seeing him on our special evening.'

'Of course.' The woman's eyes were veiled as she turned away, or Dominy might have wondered at the look which had entered them. 'If you have need of more men you know where to come. Do not hesitate.'

'If we work around the clock we might just make it with the work-force we have, but if there's an emergency I shall call on you, be sure of that. You have my gratitude, for what it is worth.'

'A great deal—to friends.'

'You look as if you could use a cup of good strong black coffee,' Beau declared when they were alone and, taking Dominy firmly by the arm, propelled her back into the coolness of the dining-room. 'And no arguments,' he added as she opened her mouth to protest her dislike of the sweet syrupy mixture he always drank. 'You look as if a breeze could knock you flat on your back.'

'Everyone is full of compliments this morning. Maisie said almost the same thing, but there is nothing wrong with me—except a slight headache. . .I suppose I must have hit my head, but I don't remember.'

Beau poured piping hot coffee into two large mugs from the large pot behind the bar and pushed one towards her. Last night it had been champagne, Dominy thought as she sipped the contents, and immediately put it down again.

'It will do you good. Clear that head,' Beau said. He came around the bar and stood in front of her, his hands on his hips. He looked. . .uncomfortable, Dominy thought, as if he was having trouble knowing what to say to her. Light though his touch was, as his fingers brushed her bruised cheek she winced. They slid lower to the tiny cut at one side of her lips. Giving her no time to guess his intentions, he bent and laid his mouth against the spot, and had quickly drawn back before she could do so herself. 'Small consolation for the discomfort—and the fright. Why did you try to protect me last night? If Gascoigne had killed me all your troubles would be over.'

'I—I don't want to see you dead!' Dominy gasped. 'How can you think such a terrible thing?'

'And there was I, unconscious and not able to appreciate the moment, the feeling of you pressed against me—and of your own free will too.' The mockery died from his voice as he said quietly, 'I owe you my life and I won't forget it. When you find out why, I'd like to know.'

Because I love you, Dominy cried out in silent anguish, and turned back to concentrate on her coffee, unable to look into those pale blue eyes any longer.

'Maisie tells me not everything was returned last night. . .is she right?'

'She. . .she should not have said anything. . .' But then, Maisie could never stay silent. 'I expect she over-exaggerated their value. . .'

'She said something about trinket boxes. . .does she mean those glass bowls and things that you women always clutter up your bedrooms with?'

'No, these were rather special—hand-painted and a present from my grandmother. There was also a silver-backed brush and mirror missing. They cannot be replaced. . .ever. They were of great sentimental value to me. . .more so than any money.' Dominy persisted with the unfamiliar coffee and, to her surprise, discovered after the first few mouthfuls that it was not as repulsive as she had imagined—and it was warming her. 'The present from my parents had belonged to my great-grandmother, and the trinket boxes, they had been in Grandmère's family for hundreds of years and were very special.' A sad smile touched her lips 'No, nothing can replace them.'

'Then I shall have to take them out of Gascoigne's hide when I find him,' Beau said grimly.

'Did he mean to burn the *Enchantress*? Maisie thinks so.'

'We found signs of it below decks, but they were too busy enjoying themselves on an orgy of destruction to hurry with the job. Thank God Weng arrived when he did. He had the men with him sounding like a full-scale army by the time he had finished.'

His arrival had saved not only the *Enchantress*, but also Beau's life—and perhaps her own, Dominy thought, shivering slightly as the memory came crowding back into her mind. The hatred on Gascoigne's face—would she ever forget it?

'I don't suppose you will take my advice and go back to bed?' Beau asked, sensing the disquiet in her.

'No. I want the *Enchantress* to open on time as much as you do—for obvious reasons,' she returned stubbornly.

'As you wish.' Beau turned on his heel and left her without another word. She leaned against the bar, weak with relief at his departure. Each time she was so close to him she was finding it increasingly difficult to contain herself. . . How she longed to throw herself into those strong arms and gain comfort from their holding her. But to admit she wanted him would place her totally in his power. . .to be used and discarded when he grew tired of her.

She was checking a new arrival of glasses to replace those smashed when a carriage drew up on the dock and Austen climbed out, smiling as he surveyed the activity going on. Beau met him at the top of the gangplank, halting his half-naked, dripping wet torso a little distance from the elegantly clad Austen to avoid water dripping on his highly polished shoes.

'A dip to cool off?' Austen enquired, taking a step to one side just to be sure he was safe.

'Someone had the bright idea of smashing the paddles, but this is a solid old girl and he hardly scratched any of them. I went down to take a look just to be sure. And what brings you here? I have a spare brush if you'd care to do some varnishing.'

'Heaven forbid. I called at the Rest first—that's where I got the news. You always said you should have called Gascoigne out that first time he crossed you. That little water rat won't be able to find a hole big enough to crawl into after what he did last night. Between you and the Chinese who are after him there won't be enough left to squeeze between two pieces of bread.'

'He'll make good shark bait,' Beau said humourlessly. 'Do you feel like being a good samaritan? Take Dominy off my hands for the rest of the morning—lunch or a drive or something. She took a knock on the head last night and she's still groggy, though she'd swear black was white before she would admit it. Use your charm. . .but not to excess. I need her back here by evening at the latest.'

'That kind of work I shall enjoy. By the way, if you are interested in the Barton place you'd better let me know in the next couple of days—or it goes up for auction to the highest bidder.'

'Buy it for me.'

'Did you get hit on the head too?' Austen was taken aback by the swift resolute answer.

'I am acting on your advice, remember? Think of the privacy—the parties. . .' Beau's eyes flickered across to where Dominy was holding a glass up to the sunlight and shaking her head. Obviously she had found some flaw in it. He recalled the sadness in her voice as she had spoken of the missing items. It had touched him more than he wanted to admit. No matter what his own personal opinion was of her, he could not deny she was a young woman of considerable determination and courage. Perhaps his judgement was at fault. . . As if sensing his attention, she turned her head and then quickly looked away again. What was wrong with him this morning? Who was he feeling sorry for—himself, or Dominy? She could not stand to look at him, let alone be near him. She trembled at his touch, hated his kisses, yet in his heart he knew she also wanted them. Now there would never be a time when they could be together and be themselves.

'You don't look too happy about the prospect,' Austen commented, and Beau realised he was frowning.

'Sorry—something just crossed my mind. About Dominy. . .?'

'It will be my pleasure. The sooner I can persuade her to leave your dubious employment, the better.'

'If you do that I'll have Weng bar you from the cellar at the Rest,' Beau threatened. 'Now go away and let me get back to work.'

When Austen made the offer to Dominy she sat back on her heels and stared at the three cases of glasses before her that still needed to be inspected.

'Lunch—now? I have so much to do, Austen. . .after last night. . .'

'Someone else can take over for a few hours. You look as if you need a break, and I will not take no for an answer. I should have thought you realised that by now. Besides, a few hours away from here will make that old slave-driver Beau appreciate you more. I am getting pretty jealous of your devotion to this job—even though I do understand your desire to pay him back his money. It can't be over too soon for me. Now go and change into something pretty and cool.'

Beau appreciate her! What a joke. The offer of lunch was very appealing, if only to take her mind off her immediate problems. She nodded and got to her feet, wincing as she straightened an aching back. She had discovered a large bruise on one thigh where she had fallen against the bar. It would be all colours of the rainbow in a few days, but luckily it was in a place where it did not show.

'Give me a few moments.'

She passed Weng as she went to change, and the thought crossed her mind that if there was one person who might be able to trace the whereabouts of the necklace it would be him—he knew so many people. Whoever had taken it would take it to the nearest money-lender and get as much as possible, with no intention of ever redeeming it. But then, she reasoned, there were probably hundreds of those men in tiny side-streets, and the chances of finding the right one were slim. And there was also the suspicion that Weng would report straight back to Beau.

'How do I look?'

Dominy swung around in front of Austen when she reappeared, aware that Beau had stopped what he was doing to look their way. Had this been his idea? She had chosen a dress of primrose-yellow, as bright as the sunlight which framed her against the side of the boat, and she had entwined a matching ribbon through the thick coil of rich brown hair.

'I think if you continue to stand there looking so attractive not a single man here will do any more work,' he replied, quickly propelling her to the gangplank. When she looked back as he helped her into his carriage there was no sign of Beau on the deck.

'May we go somewhere quiet to eat, Austen? I have something I need to talk about,' she said, opening the green and saffron striped parasol she had brought with her. She had grown to love the feel of the sun on her face, but today her aching head warned her it was not wise to leave it unprotected.

'You sound very serious. We shall go to the Savoy; it will not be crowded, and you can tell me all your troubles. I am very pleased you feel we can still talk, Dominy. Whatever it is, I shall find a way to help you,' Austen said reassuringly, patting the gloved hand that lay upon the primrose silk. When she did not draw away he held it until the restaurant was reached.

'Now, what is it that is troubling you?' Austen ordered light aperitifs for them both, reeled off a list of food from the menu and asked that the wine was well chilled before he allowed Dominy to unburden herself.

'I have lost something of value—and I do not know if I can ever retrieve it. I do not even know where to start. . .'

Austen's brows puckered into a thoughtful frown. It was obvious that he did not understand, if she had possessed something of great value, why she had not sold it to pay her father's debts and saved herself the indignity of having to work for Beau.

'It is rather a long story,' she confessed.

'I am in no hurry. Take your time and tell me everything.'

As she sipped the deliciously cold white wine which accompanied the chicken in cream sauce, Dominy explained about the necklace that had been given into her keeping. It was hers, and yet not hers, she told him. It was something that she, in turn, should have passed on to her daughter on her wedding-day. Her eyes clouded as she spoke of the promise she had made to her grandmother never to part with it.

'Before I write to tell her it has been stolen I must try to get it back, but I do not know how. Those men who were on the *Enchantress* can have no idea of its true value and could lose it in a game of dice, for all I know. It could be anywhere.'

'Dominy, my dear, I could have saved you so much heartache if you had confided in me before this,' Austen said gently. Unknowingly she had opened up for him new hopes of her becoming his wife. 'If this necklace is as valuable as you say—and I believe you, of course—then with that as collateral I could have advanced you a considerable loan, sufficient to repay Beau and find yourself somewhere more suited to your needs than your present abode.'

'But how could I have repaid you? I would have had to find work of some kind,' Dominy protested. He made it sound so simple now.

'I prefer to think we would have allowed things to take their course in the fullness of time,' he replied, refilling her glass. 'You would have been able to enter society without all this unpleasantness about your father had you not been so headstrong. . .and this foolish desire for independence. . .'

'I did not realise you wanted your women to be mere decoration,' Dominy chided softly.

'I prefer them with spirit and you have more than your fair share. That is what first attracted me to you. And, I do believe, has drawn me back to you after you spurned me so callously.'

'The only thing hurt was your pride, Austen. But you are deviating from the subject. How on earth do I go about finding my necklace? Do you even think there is a chance?'

'Beau is the obvious choice in the matter—he knows most of the villains in San Francisco, and those he doesn't know Weng will. One of them would know where to start searching—but you don't want him involved, do you? Or you would have gone to him in the first place. I can understand why you kept silent about having such a valuable piece of jewellery when you owed him so much money, and to tell him now. . .I do not think he would be too sympathetic.'

'I knew it. There is nothing I can do,' Dominy said, putting down her knife and fork, her appetite suddenly vanishing. 'Thank you for listening to me anyway.'

'On the contrary, I know certain men who for a few coins will undertake such work. You will not want to know them, believe me—they are waterfront characters—but they will know where to look, and if I dangle a reward in front of them for finding it then we do stand a chance. A slim one, I admit, but we can hope.'

'And if it is recovered I shall be in your debt too,' Dominy said, her eyes searching his face.

'Then we shall have to do what I mentioned earlier: arrange a loan on the necklace to settle your monetary problems and then give things a chance to work themselves out.'

'And you will not try to use any indebtedness to persuade me to a certain suggestion of yours?' she asked innocently, and Austen's face took on a wicked expression.

'I shall use my devastating charm to persuade you—as you call it. You will not be able to resist me when I take you to the races, wine and dine you at all the most fashionable restaurants, boast about you to all my friends. I shall even have my mother eating out of the palm of your hand.'

He sounded so sure of himself that Dominy had to smile. She was sure of herself too. Sure she would never succumb to a loveless marriage, even though she knew Austen would do everything possible to make her happy.

'Say nothing to Beau about the loss,' Austen said as the table was cleared and they relaxed over coffee. 'The temptation might be too great for him. Of course, you don't know; he only sprang it on me this morning. He has told me to go after the Barton mansion for him. Lance Beautrellis living on Nob Hill. That will set a few noses out of joint, mark my words. The house would suit him, though—a little piece of the south that is all his.'

'He is going to buy a mansion!' He had not been joking. He had taken her at her word, and once it was his he would expect her to repay him. She crushed what she knew was a momentary thrill of excitement at the thought of sharing something so important with him. She would be part of the scenery, nothing more. Always there when required, provided with everything she wanted, but not of importance.

'Yes, it does sound rather fantastic, doesn't it? If I didn't know my friend was a confirmed bachelor I would think he was planning to settle down. But Beau. . .never! At least not with any woman that I can think of and, from the delectable creatures in whose company I have seen him lately, he has a lot to choose from. He's getting his life together at last and it's time I did the same. That means you and me, Dominy—no matter how long I have to wait or how many times you turn me down. A LaMotte never accepts defeat.'

'Perhaps you should retire gracefully while the going is good?'

'I can be as stubborn as you when I want something. Don't look so sad. I admit I am thinking of the advantages of the return of the necklace for me, but I do realise how much this has upset you. It would mean a great deal for you to wear it on your wedding-day, would it not?'

'Grandmère first showed it to me when I was ten years old. She allowed me to wear it for a few moments. I have dreamed of it since that day. . .' Dominy gave a soft sigh and lifted her shoulders in a shrug of resignation. 'I want to believe I shall have it back, but part of me believes otherwise.'

If he had his way it would be returned to her, Austen thought as he beckoned for the bill. No woman but Dominy would ever own, or wear, that necklace. And the money advanced to her against its value would be a mere pittance to what he would bestow on her when she became his wife!

'Did you enjoy your lunch?' Beau watched Austen's carriage drive away before turning to the girl at his side. Her cheeks were flushed with colour, but it was a definite improvement to the way she had looked when she had left.

'It was very pleasant, and we went for a drive afterwards. I did not realise how beautiful the countryside is. Those enormous trees. . .'

'Redwoods. Most of them are hundreds of years old. They could tell stories of the conquistadors, Indians, even pirates. Are you feeling up to your first card lesson? I have a few hours free.'

'Well—yes.' Dominy was surprised by the offer. Whenever there had been time Paddy O'Neill had been showing her how to handle a deck of cards. She had discovered he could palm an ace almost as deftly as Beau, but her sharp eyes soon became accustomed to his moves and she caught him out almost every time. 'I thought you did not consider it important.'

'It's only natural that a man will lose money more

readily to a pretty face,' Beau returned with a shrug. He had washed and donned a clean shirt, and she could smell a tangy cologne on his skin. 'We'll use the gambling-room and get you accustomed to the surroundings before we open. Nothing fancy, you understand, but if you can deal a hand of poker and recognise when someone is trying to rig the roulette wheel it will be a good start. You'd be surprised what some of them will do to make that wheel stop where they want it.'

Two hours later Beau sat back in his chair and stared across the table at Dominy, watching the long ringless fingers deftly dealing the cards face down before him.

'You are a natural, do you know that?' he drawled.

'Like father, like daughter, perhaps?' Dominy would never have confessed the excitement she had begun to feel as they played. Was she like her father after all? His blood ran in her veins; was it also possible she might succumb to the same fever that had destroyed him?

'On the contrary, you have a cool head on those shoulders. And, besides, no one expects you to do anything but look pretty and deal a fair hand.'

Which will enable you to recoup the money that you have to pay out for your mansion, Dominy thought, lowering her gaze. She had been tempted to ride past it while out shopping, but balked at the last moment. That would have been almost like an acceptance of Beau's offer.

'I think you have had enough for now; you look tired.' Unexpectedly Beau pushed the cards back to her. 'You really are very good. We would have made a fortune on the Mississippi together.'

'I am sure one woman in your life is enough for you to handle,' Dominy said, getting to her feet. Instead of anger, the remark brought a chuckle from his lips.

'If you regret saving my life, why on earth did you do it—and risk your own neck in the process?' he flung back.

It was a question to which she did not have an answer. At least not one she could give him! When she reached her room it was to find there was no sign of the chaos that had prevailed after Gascoigne's men had ransacked it. Even the broken chair and the mirror had been removed and replaced with new items. Had this been the reason Beau had wanted her out of the way for a few hours? And she had been so rude to him. Had it been an act of kindness or had his conscience pricked him?

And hanging in front of the open window were the Chinese wind-bells—the present Madam Chen had brought from her father. The sound they made as they swung in the breeze was like a haunting refrain, and she relaxed into a chair beneath them, closing her eyes and listening to the strange music, which had an instant soothing effect on her.

She was so looking forward to her father being present when the *Enchantress* reopened. To walk through the crowded rooms on his arm so that no one would be in any doubt who he was or that she was proud to be at his side. She decided against telling him the necklace had been stolen, afraid he might misunderstand the promise she had made never to sell it. Had she done so upon her arrival in San Francisco things would have been so different for them both.

But when it was recovered—and she had to believe it would be—then they would be able to plan a real future together. She had discovered the true meaning of independence now; finding work would be no obstacle. Another chance for them both—how wonderful that thought was.

The day of the reopening arrived, and the *Enchantress* was chaotic—more so than ever before as last-minute preparations kept everyone aboard busy from first light until dusk began to fall and the lanterns strung from stem to stern suddenly blazed into life.

'She looks good.' Hands on his hips, Beau stood with Dominy on the dock and searched the boat for anything out of place. 'What do you think?'

'I think she looks—everything she is meant to be. . .an enchantress,' Dominy breathed, unable to keep the excitement from her voice. 'I know she is going to be a success.'

A fairy-tale world floating on calm water that danced with coloured lights, she thought, allowing herself a private moment of satisfaction. Inside the best of everything awaited those who stepped over the threshold. Tonight the restaurant was serving a cold buffet, which even her grandmother would have had trouble surpassing: thin slices of cold turkey and chicken; giant prawns fried in butter and served with a variety of tasty sauces. There was fresh crab and lobster, a multitude of small meat and chicken pasties and, resplendent in the middle of this mouth-watering array, the chef's '*pièce de résistance*'—a model of the *Enchantress*. Beneath the topping of rich cream was a soft sponge, the thick layers lavishly spread with more cream.

To drink there were wines from France, Greece and Spain—chilled white, heady reds, an enormous bowl of punch, brandy and champagne. Cigars for the gentlemen, chocolates for the ladies. Something to suit everyone's palate, Dominy hoped. The very sight of it all made her stomach groan, for she had been too busy to eat during the day.

Within the hour guests would begin arriving and she had not begun to get ready, even though Su Lin had been waiting to help her dress for quite a while. She hurried back on board, realising she must be present when Beau began to greet his customers. His attitude of the past few days had proved very puzzling to her. One moment he was full of praise for her skill at organising and her handling of the often annoying little problems which arose to disrupt the precise routine they had all adopted in order to be able to complete everything on time, the next he practically ignored her. She had noticed Weng's co-operation at times such as these—tripled, as if to make up for his employer's mode of behaviour.

'Lance Beautrellis can go to the devil,' she whispered fiercely to herself as she faced her reflection in the long mirror. This was her night too, and no one was going to spoil it for her. The silk clung to the lithe contours of her body, accentuating every slender curve and the firm, proud uplift of her breasts. Her hair, swept back from her face, was piled high in several gleaming brown coils on the top of her head. On one side Su Lin had secured two soft creamy gardenias. Dominy had arranged that each hostess would have one pinned to her dress also.

From her jewel box she took out the necklace Beau had given her, and the little Chinese girl hurried forward to help her fasten it, the soft gasp of surprise which escaped her lips betraying how exquisite she thought it to be. She could have been going to a hunt ball in Berkshire, Dominy mused as she scrutinised every inch of herself for some flaw—or one of her grandmother's renowned summer parties. She had not changed along with her circumstances—not outwardly, anyway—and tonight everyone would see what she was. A lady of breeding—of better background than many of them possessed—and proud. She would always be that and it no longer bothered her.

'Wish me luck,' she murmured, knowing Su Lin did not understand her, but the hug she received was more eloquent than a thousand words. When she left San Francisco she would ask the girl if she would like to go with her.

'Wowie!' At first she thought the piercing whistle had come from one of the immaculately clad waiters, in dark trousers and brilliant white shirts, who stood patiently waiting just below the stairs to offer drinks and hors-d'oeuvres as people entered. Instead she found Maisie confronting her. A far different Maisie from the one whom she had first encountered at the Devil's Rest that day which seemed a hundred years past now. Her hair had been dressed properly, there was less make-up than usual on her face and she had even consented to wear the restricting corset she had grown to hate. 'The men are going to swarm around you like bees around a jam pot—and the women are going to want to claw your eyes out. Dominy—you look. . .just lovely.'

'I second that. Sure, now, it does these eyes good to

take a look at the real stuff sometimes.' Paddy O'Neill added his comment from behind the bar.

'You are both very sweet. But I am terrified. My knees feel as if they are going to start knocking any moment. . .and the first guest has not arrived yet.'

'Wait until you hear the beautiful sound of money pouring into the cash register and you see those plates of food being emptied, then you will feel better,' came the mocking comment from behind.

She turned slowly, determined not to allow him to rouse her temper. Beau, seated at one of the tables, inclined his head in her direction. She could not remember ever seeing him looking so handsome. His trousers were of the best and most expensive broadcloth, dark grey to match the elegant close-fitting jacket. A snow-white jabot at his throat highlighted the darkness of his features. She wondered if he had his favourite stiletto nestled beneath the full-frilled sleeves of his shirt, easily accessible should there be trouble.

The pale blue eyes considered her with an intensity that made her grow warm. He came to his feet with the litheness of a huge cat, and came to the bar.

'Open a bottle of our best champagne, Paddy. . .and we'll have four glasses. A little courage before the onslaught begins. . .not that we need it.'

'You always were a confident devil, Beau,' Maisie remarked.

'And why not? How far does anyone get in life without self-confidence? I have more than my fair share and am damned glad of it.' Beau raised his glass and touched each of theirs in turn. Paddy considered his for a long moment, wishing he had been offered ale instead, but, acknowledging that it was going to be a very long night and hours before he would be able to replenish his vast thirst again, he relented and drank it in one swallow. 'To the *Enchantress* and all who have helped her to be the success I know she will be after tonight.'

'Miss Granville, this letter was delivered for you a few minutes ago.' Weng was at Dominy's elbow, holding out an envelope to her. She recognised her father's handwriting at once and knew instinctively something was wrong. . .but what? She had sent him the right clothes, everything he would need to appear in public without anyone knowing his lowly circumstances. How she had enjoyed shopping for him.

'Nothing wrong, I hope?' Beau was staring at the envelope; then he looked enquiringly at Weng, but the man offered no further comment.

'Excuse me.' Dominy turned away and hurried out on to the deck. Beneath one of the lanterns, she took out the single piece of paper. Her hand had begun to shake. Edwin had written,

My dearest Dominy, I know this will be a disappointment for you, but I shall be unable to attend tonight. The doctor has ordered me to rest, and if I am honest with myself I know this is best for me. This past year has taken its toll of my health, and I am now forced to admit I am no longer the active, foolish, fun-loving father you have known. My life from now on will be a quiet one. Madam Chen has my full confidence and has not hesitated to offer me a home here for as long as I wish. She has made me the manager of her new hotel—can you imagine that?—so at last I am standing on my own two feet and you can get on with your own life.

Do not worry over me. I have everything I need here and, of course, you are welcome, with madam's blessing, to visit whenever you want to. As for money, I have all I need, earned honestly for the first time since the day I drew breath. And Mr Beautrellis, strange fellow that he is, has done the rest.

My thoughts will be with you on this very special night for you, my dearest daughter.

Your loving father, Edwin.

Ill! She had thought his health greatly improved at their last meeting. Why had he not said anything to her. . .why had he agreed to come tonight, when he had had no intention of doing so? She had vowed that nothing, no one would spoil this night for her. . .no one but her father himself. Nothing but his reluctance to be with her, to acknowledge their relationship before the whole of San Francisco without shame! Had Madam Chen replaced her in his affections—was that the real truth?

'There are carriages arriving, milady. . .time to start the show.' Beau stood in the doorway behind her, a thin black cigarillo between his lips.

'What have you done to my father? Are you behind it?' She swung around on him accusingly, grasping at straws. . .anything but believe her father had let her down so cruelly. He could have come just for a little while. . .

'And what horrific deed am I to be accused of now? Can't this wait?'

'What have you to do with Madam Chen, apart from lending her money whenever she requires it?' she flung back, cheeks flaming at his nonchalant attitude. He cared for nothing but himself. . .and the success of the *Enchantress*. . .the money it would bring in. At least *she* was human. . .and possessed feelings!

'I take it the letter is from your father. He is not coming tonight. . .did you really expect him to? At least he has some self-respect left. . .enough not to embarrass you before important people.'

'How can you be so callous? I wanted him here. . .as much for him as for me. . .I wanted us to be seen together. . .'

'And ruin everything you have done for yourself these past weeks? Aboard the *Enchantress* you will become a celebrity in your own right. . .you will be surprised at the doors which open for you after tonight.' Beau leaned against the jamb of the door, drawing deeply on the cigarillo, sensing that if he pushed her too far she might rush off to see her father and not return before the evening was over. Damn Edwin for his thoughtlessness. Or was it? Perhaps this was the man's way of telling Beau he had not retired from the scene altogether—as Beau had intended. 'We can talk about it in the morning. . .'

'Now. If you want me to play hostess to your rich friends,' Dominy said coldly and seated herself in a chair. 'Is it Madam Chen who influences my father—or you?'

'Very well, if you must have the truth. . .I made a deal with him before you came to work for me. If he stayed away from you, allowed you to make a new life for yourself, then I would keep all other creditors off his back. That's why I bought up all his IOUs. . .not to put you on the spot.'

'And you lent Madam Chen money after her restaurant was destroyed?'

'On the same basis as before. She cared for your father and I cared for her,' Beau returned, choosing his words with great care. 'If you can consider it rationally you will realise it was for the best. Would you be here tonight, with a chance to solve all your problems—be your own woman, the way you have always wanted—if I had not? No! You would be living in poverty in some cheap boarding house, working all hours of the day and coming home black and blue from customers who liked the look of your rear end, wondering if you had enough money to support both of you another week and if he would be sober when you got there. Or if he had taken those few dollars you hid away to gamble. . .or cheated someone else out of their hard-earned cash——'

'Don't. . .' Dominy cried. All he said was true, but she hated him for bringing it out into the open again, forcing her to accept the truth. 'Madam Chen has given him back his self-respect, I admit that. You want to deprive me of mine.'

'Only you can do that to yourself,' Beau returned, drawn to the window by the sound of raised voices. The faces on the dock below brought a broad smile to his face. Trust Austen and his mother to be among the first to arrive. The dragon lady was in for the surprise of her life when she came face to face with Dominy, he mused, and discovered not an employee, but an equal. He turned and studied the rebellious face confronting him. 'You are a woman, not a child. And you want me as much as

I want you. We have known that since the first time I kissed you on this very boat, although only I am honest enough to admit the attraction between us. Your father may not want you, but is that any reason to deprive yourself of a better life? He has chosen his way and left you to choose yours.'

'What makes you think I could ever think of you. . .in that way?'

'Because I am prepared to give you everything you want. I'm a gambler, remember? Willing to take risks—bet against the odds. I'll make a deal with you. The day you move into the Barton mansion, should I obtain it, with or without your father—that is something you will have to work out between you—I will tear up his IOUs.'

'I see no reason to consider your outrageous suggestion. Austen has offered me marriage!' Dominy felt the breath catch in her throat. She would be free of him—yet still a prisoner! A prisoner of her own love! He wanted her, but there was not a single word of affection, of caring. She was no more than an object he desired. And her grandmother had told her that when she fell in love it would be the most wonderful, memorable moment of her life! It was far from that. 'You cannot expect me to turn him down to live as your—kept woman!'

The fact she did not slap his face and walk away condemned her. In two long strides Beau had crossed the space between them and pulled her to her feet. His eyes searched her face. Somehow she met his piercing gaze without betraying one flicker of emotion.

'I do not have a vindictive mother hovering in the background to make your life hell. Think about that.' It was not what he knew he should say to her, what cried out to be said from the depths of him, but he knew she did not expect to hear sweet endearments. Now, when he could have erased the misery in her heart, he could not find the words. For the first time in years Beau hated himself, silently cursed the bitterness in him that ruled his life. His need for peace was as great as hers! 'At least we understand each other.' Her mood perplexed him. He had expected at least a show of indignation, a pretence of anger, but she stared at him as if he were a complete stranger. He knew how to change that.

'You will never understand me.' His lips on hers were intended to rouse her, but beneath them her own refused an answer and he drew back, angry lights glinting in his eyes. 'Your guests are waiting.'

'Our guests,' Beau said, but the concession gave her no pleasure, as it would have done an hour ago. She felt drained of all emotion, all energy, as he took her arm and led her back to the main reception area, and she forced a smile to her lips as she hurried forward to greet the first arrivals, not noticing how he lingered in the background to allow her to be the main attraction.

For her father! If she accepted his offer it would be for him—not herself. She was prepared to consider residing beneath the same roof as a man she detested—sharing his bed—so long as her father's future was secure. Beau had never known that kind of love before. A love so deep and binding that no humiliation could penetrate its depths. He had believed she wanted wealth and comfort for herself! And when she had thrown the challenge to provide her with it in his face he had been unable to refuse. Hating himself for taking up the gauntlet, and her for not changing his mind about her. And now. . .

Now everything was turned about. Lucky at cards, unlucky in love, Beau mused as he watched her with the couples arriving, moving among them with an easy grace that turned many heads and caused eyebrows to be raised. How easy it was to imagine her in a setting more befitting her needs. The Barton mansion could be part of his world and she could belong. He frowned down at the empty glass in his hand and a passing waiter, thinking he needed a refill, promptly took it and handed him another, not realising his thoughts were hundreds of miles away on a quiet stretch of backwater not far from Savannah. It would have changed in the years he had been away. Seven long, bitter-filled years, yet he suspected two things had remained the same: the plantation and his father. Both had weathered many storms and would never change, despite Julia's promises. The house had survived Yankee invaders and carpet-baggers who had sought to destroy what was left of the south after the war. His father had lived through famine and hardships that would have broken a lesser man—the loss of the woman he adored and the son he had idolised to the exclusion of all else—and now, as the years took their toll of his strength, he faced a bleak future, with no grandson to carry on the family name.

He tried to visualise Dominy walking on the lawn on Nob Hill, her lovely face shadowed from the sun by a silk parasol. . .instead the old house was behind her, resplendent, as it had been since the day it had been built, tall white columns rising upwards, bougainvillaea trailing along the walls, entwining in the wrought iron-work of the balconies. The magnolia trees were in full bloom—how his mother had loved those flowers—and the borders alongside the winding path were ablaze with colour.

'Mr Beautrellis?' Weng was at his side. How long he had been there Beau did not know, but he discovered the room was suddenly full of people. 'Senator Lemming is in the gambling-room; he wishes to know if you would care to play with him and a few other gentlemen. They seem very eager to take your money tonight.'

'Then I must let them believe they can,' he replied with a smile. 'Have some chilled champagne sent up and a bottle of brandy for the Senator. You know what kind he likes. When milady is free tell her where I am.'

'I do not think you will see her for a while,' Weng replied, and Beau was astonished to hear a note of surprise in the usually toneless voice. 'She is managing rather well, do you not think so?'

'Yes, I do, but keep an eye on her anyway. Have we men outside just in case?'

'They are as silent shadows all about the boat. There will be no trouble tonight, Mr Beautrellis,' Weng assured him, and for a moment Beau's hand rested on the man's shoulder. He looked as if he was about to speak, then, changing his mind, turned away and went up to the gambling-room. There was a great deal on his mind tonight, Weng thought as he watched the tall figure mount the stairs, and it was not all to do with the *Enchantress*. It had been a mistake to give him the letter that had arrived early in the morning. He always seemed moody and not himself after receiving one of those. Whoever the woman in Savannah was, she was no longer part of his past. With every fresh letter he was changing, drifting away from the life he knew now and had once loved. From the people who loved him. . . Weng's eyes were drawn to where Dominy was shaking hands with Mrs Elizabeth LaMotte herself. Yes, even from those very close who loved him!

'Please excuse me, Austen, perhaps I shall see you later on?' Dominy could not get away quickly enough from the odious presence of his mother, who had condescended to shake her hand, then had rudely turned her back, indicating to the watching eyes that she wanted nothing to do with such a person. A fact which had been well noted by all her friends.

'The chicken over there looks delicious, Mother. Shall we try some?' The fingers which closed around Elizabeth's arm bit tightly into the skin beneath the jewelled glove, and she barely held back a grimace of pain.

'You are hurting me, Austen. Release me at once.'

'There are times when I think I would like to throttle you, Mother, dear, and this is one of those times. It's a wonder your husband did not do it long ago. . .'

'Your father.'

'He was not my father. I thought we had discarded that charade years ago. My father was a common seaman, who was killed by your husband when he found you in a compromising position. . .and then he had the good sense to take himself off to New Orleans and lead a decent life.'

'I refuse to discuss any of this!' Elizabeth had grown pale beneath her rouge. The subject always distressed her. But only because she was afraid that Austen would one day keep his word if she provoked him too far and leak the disastrous story to her friends. It would kill her!

'I forgave you your interference when Dominy tried to get work, but tonight you have gone too far.' Austen accepted a plate of sliced chicken and thrust it into her hands.

'One look at that. . .slut must tell you she can not be trusted! Working here—a girl of so-called breeding. . . You are blind, Austen!'

'Breeding! She has more breeding in her little finger than you have in the whole of your body. You forget, Mother—I know where you came from. . .what you were before you found a rich man to take you away from the squalor you lived in, who gave a name to your child, not knowing he had not fathered it! The poor fool! And you look down your nose at Dominy! You have pushed me as far as you are going to. I am going to marry that girl and there is nothing you can do about it, unless you want me to start a little rumour among your friends. . .about a certain very accommodating place I know in New Orleans, whose owner bears a remarkable resemblance to your late husband. You did tell everyone he had an accident at sea, didn't you? Fell overboard or something like that—and no body ever discovered. What would your friends think of you. . .?'

'Austen, please, take me to a chair; I feel quite faint. . .' Elizabeth pleaded.

'Eat your chicken, Mother, and smile. Mrs Freemont is coming our way. . .and I am going to find Dominy. Tomorrow I may very well bring my fiancée to the house, so be prepared to receive her cordially.'

He delivered the final blow to his mother's pride with a triumphant smile. She did not like the ultimatum, but she would accept it because there was nothing else she could do. It might take her all of an hour to accept that he was serious and that Dominy was about to become part of the LaMotte family, and then she would begin to plan the most elaborate wedding San Francisco had ever seen, to soothe her wounded vanity. And if he knew his mother everyone on board would be aware of the forthcoming nuptials by the end of the evening—the news delivered with the utmost discretion and everyone sworn to secrecy until it was formally announced.

'You look like the cat who has just stolen the cream,' Dominy said with a soft laugh as Austen appeared through the crowd, excused them both and guided her towards the door. 'I cannot leave! Where are you taking me?'

'We have to talk before my courage fails me. . . No! It won't do that—but it is time we talked. A moment, that's all, and then I'll let you return to your guests.'

'I shouldn't. . .I cannot see Beau,' Dominy protested.

Austen skilfully collected two glasses of champagne as a waiter passed them, and propelled her firmly towards the door. She gave in and led him to her rooms. How peaceful and quiet it was after the hubbub of voices.

'If I know my friend he will be in the gambling-room already and he won't leave until the early hours,' Austen assured her. 'You look pale. Are you feeling up to this? Here, drink a little nectar.'

She was grateful for the iced champagne to cool her. All the doors and windows on the *Enchantress* were thrown wide open, but there was no air. No breeze from the sea to ease the stifling atmosphere.

'Tonight I shall sleep as I have never slept before.' Dominy sat on the edge of a chair with a sigh, knowing she must not be away from her guests for too long. 'How do you think it is going, Austen? I know it is still early, but so many people have arrived. . .'

'All eager to get a look at you,' he chuckled. 'I am quite jealous of all those looks coming your way, do you know that? Perhaps I should warn them you are spoken for.'

'What—what do you mean?' Dominy looked at him sharply, but it seemed to be a casual remark with no reference intended to her and Beau. For a moment she thought they might have discussed her and his offer. 'I am not spoken for, Austen.'

'I hope you will change your mind—after tonight. I have something important I want to ask you.'

Dominy came quickly to her feet. She knew what it would be and wanted no more complications in her life.

'You have reminded me I too have something important to ask. Is there any news of my necklace?'

'I wish I could give you good news, but at the moment. . .I'm sorry, I know how worried you are about it. . .and the need for its swift recovery. You will want to borrow money on it as soon as it is found, and you shall; have no fear about that.'

And on her wedding-day when she stood at his side she would be wearing it and keeping the promise she had made to her grandmother.

'Within the week we should have some news.' He had offered enough of a reward to tempt even the most cautious of men. He was hoping against hope that one of Gascoigne's own men would provide him with the answer. 'Perhaps you would prefer we talk then. Dominy, you know what I am going to ask you.'

'I cannot marry you. It would not be fair—on either of us. I am in love with someone else and I will never think of another man as I do him. I would hurt you and I do not want to do that. You have been so good to me.'

'Good! You speak to me as if I am a little boy. I'm a man, Dominy. What I feel for you is more than I have ever felt for any woman before, and I am not prepared to let you go. Once you have settled this monetary difference with Beau you will be free. Free to do as your heart dictates.'

'And I am thinking seriously about returning to my grandmother in France.' The safe haven of the château, where she could forget Lance Beautrellis.

'I thought at first this man was someone you had left behind there, but now. . .' Austen regarded her from beneath furrowed brows. 'There is no reason I can think of why you should leave San Francisco.'

'It is impossible for me to stay. I must go back before I am missed.'

Austen caught her by the arm and stared long and hard into her face. At the intensity of his gaze she felt the colour slowly begin to mount in her cheeks.

'If you had been seeing another man I would know about it. My mother would make sure of that. Beau and I—we are the only two, I'm sure of that. Now I think of it you were not as surprised as I was at Beau's bid for the Barton place. Why, after all these years, and knowing how he feels about Nob Hill society, has he decided to go and live among them? It's for you, isn't it? He wants a fine house for you! Devil take me for a fool—and all along I thought our wagers were in jest. They were real. I cannot believe he has made such a commitment.'

'He hasn't. You are right, he does want me to live in that house. He has promised that the day I move in he will tear up my father's IOUs. My father could even come with me if he wanted to. A magnanimous gesture, do you not agree, considering how he feels about him?' she added, and the bitterness in her voice caused Austen's frown to deepen. His own immediate anger dissipated when he realised she was miserable when she should have been ecstatic.

'And you have agreed? I don't understand. . .why are you talking about a loan on the necklace to repay the debt you owe him?'

'He wants me, Austen. There has been no talk of love. With that money I could be free of him. Without it. . . I love him so much. I am sorry.'

'He doesn't know how you feel? He is a blind fool!'

'Blinded by the past, perhaps, and the woman from it whom he still loves with all his heart. Or what she left intact, which, I suspect, is very little. He has been receiving letters from her, and each time he does part of him leaves. . .returns to wherever it is he is from. It is her he really wants. I would merely be a substitute—perhaps until he could find some way of having her. I pray you find my necklace soon before I weaken. . .'

'You would go to him—on those terms—but not to me?' Austen declared, shaking his head in disbelief. 'Dominy, consider what you will be doing. You say you do not love me now, but I believe that could come in time. I am willing to take the risk. Please, give him no answer until you have thought again about my offer. I will do anything you ask of me. . .'

Beau and Dominy. It was a relationship he had never considered feasible. One he would fight with every breath in his body. She would belong to no one but him! It was the first time he could ever remember being glad he had been so open with his mother. She would set in motion a train of events that even Dominy would find herself unable to fight against. . .a word here and there in the ears of her closest friends, many of whom were aboard the *Enchantress* at this very moment. A hint that he, Austen, had found himself a suitable bride and that she, his mother, approved. She had little choice, he thought, a little sad at the lengths he was prepared to go to to have Dominy. Enlisting the aid of his own mother. . .! But never had any woman been so elusive.

CHAPTER TEN

WHEN Su Lin brought her a breakfast tray the following morning Dominy thought she had been awakened in the middle of the night. Her feet still ached from the new high-heeled shoes she had worn, and her legs felt like lead. She pulled herself up on to the pillows and reached for the cup of lemon tea in the desperate hope that it would revive her. It could not be one o'clock! But the marble clock on the table beside her confirmed that it was.

It had been almost dawn before the last of the guests—apart from four men still playing cards with Beau upstairs—had drifted away. Even Mrs LaMotte had been among the last to wander down the gangplank and stand talking to friends beside the waiting carriages for over half an hour before being driven away. Austen had been the last to leave, and not without reminding her that she was to have lunch with him again. She had refused his offer to dine with him at the family home, despite his insistence that his mother would receive her. There was too much to be done aboard the *Enchantress* before she opened again the following day, she had told him, and had been relieved when he had accepted the flimsy excuse.

She wanted nothing to do with Elizabeth LaMotte. Or to do with anyone who would try to sway her from the decision she had made. . .and Austen, sweet, kind Austen, might have the power to do just that if she allowed herself to weaken. He knew she did not love him, but it did not matter; he wanted to marry her, and she at last believed that he did love her. Had Lance Beautrellis not entered her life to turn it upside-down she knew she would have been proud to accept Austen, despite his mother. It would have been the kind of marriage her parents would have wished for her. . .but not her grandmother, who had always insisted she should marry for love.

Love was for fools—or for those who could afford to indulge themselves with dreams that would never come true. Love for her was Beau. Arrogant. . . ruthless. . .dangerous to those who fell foul of his temper. Just once, could she not have looked into his eyes and seen something other than mockery or contempt there? Could the kisses which roused her so shamelessly not have come from the heart?

And yet he could be gentle, she remembered. He had been last night when he had encountered her on deck. She had not gone to bed, but had lingered to watch the sunrise, tired as she had been, reclining in a chair beside the rail and recalling that was how she had first encountered him! The first stirrings of a breeze wafted across the water to cool her flushed cheeks. She felt herself relax and begin to grow drowsy, but was too comfortable to move when she realised she was not alone. Beau was leaning against the rail, watching her, his jacket thrown over one shoulder, his jabot discarded, his shirt open. He looked more like a labourer than a gambler—who was about to become very rich, if she was any judge of the complimentary conversation she had overheard all through the evening. The *Enchantress* was a success. Their success. How she wished he would share it with her.

'I thought you would be in bed.'

'It is cooler out here. Did you win?'

'Of course, but I allowed the Senator to do so also. . .he was so pleased with himself that he is coming back as soon as we are open again,' Beau chuckled. He leaned over the rail for a moment, watching the first pinpoints of light drift across the calm surface, before turning to look at her again. 'You were a great success. I told you it would happen. If you don't get to bed you will fall asleep where you are,' he added as Dominy smothered a yawn. 'And you would wake up stiff in places you cannot imagine. I know—I slept like that for weeks while I was first renovating the old girl. Those were good days. . .sometimes I forget how good. . .'

Dominy did not move, hoping he would continue, but he leaned down and helped her to her feet and followed her to the state-rooms. When she entered she found him directly behind her. His eyes travelled slowly about the room, noting that Su Lin had turned down the bed in readiness for her mistress to retire. There were fresh roses in two large vases, and the air was filled with the sweet aroma of musk. Su Lin again, he mused, playing Cupid.

Not knowing what to expect next, Dominy sat down before the dressing-table and, unpinning her hair, began to brush it with the ebony-backed brush Su Lin had bought her, together with a matching mirror. Through the mirror she saw his eyes narrow at the intimate atmosphere she was unwittingly creating. He did not know the effort it cost her to remain so casual beneath his scrutiny.

Tossing his coat to one side, he came to stand behind her. She felt his fingers lift a thick lock of hair and saw him smile.

'My mother's hair was soft like this—and as long. I used to creep into her room sometimes when the maid was brushing it. It was a ritual she never neglected. One hundred strokes day and night.'

'She was very important to you,' Dominy said softly, touched by the memory. She knew it was rare for him to share his past with anyone—except, perhaps, Austen, who, she suspected, knew far more about his friend than anyone imagined.

'Once she was the most important thing in my life. No—that is not true. I loved her with all my heart. It all but broke when she died, but there has always been someone else I cared for more.'

The girl called Julia, whose letters had reopened old wounds. How much of himself had he shared? All, she suspected—to make him so bitter. What girl in her right mind would spurn a man who could offer her everything?

Beau stepped back as she rose, sweeping the long

brown hair back from her face, and suggested casually, 'Why don't you get undressed and into bed, and I'll bring us a nightcap? I think we have earned it.'

'I really am very tired. . .' Dominy protested, and yet her traitorous heart missed a beat at the proposal. What more did he have in mind—and would she be able to refuse him? She ached just to be near him!

'A last glass of champagne, and then you can sleep around the clock.'

He was gone before she could protest further. She thought of locking the door after him but decided that would be childish. Was he expecting an answer from her tonight—or perhaps anticipating it? For the first time she was struck with the realisation that to agree would mean she became his mistress!

His mistress! Her hands trembled as she quickly slipped out of her dress and petticoats and reached for the nightgown upon the pillows. It was one she had brought with her from France, she recollected as she slid it over her head. Sheer white silk with wafer-thin straps. Hurriedly she grabbed up the wrap beside it and put that on too.

She had hardly pulled the covers over her when Beau returned with champagne and two glasses.

'Do you know, we went through every case of this stuff? I hope the next time our customers remember they pay for everything they drink—and eat. Did you see the way that table was cleared? Vultures!'

'Is that any way to speak of future clientele?' she reproved, unable to suppress a smile. She too had watched the way people had sampled everything and anything. . .comparing, criticising. . .suggesting the way they would have done things had they been the hosts, but she had allowed the frequent comments to pass over her head. Beau was right. The next time they came they would be more selective—and probably less gluttonous, although she had no doubt that the restaurant would be a success. The chef, she had found, was a superb cook, and if she was satisfied with what he presented then it was certainly good enough for the inhabitants of San Francisco!

Austen had to find her necklace and resolve her problem. She would miss the *Enchantress* and all those aboard her. She had come to love them—without exception. Maisie, Paddy O'Neill, Weng and Su Lin. . .and Lance Beautrellis!

'Now what are you thinking to bring such sadness into those lovely eyes, milady?' he asked softly. He had seated himself on the edge of the bed after filling their glasses, the bottle on the carpet between them.

'I was thinking that when—when I have paid you back all Father owes you I shall be out of a job.' She told the lie with wildly beating heart.

'Never! The *Enchantress* is in your blood now. . .I saw that tonight. You were as excited as I was at the people who turned up. I noticed a few gatecrashers too, but I told Weng to allow them in, as they own most of the houses on Harbour Street,' Beau told her with a grin. He showed no signs of tiredness, yet she knew he had been playing poker for over five hours. 'Soon I shall have. . .other objectives on my mind, and I expect my time to be fully occupied, so I shall keep the *Enchantress* and sell the Devil's Rest. It goes without saying that you will run this place for me. No one could do it better.'

Three choices presented themselves to Dominy to set her brain racing: he had given her the chance to stay and always be close to him; Austen offered her marriage and a place in his society world; her grandmother offered an escape from both, for both were impossible. She was too fond of Austen to launch into a loveless marriage, and too deeply in love with Beau to remain in San Francisco, knowing that each time he held her in his arms and made love to her another woman would be in his thoughts.

'Why, Mr Beautrellis, do you realise you have just paid me a compliment?' Dominy murmured, and he leaned closer, a wicked gleam springing to his eyes.

'And I feel very comfortable with you tonight, milady, so beware. Remember the last time we found ourselves in such a situation. . .? I might be tempted to finish what I started that night.'

The colour surged into Dominy's cheeks. She remembered only too well!

'I suppose if I kiss you there will be protestations of outraged dignity,' he mocked. His gaze rested for a second or two on her mouth and she knew he was going to kiss her, whether she wished him to or not.

He took the glass of champagne, which she had not touched yet, and put it to one side. Dominy quivered as his lips touched her cheek, and then his fingers, as light as a breath of wind, trailed along her arms to her bare shoulders. How cool they were against her warm skin, she thought, unresisting as he drew her into his embrace.

Not so the lips that scorched hers with a hunger so intense that her senses swam. Was he thinking of Julia as he kissed her, wishing it were she in his arms? What did it matter? This was her moment and it might never happen again. Her hands slid slowly up to his shoulders, feeling the hardness of his muscles beneath her fingers, reminding her how powerful he was, how capable of defending himself—against everything but love. . . How ironic that it had trapped them both!

'Beau. . .' His name broke from her lips. She felt him stiffen, and then he drew back, holding her away from him.

One strap of the diaphanous nightgown had slipped from one creamy shoulder, revealing the rise of her breast. She caught her breath as Beau returned it where it belonged, puzzled by the strange look on his dark features. And in his eyes, such tenderness as she had never seen before.

'I want you very much, Dominy. I have never lied about that, but if I do not leave now. . . We are both too tired to think clearly. . . Goodnight. Sleep well.' He kissed her once more upon the mouth, but there was no passion in it. . .nothing to betray the fierceness of the kisses that had seared her own a moment before. He stood up, reaching for his jacket, a smile deepening the corners of his mouth. 'Besides, whatever you think of me, I was raised a gentleman and I never take advantage of a woman—not even one as attractive as you. Well—hardly ever.'

Dominy watched him go into his own room, watched the light disappear from under the door moments later, but it was an hour before she turned down the lamp and attempted to sleep. It was impossible.

'I didn't expect to see you up this early,' Beau remarked from the table where he sat, adding figures from the takings of the night before. He looked as fresh and vital as if he had slept the whole night, Dominy thought as she accepted his invitation to join him.

She lifted her eyes to his face as Weng brought her coffee, wondering if last night had been a dream. He was more concerned with how much they had taken than the wonderful moment they had shared. Wonderful for her, not him, she reasoned. He loved another woman, but he wanted her! And had he stayed with her Dominy knew she would not have refused him. In the light of morning—and with the return of sanity—she was swept with shame that she could have given herself to a man who cared not one iota for her.

'These are good—very good,' Beau sat back in his chair with a nod of satisfaction, 'but I shall have to finish them later. Weng, what time am I to meet Mr LaMotte? Was it two or two-thirty?'

'Two, Mr Beautrellis. I have laid out your clothes and ordered the carriage for one-thirty. That will get you to the mansion of Mr Barton in plenty of time for the appointment.'

'As efficient as always, Weng. What shall I do without you?' Beau thrust a cigarillo into his mouth as he rose, handing his books to the man who stood beside the table. When he turned to look at Dominy she thought he was about to enlighten her as to where he was going; instead he said matter-of-factly, 'I may be back tonight. . .but probably not. Weng's men are still aboard, so you have nothing to worry about. Can you handle things alone?'

'Of course.' What was so important that he would absent himself from the *Enchantress* only one night after the opening? Or who?

Twenty minutes later as she walked on deck she saw him leave. He climbed into the waiting carriage and was driven away without a backward glance. At her side Maisie remarked, 'Where's Beau off to, smelling so delicious?'

'He has an appointment with Mr LaMotte.' Dominy supplied the answer with reluctance, not wanting to be drawn into conversation about his private affairs, but Maisie's curiosity had been aroused.

'About the house, I expect. . .and then, I bet, he's meeting a woman. No man looks that good to go and buy a house. Besides, he received another letter this morning. . .you know, those in the scented envelopes. And this one was hand-delivered. Do you know what that means?'

'Yes, that we should mind our own business.'

'Aren't you just a little bit curious to know who she is? What she looks like—this woman who is going to steal your man unless you do something about it?'

'He is not mine,' Dominy replied, cheeks burning. 'Please do not refer to him that way. You have not mentioned the way I feel to anyone, have you?'

'Of course not. It's our secret. But if it were me I'd fight for him. I shan't let mine get away from me. Did you see him?' Maisie's expression grew dreamy as she contemplated the tall, slow-speaking Texan with whom she had spent all the evening. Out of all the hostesses he had picked her, and had not allowed her to leave his side. 'He has a ranch near Los Rios, not a big place, about five thousand head of cattle, a house with ten rooms. . .and all empty because he has no wife and family. I think this could be love at first sight.'

'Five thousand. . .' Dominy found it impossible to imagine so many animals together. Maisie had set her sights high. She hoped she would be luckier than herself and be swept off her feet by a man who really cared for her. 'I wish you luck.'

'Luck has nothing to do with it,' Maisie returned with a shrug of her shoulders. 'He's looking for a wife—and I'm a farm girl, born and bred. I'm just what he is looking for.' She patted Dominy on the arm before moving away. 'Fight for him. . .if you think he's worth it.'

But Beau was not the most important thing on her mind that afternoon. She had to see her father and tell him what she intended, and she was not looking forward to it. . .not with Madam Chen hovering just out of sight, listening to every word they said. She doubted if she could persuade him to leave and return to France with her, or even go elsewhere—the influence of the Chinese woman was too great—but she had to make her peace with him and reassure herself that he would always be looked after.

She returned to the *Enchantress* late that afternoon. Most of the staff had already arrived, and a delicious smell of food being prepared wafted to her as she stepped on deck. As always when she went out, Maisie was awaiting her return, eager for news of where she had been—-and who with! But Dominy was not in a talkative mood. Each time she saw her father she was forced to admit that not only the surroundings in which he now lived, but also the company seemed to agree with him. And reluctantly she had admitted at last that she had become jealous of someone else being the centre point of his affections and it had clouded her reasoning.

He had greeted her with all the affection he had once shown her, but had remained resolute in his decision to stay as Madam Chen's manager. She knew it was useless to argue. There was something in his manner she had never known before, a self-assurance that stirred pride in her. He had endured so much. Whether it had been of his own making was no longer important. He was his own master again and no one would ever change that.

She did not tell him about Beau's offer. She had considered it only because of her father. Now that she had only herself to think of she knew it was impossible to accept.

Maisie had the habit of draping herself over a chair in a most unladylike manner whenever she relaxed in Dominy's company. As she saw the latter frown at her through the mirror she drew herself up, smoothed out her skirts and folded her hands demurely in her lap.

'A little overdone,' Dominy commented, a smile replacing the stern look of disapproval.

'I had to do something to cheer you up. I suppose you have been to see your father. You go out happy and come back miserable every time.'

'I was feeling sorry for myself, and I should not. He is happy, and soon our problems will be solved.'

'Which ones are those?' Maisie asked, examining her long nails. 'Money or the men in your life? Mr LaMotte was here this afternoon asking for you. I thought you said he was meeting Beau.'

'I thought he was. I really would love to sit and talk, Maisie, but I have to change. . .' Dominy added, and her companion got ruefully to her feet. Something was going on that she did not know about—and that was unusual!

Wherever Beau was, it was none of her business, Dominy told herself as Su Lin brushed and arranged her hair, but if he was not with Austen then where had he gone, looking so smart? Who was he meeting? It was no coincidence. The letter delivered that morning, which bore no postmark, and Beau's absence from the *Enchantress*, not only for the afternoon, but probably all evening too, were linked. Julia was in San Francisco—and he had gone to see her!

After the success of the previous evening Dominy had expected a large number of people to appear, but she was amazed at the throng that swelled the dining-room and out on the decks, taking advantage of a cooling of the temperatures that had reduced them to little more than limp lettuces during the day. She was greeted most cordially by couples she suspected would not even acknowledge her in the street or invite her into their homes, but it no longer mattered. She had found something infinitely rewarding in the work she was doing, and it was a feeling she had not known before. The lifestyle of these people was as shallow as the one she had led before she had left England, and she did not miss it any longer. But she could not deny she would miss the *Enchantress*—and the man who unknowingly possessed her heart and soul.

She looked for Austen, but could not find him among the sea of faces. She saw Mrs LaMotte amid a group of heavily jewelled women, their fans fluttering in the sultry evening heat. She acknowledged her as she passed, but did not linger, and was conscious of the woman's eyes following her about the room.

Maisie and her Texan were sitting on one of the couches, watching the roulette wheel. Dominy deliberately paused beside them so that she could be introduced and get a look at him for herself. She liked what she saw. A hesitant, rather shy young man in his late twenties, who, despite the new suit, was out of his depth among the cigar-smoking, elegantly clad men around him. When she shook hands with him she felt as if her fingers had been crushed.

As she lingered at a distance from the main table, where a game of five-card stud poker was in progress, she became aware that she was under observation. Lifting her eyes, she encountered the gaze of a middle-aged man a few feet away. She inclined her head in his direction with a faint smile, wondering who he was, and immediately he came to her side.

'I didn't think I'd find anything as pretty as you outside of South Carolina, my dear. Would you be insulted if I asked you to have a drink with me?'

'You are too kind, sir. But I do not drink with the customers. Would you like one of the hostesses to keep you company?' Dominy replied, and the man's eyebrows rose a fraction.

'That is a charming accent—English, isn't it?'

'Yes. My name is Dominy Granville. I am in charge of the *Enchantress*. We are open from six in the evening until the last customer leaves, if you wish to risk your money on the turn of a card.'

'If you deal them, my dear, I shall be unable to stay away. I hear the young buck who owns this place is quite a gambling man. I don't see him about.'

'He will not be here tonight, but I am sure we can arrange something whenever you wish. Are you visiting San Francisco, Mr. . .?'

'For a few days. I am sure I shall catch up with him before I leave again.'

Obviously a married man with possibly a jealous wife, Dominy mused as he left her. Not only had he pointedly withheld his name, but as he wandered downstairs he scanned the faces of people passing by, as if searching for one in particular. The night before many men had brought their wives, paying lip-service to the society that demanded that, on the surface at least, all should seem normal. It had not taken long for them to shed the cloak of respectability once out of sight of them, she thought, noticing that every hostess was being monopolised tonight, now that the husbands were alone.

Dominy was enjoying a few moments' solitude on deck the following morning, reclining in a chair, her legs and head resting on comfortable cushions. The warmth of the sun on her face made her feel drowsy, even though she had slept fitfully since tumbling into bed in the early hours. Beau had not returned to the *Enchantress*, and Weng denied any knowledge as to his whereabouts, although she doubted if he would have told her if he had known.

'What do you think of that, then?' a voice declared in her ear, and, opening her eyes, she found herself staring at the largest sapphire she had ever seen.

Startled, she shaded her eyes and found Maisie grinning down at her.

'Isn't it something? And it's official. Where's Beau? I have to tell him I am getting married next week! Isn't it wonderful?'

'Maisie. . .wait, you are going too fast,' Dominy intervened. 'Are you trying to tell me you are engaged—to your Texan? But you have only known him a couple of days. . .and married—next week! I cannot believe it.'

'So? He says he loves me! Just like that. He saw me and he loved me! You could have knocked me over with a feather. . . And before he takes me to his home we are going to the farm to collect my mother. She's coming to live with us. . . Dominy, it's a dream. A fantastic, unbelievable dream, and I never want to wake up. Imagine me, in Texas. You can come and visit us.'

'I am so happy for you. Tonight you are both guests of the *Enchantress*. . .dinner and wine and anything else that takes your fancy. I know Beau won't mind,' Dominy said, experiencing a twinge of envy at Maisie's happiness. Love did happen for some people after all.

'I hate rushing off at such short notice; you'll have to find another girl. Beau might get mad. . .I'd best talk to him.'

'He isn't here. He did not come back last night. I expect he encountered some gambling friends—you know how it is with him.' Dominy somehow managed to keep her voice unconcerned.

'That was no gambling friend I saw him with this morning,' Maisie returned, leaning back against the rail and holding her hand up to the sun to watch it dance over the huge stone there. 'An hour ago he was coming out of Del Cortes with a real good-looking woman on his arm, and when Tex and I came out of the jeweller's we saw them loaded down with parcels, climbing into a carriage. I heard him tell the driver to take them to the Majestic.'

Where he had installed her when she had first arrived in San Francisco, Dominy thought bitterly. Julia also was being given the royal treatment.

'Do you think he bought that mansion—for her?' Maisie tried to gauge her companion's feelings, but Dominy's gaze was centred on the water and her expression betrayed nothing. 'So you've given up on him.'

'He was never mine. And the subject is closed. We were discussing you.' She got to her feet, already planning the special evening in her mind. 'You go and do whatever you have to. A week is no time at all. If you need anything, like money. . .let me know. Now go away and enjoy yourself, and don't forget to bring your Texan here tonight. The champagne will be well chilled.'

'Would you believe he prefers root beer?' Maisie giggled.

'I will see what we can do. He will get on well with Paddy if that is what he likes.'

'And what can I do for you?' Maisie was suddenly serious as she took Dominy by the hand. 'I shall miss you. We have become friends, haven't we?'

'Yes, we have. What can you do for me? Go away and make every moment that you are together count. I mean it. I don't want to see you back here before this evening.'

Dominy's smile vanished as she turned away and went to arrange a table to be reserved for the newly engaged couple. Beau and Julia! He had deliberately lied, pretending the woman meant nothing to him, yet here he was, openly showing her off to all of San Francisco! How would her arrival change what he had planned? Who did he intend would reside in the mansion now—Dominy or Julia? Of course, that was assuming she stayed and did not go back to Savannah.

'Do you think we could do something nice for Maisie before she leaves? I was wondering about the reception—here on the *Enchantress*,' Dominy said, looking across the breakfast table to the silent man who had been stirring a cup of coffee for the past five minutes, his mind obviously a thousand miles away.

It was the first time she had seen him in three days, and she thought how tired and preoccupied he looked. As if the weight of the whole world were resting on those broad shoulders.

'I was thinking along those very same lines, but not here. We shall have a house-warming and a going-away party at the same time. . .at the mansion. Have you given any thought to my offer yet?' His gaze narrowed as he watched the colour ebb from her cheeks, and knew the answer before she spoke.

'I cannot possibly accept. It was madness for you to

ever believe I would. I shall continue to work for you, of course, until I have paid back all your money—then. . .' She shrugged her shoulders. 'I am not as helpless as I used to think. I shall manage to support myself.'

'Strange how unimportant the money seems now—not that I cared about its loss, only the deception involved. On the part of your father,' he added as she looked daggers at him. 'There is always work for you here, you know. It would be nice to know the *Enchantress* was in good hands, but I expect, with your nose back amid the nobility again, you will not have time for her. A pity. Anyway—Maisie. . . She's asked me to give her away, and I have said I would. I am also going to give her the best wedding any girl has ever had in San Francisco, and I want you to go out and buy her the fanciest wedding dress you can find. I want that Texan of hers to know he is getting the best. Send all the bills to me, naturally, and don't spare any expense with the reception. I'm going to show Nob Hill a party such as they have never seen before. I might even invite the dragon lady to come and mingle with the lower classes. I guarantee she would come out of sheer curiosity.'

'You are going to make life very difficult for yourself if you antagonise them before you have even moved in,' Dominy warned. 'This does mean you have bought the place?'

How sure he had been she would accept him to do so, she thought bitterly, and yet he did not seem too put out that she had not. After all, there was now someone else far more important to him who, she was sure, would be more than willing to reside there.

'The Colonel heard my southern accent and didn't argue about the price,' Beau returned, wondering what her reaction would be if he told her the truth. 'It is quite a place. You might change your mind when you see it. Magnolia trees on the lawns, doves fluttering behind the house, large, airy rooms. A touch of home.'

'For you perhaps, but not me,' Dominy said firmly.

'You said you wanted a fine house on Nob Hill, with all the trimmings. It is yours for the asking,' he said, getting to his feet and reaching for his coat. 'But I am obviously the wrong person to share this idyllic place with.'

'You are the last person in the world I would think of sharing it with,' Dominy said through stiff lips, and instead of anger the oddest smile flitted across the sun-bronzed features.

'Yes, I have rather misread the cards, haven't I? But all is clear now. So now I am stuck with a house and no one to live in it. It's of no use to me. I suppose I could give it to you and Austen as a wedding present. You have accepted him, haven't you? All of San Francisco is talking about what is to be the wedding of the year. The dragon lady is making the most of her defeat. I wonder how Austen managed it?'

Dominy was silent—dumbfounded by his words. She had dismissed the speculation, which had been rife since the opening, as mere gossip—and determinedly avoided Maisie's none too subtle hints on the subject. After all, Dominy had reasoned, she knew there was no substance to any of it. But now it was beginning to look as if—amazing as it seemed—Austen and his mother were working together, determined to push her to the altar. It was her way out! Her escape from Beau. Yet the words stuck in her throat. Confirm it, a voice cried, and she heard herself saying lamely, 'Did you ever expect me to do anything else?'

Again that strange smile, as if he was in possession of some knowledge unbeknown to her. Then, with a shrug of broad shoulders, he said, 'Our little dispute—shall we call it?—will not stop you taking care of the arrangements for the reception, I hope. And you will come. . .'

'Maisie will expect me to be there. . .I will do nothing to spoil her day.'

'At least we can agree on that. A formal guest list will not be necessary under these circumstances. You pass the word to anyone you think would enjoy good food and liquor, and I will do the same.'

'Anyone?' Dominy queried as he turned away towards the door. 'Paddy? Our people here?'

'My dear Dominy, Maisie is going to want to be surrounded by her friends. I will take care of the other faction—with Austen's help. I think it will turn out to be quite an interesting evening.'

'But where will you be—if I need you, if there is a problem?' she added as one dark eyebrow rose mockingly at the question.

'You will not. You will have to deal with it yourself. Ask Weng if you cannot cope. He can deal with any emergency, but, as you yourself said just now, you are not as useless as you thought you were. Far from it, milady.'

And that left her in sole charge of organising everything, she thought, which was not such a daunting prospect after all the work she had put in to ensure that the *Enchantress* opened on time and in all her glory. How long she sat in her chair she did not know. His attitude perplexed and confused her, made her realise how impossible it would be to remain in San Francisco if he and Julia came together again for good. She could not bear the thought of his holding another woman, let alone seeing them on the streets together, or on the *Enchantress*. He would have eyes only for her, as he now had thoughts only for her, or he would have assumed some of the responsibility for the arrangements himself. But he had indicated that he had no use for the house. Was he leaving San Francisco, going home to the woman he had once abandoned?

But, as she went in search of Maisie to break the wonderful news to her, her own problems were of minor importance. She had discovered she had a flair for organising and was sure she would be fully involved until after the wedding. Julia's arrival gave her no choice now. She would go back to France as soon as it was all over.

The following days were crammed full to capacity with finalising the wedding details. Dominy was delighted when she was asked to be the sole bridesmaid. At last a very special occasion, where she could wear that very special gown which hung in her closet. Beau was to give the bride away and, as the groom knew no one in San Francisco, Paddy was elected to be the best man. Only the thought of all the free beer could have induced him to wear a stiff white collar, Maisie joked when she heard he had accepted.

The bride-to-be was in seventh heaven as she went from shop to shop with Dominy, complaining only once of her aching feet. In the end she chose a dress of frothy white tulle and satin, with a train so long that Dominy hoped there would not be a high wind on the day. But she looked lovely and she was really in love. She knew it from the way Maisie's eyes shone each time she mentioned her Texan, whom she had at last remembered had not been properly introduced to everyone—although to most he had become just Tex, and so it was of no importance. When they were together he always held her hand and barely took his eyes off her. More than once Dominy felt a tug at her heart-strings.

She did not begrudge them one moment of the happiness they had discovered, but how she wished she could have just once experienced love such as they knew, which had come upon Maisie as swiftly as it had Dominy herself. Without warning—and, in Dominy's case, without compassion. Maisie's hints that she herself would soon become a bride were ignored or laughed aside. Dominy was beginning to believe there was not a single person in San Francisco who did not think she would soon marry Austen LaMotte!

Eight days later Maisie became Mrs Abraham Edgar Clovis the third, and proudly walked out of the tiny church on Dempsey Street on the arm of her new husband and was showered with hundreds of multicoloured rose petals thrown by the six little girls Dominy had paid to be waiting at the entrance.

'Is she not a picture?' she said, a wistful note in her voice as she watched the couple being arranged for the first photographs, and Austen leaned to whisper in her ear with a smile,

'Enchanting. I think you look stunning in that dress.'

'I was talking about Maisie,' she reproved, aware of

Beau half turning to look at them. He was the most handsome man at the ceremony and, even though she tried to steel herself against fantasising, Dominy found herself indulging her dreams as she watched the Texan slip the gold wedding band on to Maisie's finger. It was she in the beautiful gown with Beau at her side, turning to look at her with love and tenderness in his eyes as he made her his wife.

'There is not a woman here to hold a candle to you—not even Maisie. I agree—she is something. I can hardly believe it is the same girl who used to be in the Devil's Rest. I didn't realise how clothes can change an image.'

Dominy wondered how she would have been treated had he first seen her in the same apparel as Maisie used to wear, instead of aboard the *Enchantress*, with the appearance of a lady?

This was the poor part of the town, where none of the families, mostly immigrant workers who barely earned enough to keep body and soul together, could afford to give their daughters such a lavish wedding as Maisie was enjoying, but she had insisted she wanted to be married in a simple little church such as she had known back home. Dominy understood why—and why she still held such affection for her old home, where, she maintained, no one was ever a stranger—when complete strangers, passing by in the street, stopped to congratulate the couple as they posed for photographs. One old lady, bent with rheumatism and with tears on her cheeks, stopped to embrace the bride and admire the tall young man at her side, and pressed into Maisie's hand a piece of dried heather. A memento of happier times, Dominy wondered as she limped painfully away—perhaps something treasured from her own wedding-day, when the world had been perfect and the future had glowed with prospects?

'You have a strange look in your eyes,' Austen whispered as they watched the carriage, taking the newly-weds to their reception, drive off. 'I hope that means you are taking my proposal seriously.'

'This is not the time or the place,' Dominy said in a

fierce whisper. He had not wasted one moment, even during the ceremony, to remind her he was still awaiting her answer. She did not want to spoil the day for either of them by accusing him of trying to manipulate her.

'I have some last-minute wedding presents to pick up from the *Enchantress*.' It was an excuse to get away, but Austen immediately seized on her words to be alone with her.

'We can take my carriage. Don't worry about Beau,' he added as she sought his face among the gathering to tell him she was leaving. He had done a wonderful job with the organisation at the church and, if the bride had drawn attention, so too did the array of carriages continually drawing up outside the church to convey the guests to Nob Hill. The dragon lady would think there was an invasion of the lower classes, Dominy thought, unable to suppress a smile. But that was Beau—in at the deep end and the devil take what anyone thought. But it would have needed more to brazen it out among the gentry on the hill if she had accepted his offer. More than courage. . .she had enough of that. What she did not possess was the ability to ignore what others said about her. She had tasted the sting of their resentment before and it had wounded her deeply. She turned and looked enquiringly into Austen's face as he assisted her into his carriage. 'He has to pick up a couple of extra guests on the way—and one of them is almost as lovely as you, my dear Dominy.'

'Julia,' she said, and was shocked at the sudden tremor in her voice.

'Yes, I believe that is her name. I was only introduced to her yesterday. Beau has been keeping her well out of my way. As if I could have eyes for any woman but you.'

Julia at the reception! She balked at coming face to face with the woman who was about to take away from her the most important thing in her life, but for Maisie's sake she knew she had to be there.

As he watched the agitation his words had brought about die from her face Austen felt the taste of victory turn sour in his mouth. He had been so sure he was doing the right thing. . .for himself. . .for Dominy! But if there was sadness in her heart to match that in her eyes then he had been wrong. Because of what he felt for her he had betrayed a close, binding friendship, deceived a man who had never lifted a hand against him—and in doing so thought he had paved the way for her to come to him. But had he? How could he have been so wrong?

'Weng, what are you doing here? I thought you would be helping Mr Beautrellis with the reception,' Dominy exclaimed in surprise as through the door of her state-room she saw the man arranging some flowers. With Austen close on her heels, she stepped through and gave an exclamation of delight. 'Oh, Weng, this is lovely! Maisie will think she is a queen tonight.'

'Then tonight she will be,' Weng returned solemly. 'I just wanted to be sure everything was in order before I left. It is to your satisfaction, Miss Granville?'

'It could not be more perfect. Thank you for going to so much trouble,' Dominy said with a warm smile. For one night she and Beau were returning to the Devil's Rest and allowing the married couple to use his rooms. There were fresh flowers everywhere, night attire folded and laid upon the pillows, glasses all ready upon a table, awaiting the ice-cold champagne Dominy had ordered for them.

'Perhaps one day I hope I shall be able to do the same for you. If there is nothing else I must take these things to the other house before I go on to the reception.'

'But why are you removing all Mr Beautrellis's clothes?' Dominy experienced a brief moment of unease as she watched him close the large travelling valise. As she lifted her eyes and looked about her she realised nothing belonging to Beau remained in the room.

'He will not be returning to the *Enchantress*, Miss Granville. He intends to stay at the Rest until. . .' Weng paused, watching her cheeks grow pale.

'Until he moves into the mansion—of course, how silly of me.' Why was it she felt that was not what he would have said?

'In time all will be made clear.' As he passed them

Dominy was aware of the penetrating look he cast at Austen. As if they shared some secret of which she was unaware.

'Things happen quickly when they happen around here,' she said with a short laugh that brought a frown to Austen's face. 'Did you know Beau wants me to stay in charge of the *Enchantress*? He is going to sell the other gambling house. I shall only stay until my father's debt has been cleared, of course; then I shall leave San Francisco as soon as possible. I have given up all hope of ever seeing my necklace again. I must write to Grandmère and tell her of its loss and ask her for money for the passage home. It will be the hardest letter I shall ever have to write.'

'I shall spend every moment of every day trying to convince you how wrong you are,' Austen declared. 'Why can you not lie to me, tell me you care?'

'I do care,' Dominy protested gently. 'Too much to lie. I will always have a special place in my heart for you, Austen.'

'If I took you in my arms now and kissed you I could change your mind,' he said fiercely, and she took a step backwards as he made a move as if to keep his threat.

'You are too much of a gentleman to force me to do something we both know would be wrong—and which I am sure you would regret.'

'Gentleman! Honour!' She was taken aback by the harshness of his tone. 'Do you know what I have done in the name of love? Thrown honour to the wind! Lied to my best friend. Deceived the only man I have ever been able to call friend. Because I am in love with you.'

'I—I don't understand,' Dominy whispered, a hand unconsciously resting over the spot where her heart had suddenly begun to beat faster. 'What do you mean?'

'I think you had better sit down and read this.' From an inside pocket Austen took a bulky envelope. He stared at it with angry eyes for several minutes before handing it over. 'I was supposed to give this to you after Beau had left. He's going back home—for good. So, you see, there is no reason for you to leave. He won't be around, but when you know what I've done you won't want me in his place. I was a fool to ever think I could fit his shoes. Go on, open it,' he ordered as Dominy looked at the envelope in her hands, wondering what on earth it could contain. There was something inside besides paper; she could feel it. 'Beau has done the gentlemanly thing too. We are a fine pair. Both wanting the same girl, both willing to give her up in the name of love.'

As he turned away from her with something that sounded suspiciously like a groan Dominy tore at one end of the envelope in a feverish haste, inverting it so that the contents fell into her lap. A single piece of paper and a pouch like those used to contain jewellery lay upon the burnt-orange silk. Austen wheeled about as she gave an exclamation of delight.

'My necklace. Austen, you have found it!'

'No. Beau had it all the time. He recovered it the same time as your other pieces that were stolen,' came the reply, which brought a gasp of disbelief from her lips.

'Then why did he not return it to me then?' Had he known that in keeping it from her he had been depriving her of her only chance of escape from him? The idea was too absurd to consider.

'That is something you must ask him. Read the letter.'

Austen turned away from her again and helped himself to a large glass of whisky from the full decanter on the nearby table. Slowly Dominy lowered her gaze to the single sheet of paper, her thoughts reeling. The bold handwriting stood out against the whiteness of it, the words she read only serving to confuse her more.

> I am returning what is rightfully yours so that you may wear it at your wedding. My blessings on you both. I am sure you will be happy. I have returned the IOUs to your father and told him I consider the debt paid in full. When you read this I shall be back where I belong. Where I am needed. Take care of the *Enchantress* for me; consider her a wedding gift.

It was signed simply, 'Beau.'

'Wedding! I don't understand. Austen, what does he mean, he has given me the *Enchantress* as a wedding gift? What have you told him. . .?'

As a dull flush of embarrassment crept into Austen's face it became clear to her what had been said, of the lies he had told his best friend. 'He believes you and I are to be married! How could you?'

'He intimated that you yourself might be considering my proposal. Marriage against. . .what you thought he was offering you.'

'Thought he was offering,' Dominy repeated, and he took a large swallow of his drink before answering.

'Beau wanted the Barton mansion for you. He told me so the day we went to look it over. He wanted to try and give you back a little of what you had lost, and it was also his way of repaying his debt to you. He owed you his life, and Lance Beautrellis owes no one, believe me. I discovered that very early on in our friendship.'

'But if you have made him believe we are to be married, why did he still buy it?' Dominy asked, clutching the ruby and diamond necklace against her heart.

'He didn't. I did. For us.' Austen supplied the answer reluctantly, knowing with each word she was slipping further and further out of his reach. 'I told him about the necklace. He didn't tell me he had it. It was his way of keeping you close to him, I suppose. Without it you were penniless—tied to him. In time perhaps he thought you might think of him in a different light.'

'You knew I loved him, yet you said nothing,' she breathed. 'Austen, how could you?'

'Love does strange things to people—even gentlemen. I couldn't think about anything except having you. . . Once I explained to him how in love you were with me, but that you would not marry me until you were free of his debt. . .' He shrugged, and for several minutes silence hung between them, neither knowing what to say. 'He was very decent about the whole thing. Said at least he could go back to Savannah, knowing you would be taken care of. His father has been ill, you understand, and needs him back to run the plantation.'

'Julia needs him too,' Dominy whispered.

'But of course. Now her husband is dead there is no reason for Beau not to return.' As he saw the pain that entered Dominy's eyes Austen gave a low oath. 'They are friends. . .only friends. She was his brother's wife. There was bad blood between Beau and his younger brother—some scandal about a duel he was too cowardly to fight. Beau took his place and the blame for the aftermath.'

'The duel he told us about at dinner that first night? He made it sound so unimportant!' His brother's wife! Friends! Bright tears glistened in Dominy's eyes. The sight of them was like the turning of a knife in Austen's chest. And then through the shimmering haze there shone such a look that he knew he would never have received from her if he had waited for her until he was ninety.

The enmity he had harboured towards Beau died in that moment. No man or woman could tell what moment in time they would fall in love—or who it would be with. Once fate had intervened nothing could be altered. Beau had kept his secret well, rejecting love as he had been rejected as a child. Afraid to trust the feelings which plagued him. Austen, on the other hand, had always gone where his instincts dictated—very often in the wrong directions, as his mother so acidly reminded him on frequent occasions. He had known more women than he cared to remember—not that he could remember many. If only it were possible to forget Dominy as easily as all the others who had passed without meaning, without commitment, through his life.

'What are you going to do?' he asked quietly. He watched Dominy get to her feet, acknowledging that she was still very shaken by what had been revealed to her, and stand before the mirror, holding the necklace against her creamy skin. He moved behind her, took it from her lax fingers and fastened it around her throat. 'The answer is simple, you know.' She looked like a fairy-tale princess, waiting to be awakened by her prince.

'Is it?' A sad smile touched her face as she looked up at him. 'He would not believe I love him if I went to him now, only that I was having second thoughts about marrying you. He does not trust me; he never has. He has never known love and so he has no conception of what I feel. . . Oh, Austen, it is too late for us!' she cried and turned her face against his shoulder. For a moment he held her, pretended she was still his—had she ever been—as she trembled in his embrace, and then he put her firmly from him.

'Is this the same determined creature who refused to accept charity from me when she first arrived in San Francisco? Stood proud and resolute in her decision to repay her father's debts, even if it meant working like a saloon girl? Who reminded my mother that breeding does not come out of a closetful of Parisian clothes? Dominy, I am ashamed of you. Shall I tell you how to get Beau? Easy, my dear—you are coming with me to the reception and we are going to make the man so jealous that he will drag you off to a preacher by the hair.'

'Do we have to go to such drastic measures?' Dominy tried to joke, but the words stuck in her throat. She could not believe Beau cared for her. . .and yet. . .

'Beau is still vulnerable as regards his family. His father for years ignored his elder son in favour of the younger—a wastrel, from all I have heard from Julia. She took tea with my mother the other day and is now regarded as potential marriage material,' he added with a rueful grin. Thank heavens neither of them would be around long enough for her to make plans on how to bring them together. He had been through that too many times before. 'Now what do you think Beau would do if he found you deep in conversation with his father? I know the old man would like you. . .'

'The other night I met a man who I am sure knew Beau. He was rather mysterious about himself. It is possible he was. . .?'

'It was Beau's father. Apparently when Julia's letters had no effect he made the journey himself to ask his son to return home. The old man is lonely. . .'

'You seem to know a great deal about Beau's background all of a sudden.' Dominy moved away from him, wanting to believe a miracle could happen—and yet dreading the outcome of an encounter with Beau.

'Once he believed we were to be married he talked quite a bit about himself. From our talk I've pieced a lot together, and it's made me realise what I am doing to him. I can't deprive him of happiness. I'm his friend. . .although at this moment I wish I weren't. It's getting late; Maisie will be wondering where we are. We have to launch an all-out assault.'

'You make it sound as if we were at war.'

'We were, but not any more. I have conceded defeat. This time the south has won.'

CHAPTER ELEVEN

THE BARTON mansion could have been lifted out of the very depths of the deep south and deposited on the gentle slopes on the far side of Nob Hill. Afternoon sunshine softened the brilliant white of the woodwork, and deepened the reds and yellows of the flowers bordering the wide path that led up to the house.

Dominy smelt the fragrance of magnolias and roses as the carriage came to a halt and two liveried servants hurried down the steps to help the occupants alight. As she passed through the wide brass-hinged door, turtle doves cooed overhead and then fluttered back down to the lawn, unperturbed by the noise and activity.

The reception was in full swing, with the sounds of popping champagne corks and happy laughter filling the air. In front of her the doors to all the downstairs rooms had been thrown open to allow the guests to wander around freely. And the double french windows in the long drawing-room had been opened on to the gardens, where a marquee had been erected. And there on the lawn, dancing with the bride, was Beau. His head was thrown back and he was laughing at something she had said. Maisie looked flushed, breathless, ecstatic. And with good reason, Dominy thought as she looked around her at the tables lined with food and drink and at the jewelled women in their latest fashions who today were brushing shoulders with some of the poorest people on the waterfront. Nob Hill would not forget this in a hurry!

'I do not think this is such a good idea after all,' Dominy whispered as Austen tucked her arm beneath his and propelled her firmly in the direction of the man she had talked with aboard the *Enchantress*. He was standing behind a sofa, where an elegant Elizabeth LaMotte reclined beside a young girl in her early twenties. A very pretty girl, Dominy acknowledged as they reached them. This had to be Julia.

A mass of dark brown curls framed a small round face. The soft pink mouth deepened into a smile as she looked up and recognised Austen, and there was a warmth in the brown eyes which hinted that she found him more than a little attractive. That would please his mother, Dominy thought as she greeted the woman politely, and received a forced smile in return. Nothing would ever make Elizabeth LaMotte like her, Dominy thought, except perhaps the news that she was not to marry her son!

'Mr Beautrellis, I believe you have met Dominy Granville, the daughter of Lord Edgemont. Recently arrived from England,' Austen said, and felt Dominy start as he used her father's title. She never had.

'Indeed I have, and you are even more beautiful than I remember, my dear. Robert Beautrellis. . .' He touched the slender hand outstretched towards him to his lips, and blue eyes—not as pale as those of his son, but still possessing their intensity—scanned her from head to toe. From the open admiration which crept into them, he liked what he saw. 'And this is my daughter-in-law, Julia.'

'Mrs Beautrellis.' As she spoke Dominy wondered if Beau had ever mentioned her and their strange relationship. One moment friends, the next adversaries. Wanting love, yet afraid to reach out and take what at times had been at their fingertips.

'Julia, please. I feel as if we are already friends. Beau has told me so much about you,' the girl replied in a heavy southern accent.

'I am flattered.'

'And so you should be, my dear. My son does not give out compliments without good cause,' Robert Beautrellis told her, a touch of pride in his voice. Whatever had been between them to drive Beau from his home, it was gone now, Dominy thought. 'Mr LaMotte tells me you and Beau have worked very closely together over this new enterprise of his. Perhaps I should try and persuade you to come back to Whispering Pines with us and put your talents to good use there. Although Beau has agreed to come home with us, I sense a reluctance that does not stem from our old disagreements. I think perhaps he has found something worthwhile to keep him in San Francisco,' he added, and Dominy was horrified to feel her cheeks begin to glow with colour.

'You are rather jumping the gun, sir. I don't think Beau has got around to asking the young lady yet. . .' Austen interrupted with a meaningful smile. 'There has been rather a tug of war on the poor thing's heart-strings, but I think she has made a fine choice and I have conceded defeat.'

'Austen. . .stop!' Dominy begged. She did not know who looked more astonished at his statement—Robert Beautrellis, or Elizabeth LaMotte! Or the man who now stood at the side of his father, those pale glittering eyes locked on the necklace around her throat. Slowly they lifted to her crimson cheeks, and the accusation there made her inwardly tremble. Did he think she had arranged all this to embarrass him?

'Where the devil did you get that?' Beau demanded harshly.

'Where else, but from me?' Austen returned casually as Dominy's fingers trembled upon his arm. 'I made one last bet—with myself. That the sight of it would bring you running—and it has. Now what could that mean, I wonder?'

'That you will be lucky if I do not knock that infuriating smile off your face,' Beau said. 'I am not a good loser, my friend. Not in this instance.'

'I was not aware you were—the loser, I mean. In fact, the opposite applies.' Austen extended his hand to Julia with a disarming smile. 'I think these two have something that needs to be talked over. Shall we go and enjoy ourselves while they engage in a last battle before sanity prevails?'

'I declare, Mr LaMotte, I do not have the faintest idea what you are talking about,' Julia said with a puzzled smile as she rose and allowed him to lead her outside.

'And neither do I,' Robert Beautrellis said, frowning at his son as Dominy turned quickly away in the opposite direction and sought sanctuary at Maisie's side. 'We have just been given to understand that you and Miss Granville are. . .involved. . .or will be as soon as you find the nerve to ask her.'

'What?' Beau stared at him as if he had taken leave of his senses.

Elizabeth LaMotte, listening intently to every single word, was totally ignored. Her fan fluttered faster and faster as she looked from one man to the other, with only one thought uppermost in her mind: her son was free! And his interest in Julia Beautrellis was worth indulging.

'Did Austen intimate that?' What was he playing at? Why had he not done as he had been asked and kept the letter and necklace until Beau had left San Francisco? The flood tide of hope which suddenly unleashed itself upon him momentarily robbed him of speech.

'Now that is what I call a real lady,' his father murmured, his gaze following the figure in orange silk as she disappeared on to the flower-covered patio.

'Good enough to be the mother of your grand-children?' Beau asked, and the fire that leapt from the depths of his eyes caused Robert to remember days long gone when he had been young and in love and there had been no bitterness between them.

'You have to snare her first, my boy.'

'Consider her snared.'

'Let me go. Mr Beautrellis, I insist. Everyone is looking at us. You are embarrassing me,' Dominy cried indignantly, but not loud enough to cause more people to turn and watch her being dragged unceremoniously from the side of Maisie and her husband, across the lawn to the shelter of a magnolia-strewn arbour—enough curious eyes had followed them as it was. 'Beau, please. . .I am out of breath and you are hurting my wrist.'

'Not until you tell me how you wheedled that necklace out of him,' Beau demanded, tight-lipped.

Dominy's breath caught in her throat at the fierceness

of his expression, the possessive way he pulled her close against his chest and stared down into her apprehensive face with glittering eyes that made her tremble. He was like a man obsessed—but by what? Feelings that he had never allowed himself to contemplate until this moment because he was afraid to fall in love? If only she could allow herself to believe that!

'I told him I was leaving San Francisco as soon as your money had been repaid,' she said, and then demanded an answer to a question of her own. 'Why did you keep my necklace?' He could have extracted an explanation from her or sold it to recoup his losses, yet he had done neither!

'As—security, you might say,' Beau mocked.

'Against my failure to repay you?' What other answer should she have expected?

'What else?'

'For a moment I thought there might have been a simpler reason, one not motivated by money,' she flung back, and the pale blue eyes gleamed with derision. And Austen had been foolish enough to think he cared!

'Please do not endow me with virtues I no longer possess.'

'You enjoy controlling other people's lives,' Dominy accused. 'Is your own so perfect that you think you have that right?'

'On the contrary, mine has been in shambles for a considerable number of years, but now it has been made possible for me to rebuild the ruin I left behind.' The mockery dropped from him like a cloak. A look crept into his eyes such as she had never seen before. Unconsciously she allowed herself to relax in his grasp, needing desperately to know what thoughts were in his mind. Sadness, longing, resignation—in the space of a moment they were all there for her to see. 'You will be very happy here, I know it. When I am back home, working all hours that God put into the day to get the plantation back on its feet, I shall think of you as you are now, in that orange gown, with the sunlight on your hair, turning it to fire, wandering across the lawns with the fragrance of magnolias on the breeze, as it is now.'

'Austen lied to you. I told him in the beginning that I could never love him and that I did not think it fair to marry him. He told you otherwise because he discovered I was in love with you. We both thought you were in love with Julia because of the letters she sent you. . .I thought you wanted to set me up in this house as your mistress because you could not have her. . .and that Father's IOUs would be held over my head until I agreed. . . I hated you! And I loved you too, and I did not know which was stronger until she came to San Francisco and I thought you were going back to marry her. I knew then I could not stay here. . .'

The words tumbled so fast from Dominy's lips that they were barely audible as her voice at last trailed off and she remained against him in a miserable silence. As the shock of her words slammed into him she felt him stiffen, and his grasp tightened until it was quite painful. Then his fingers were sliding over the satin smoothness of her bare shoulders, bringing her back to life, and she began to tremble again—but this time it was from the feelings he awakened in her which could no longer be denied—or suppressed.

'Dear, sweet, confused milady, I thought I had given myself away a hundred times,' Beau murmured in a voice so gentle. She was his! She always had been! Somehow, safe in that knowledge, he could feel no anger towards Austen. Love had made them opponents for a brief time, but they would always be friends. Nothing on earth could change that. 'Julia's letters were to try and persuade me to go home because my father was ill and needed me. I could not believe that. . .not until he came himself. . .dragged himself from a sick-bed to beg my forgiveness. How could I refuse? I thought the bitterness still lingered in my heart until I saw him, and then I realised the hatred that had almost destroyed us both was gone. Let me take you home—to the Beautrellis plantation. You will be mistress of a fine house and you will want for nothing, I swear it. Of course, you will be expected to provide Father with dozens of grandchildren. . .'

'Will I have your love?' Dominy asked in a tremulous voice, raising her face to his. His mouth descended on hers in a kiss so passionate, so heart-searching, that she felt as if the ground moved beneath her feet. The fire that had always been awakened by his merest touch, a kiss, was brought to life now with a fierceness that left her weak and drained when he at last drew back and smiled down into her bright flushed cheeks.

'You have had my love since the first day I saw you. If you need additional proof there is more where that came from, and I don't care if I have to keep you out here all night in order to convince you,' Beau chuckled, and felt her heartbeats quicken beneath his hand at his words. 'I think you would like that as much as I would.'

'Yes,' Dominy sighed. 'I need you to kiss me all night long and tell me this is not some wonderful dream.'

'I intend to use every opportunity available, providing you do not bar your door tonight with the usual chair. . .and provided we can escape from my father's gaze long enough to get to the Rest,' Beau murmured. He had sensed they were not alone for several minutes.

As Dominy looked around Robert Beautrellis emerged into view. At the sight of her in his son's arms the leathered features split into a look of sheer joy.

'Do I hear wedding music? Is she coming with us?' he demanded eagerly, and Beau's brows creased into a fierce frown. Not until she glimpsed laughter in the eyes beneath them did Dominy realise he was not annoyed at the intrusion.

'Don't plan my life for me. I am a big boy now, Father. Dominy and I will not be rushed—into anything.'

'You are not so big that I can't give you a walloping if you sass me,' came the indignant answer. 'I've missed our—discussions.'

'Arguments,' Beau corrected.

'Exchanges, then. You owe me the chance to make up for the years we have lost together—and you owe this girl a decent wedding. A Beautrellis wedding! It's time the house came back to life again.'

'I think she might like that,' his son replied non-committally.

'Of course she would! She's a lady, from good English stock. She deserves the best we can give her.'

'We?'

'Don't shut me out, boy. I've said you come back on your own terms and that's the way it will be.'

'You old fraud, all you are thinking about is a grand-child,' Beau chided, still disbelieving that he could be standing here joking with his tyrant of a father. They had both changed so much. 'I've told you I will come home, but Dominy and I need time together. . .' The look he gave her was wicked, reminding her of the night of love which awaited them at the Devil's Rest, where they would be totally alone and able to confess to each other without restraint what was in their hearts. 'Expect us home in a month.'

'A month. The two of you alone. . .before the wedding! Lance Beautrellis, you never did abide by convention, did you? I know. . .I know. . .stay out of your lives. A month, you say?'

'Go away, Father,' Beau groaned. 'For the love of heaven!'

'Remember it is a lady you have there,' he was reminded as his father turned away. 'In my day. . .'

'Mother told me all about those days. . .when the two of you would slip away from the church socials. Nothing has changed, I assure you!' Beau's mockery floated after him, together with Dominy's soft laughter, abruptly curtailed.

As he peered back over his shoulder at the two figures entwined in each other's arms and caught a whispered acknowledgement of love—and heard a sighing answer in return—a twinkle sprang to his eyes. His son was right; nothing had changed. . .thank goodness!

HESTER

Marion Carr

Trapped by the British blockade of Charleston, life was becoming difficult for the inhabitants, none more so than for Hester Mackay and her Aunt Kizzy. With brother George presumed dead, their only recourse would be to take in boarders, but the only prospects were the British themselves. When privateer Benjamin Blake requested rooms for himself and some of his men, Hester's instinctive response was to say no, for this tall handsome man upset her equilibrium. But Aunt Kizzy said yes, and that set on course a surprising chain of events . . .

AN IMPROPER DUENNA

Paula Marshall

Miss Chloe Transome, impoverished dependent of her cousin Serena, Lady Marchingham, knew that at nearly thirty, her drab life was not likely to change. But she was wrong. Her old governess wrote offering a home in Northumberland, and Sir Patrick Ramsey visited Marchingham. Sir Patrick was intended for Chloe's charge, Miss Marianne Temple, but Patrick found he had a marked prediliction for Chloe's company, though they had to be circumspect, for both Serena and Marianne were jealous of him.

Knowing Patrick had no thought of marriage, nevertheless Chloe decided to throw her cap over the windmill, and stand the consequences . . .